LIKE ...
SHE FELT
FINGERS

With brutal assault, his mouth claimed hers, and she welcomed the bruising sensation of such pressure, such hunger. Then he moved his lips to her neck and began to suckle gently against her throat.

"Please, no . . ." she whispered through the fog that clung to her like a spider's confining web. "Don't go . . . not yet . . ."

Abruptly, the searching fingers moved up to trace her face.

A masculine voice, slightly accented, hoarsely uttered a curse.

She could no longer feel his touch.

She sat up, groping about her, realized she was awake and felt a wave of terror. Was there someone in the room? Did she actually hear the sound of ragged breathing fading as someone retreated?

No.

A dream.

Nothing more.

Other Avon Books by
Patricia Hagan

LOVE AND HONOR

LOVE AND TRIUMPH

PATRICIA HAGAN

AVON BOOKS ◆ NEW YORK

AVON BOOKS
A division of
The Hearst Corporation
105 Madison Avenue
New York, New York 10016

Copyright © 1990 by Patricia Hagan
Published by arrangement with the author
Library of Congress Catalog Card Number: 90-93192
ISBN: 0-380-75558-0

First Avon Books Printing: January 1991

AVON TRADEMARK REG. U.S. PAT. OFF. AND IN OTHER COUNTRIES, MARCA REGISTRADA, HECHO EN U.S.A.

Printed in the U.S.A.

RA 10 9 8 7 6 5 4 3 2 1

For Prudence,
who was with me through it all . . .
and lives forever in my heart

Chapter One

Spain
Late summer, 1917

MISTY lavender fingers of dawn crept stealthily upward from the dusky horizon, gently brushing away the last vestiges of darkness in preparation for the birth of a new day. Gently sloping pastureland, quiet shadows of night dredges, disappeared into the jutted ledges and beyond to the sleepy Mediterranean waters, a murky purple ribbon to the distant horizon.

The opulent Coltrane Casita, reminiscent of the era of El Cid, stood as regal lord of all, as though nature were merely its serfage.

Within the house, Colt Coltrane awoke with a start. He sat up in bed, groggily tried to fathom what had jolted him from such a sound sleep.

Then it came to him.

This was his son's wedding day.

He felt no particular elation, and chided himself for that. He knew he couldn't ask for a finer daughter-in-law than Valerie. And there was no doubt in his mind that she loved Travis to a fault. After all, she

1

had waited four years for him to graduate from the military academy at West Point, which had to have been hard on them both. They'd seen each other maybe half a dozen times during that period, because Valerie had been living in Spain with Kit and Kurt.

Valerie was a pretty girl, Colt mused, intelligent, charming. He had nothing against her personally and reminded himself once again that she couldn't help her family background.

With a deep sigh of resignation, he got out of bed and crossed the pink marble floors to the balcony. He could see the vaqueros as they began their morning chores, tending the cattle and horses.

He yawned, stretched, drank in the sweetness of the jasmine and roses in the garden below. Once again he thought how glad he was he'd kept the ranch during those years he and Jade had roamed the world in search of peace, because when they realized they wanted to return to Valencia and settle down near their grandchildren, it was all there waiting for them.

Grandchildren!

He laughed softly. Yes, he *was* a grandfather, all right, and proud of it and them.

Kit and Kurt had named their little boy after Kurt's father, Joseph. But little Joe, at three years, was a Coltrane through and through. No doubt about that. And little Natasia, two years old now, was named for Jade's mother but was the image of her grandmother, blessed with those same, awesomely beautiful eyes, a radiant shade of green that could only be described as jade.

Jade. . . .

Thoughtfully, he turned to look back inside the

bedroom, where his wife lay sleeping on the straw-
berry satin sheets. She was still the most beautiful
woman he'd ever met, and he loved her as much as,
if not more than, when he had asked her to be his
wife, twenty-four years ago.

Colt went to her now, to lay down beside her and
gather her in his arms. And with merely the gentle
brush of his lips against hers, she was coaxed easily
from sleep and eagerly on to the passion that always
left them shaken and awed with wonder.

Afterward, their naked bodies entwined, she was
strangely quiet, and Colt could sense her tension, suspected the reason. He waited a few moments, then
gently asked, "Do you want to talk about it?"

She sighed, rolled away from him and onto her
back. Dully, she replied, "Would it help if I did?"

"Probably not. We've had over four years to talk
about it. What's to say, anyway? She's going to make
him a good wife. He loves her. She can't help it if
her father is a son of a bitch who nearly destroyed us
once. That was a long time ago, and we've got to stop
thinking about it. Besides, he's disowned her, and it's
not likely any of us will ever hear from him again."

"Maybe he's dead by now." She felt no guilt in
hoping he was . . . even though she knew he wasn't.

Colt didn't comment, was not about to tell her that
he knew Bryan Stevens was very much alive, that he'd
had the Pinkerton Agency on retainer to keep him
informed of the bastard's activities. Stevens was living
the life of a recluse on the island near Bermuda he'd
named "Isle of Jade," back when he'd so cunningly
convinced Jade *he* was dead, manipulating her into
marrying him, nearly twenty-two years ago. Valerie's

mother, Lita, had died the year before, and Stevens had not sent word to Valerie. When he had disowned her for running away from a prearranged marriage to wait for Travis, he had obviously put her out of his mind and heart forever, even though he knew where she was and how to reach her.

"Instead of brooding about the past, I should be giving thanks you were able to use your influence to keep Travis from being sent to the front," Jade said. "It's a miracle he wasn't sent over with the first soldiers to France in June."

Colt turned away. He couldn't tell her that their son wanted to do his duty and fight for his country. So, after a brief honeymoon, he *was* going to the front. Valerie knew, of course, and agreed that Jade should not be burdened with the news till absolutely necessary.

He reached for his robe, then walked over to the velvet cord that would bring Carasia with morning coffee. Reminding Jade that the wedding breakfast was at ten, he headed for the bathroom to get ready.

There was much he was having to keep from Jade these days. Damn, he dreaded the time when he would have to tell her *he* was going into the war, too—not in the infantry but to the diplomatic corps.

Jade was not going to react well to both the men in her life going off to war. She was already distressed over the trouble in her native Russia, where a revolution had led to the abdication of her distant cousin, Czar Nicholas, and the disappearance of their close friend, Drakar, who had also been the husband of Colt's deceased half sister, Dani.

So, no matter how deceitful it might be, Colt wanted to delay giving her further cause for anxiety.

Jade did not move, merely stared up at the ceiling, lost in painful ghosts of the past. Colt did not know she'd had detectives make sure she received periodic reports of Bryan's activities. It had been horrifying to learn he was alive four years ago, after thinking him lost at sea all that time, and added to the nightmare then was the ghastly possibility her son might be in love with his half sister. She had been tortured by that fear for years and, seeing no other way, had confided her past to Valerie, how there was a chance Bryan could have fathered the twins, Travis and Kit, because the night he had kidnapped her, attempting to prevent her reunion with Colt, he had raped her.

It had been so terribly painful to confide the horror, to actually put all her anguish into words to another, but Valerie had quickly dissipated her fears. She could not, she vehemently assured Jade, be related to Travis, because Bryan Stevens was not her real father!

She had then gone on to explain how she found out the truth one night when Bryan was in a drunken rage. He'd screamed at her that she was not his daughter, condemned her as a bastard, taunted her that her mother had been a waterfront whore and couldn't remember the names of all the sailors and bums she'd taken to her bed. He'd married her out of pity and regretted it ever since. And the whole time he ranted, Valerie sadly recalled that her mother had just sat in shameful silence, head down, tears of anguish trailing down her cheeks.

Jade's heart had gone out to Valerie, and the two

had become close since, each carrying the other's secret. So she had no real trepidation about the marriage, except that Valerie would always be a reminder of those dark, ugly days.

The last report on Bryan was like all the others—he never left the island. She knew Lita had died but had no intention of telling Valerie, did not want her to know she felt it necessary to keep her father under periodic observation.

Hearing that Colt was finished with his bath, she hurried to take her own.

When she came out, he was having coffee and juice on the balcony. She joined him, noticed his mood had become somber, and decided it was her turn to prod. "Maybe *you* need to talk about it."

"It's not the wedding."

Jade did not have to guess what he meant. "Marilee."

"Right." He poured a cup of coffee as she sat down opposite him. "She showed up for the wedding. I'm surprised. I thought once she got out of that school she hated, she'd go her own way. She can sure afford it, with the trust fund Mother left her."

Jade had always sensed that Colt had never been able to feel any true affection for his stepniece. His feelings, or lack of, had apparently also rubbed off on Travis and Kit. Oh, not that anyone was ever *mean* to Marilee, or unkind. They just subconsciously regarded her as an unpleasant reminder that the late family patriarch, Travis Coltrane, had once been married to someone other than Kitty. No matter that at the time he had believed Kitty was dead. The scar was there, and Marilee was living proof—for the "other woman" had been her grandmother.

Ironically, it had been Kitty who adored Marilee and had taken it on herself in widowhood to raise her as her own after fate cruelly repeated itself. Marilee's mother, Dani Coltrane Mikhailonov, had died in childbirth, as her mother, Marilee Barbeau Coltrane, had when she was born. Ironically, it happened the same day Travis Coltrane died.

Drakar, Marilee's father, had been so distraught that he'd placed his infant daughter in Kitty's arms and returned to his homeland to try to lose his grief in service to his Czar.

Jade, however, felt a special affinity for Marilee. After all, she had loved Drakar like a brother for as long as she could remember, and Colt's remark now inspired her own displeasure over the way Marilee had never truly been accepted. "It doesn't make any difference how much money she has," she said irritably. "She's still a young woman, and there's a war going on. And need I remind you no one has heard from Drakar in months? We're all the family she has."

"Okay, okay, so she doesn't have anywhere else to go," he conceded, "but she acts so depressed, it's contagious. This is supposed to be a happy time."

"She's worried about her father. We all are."

"I thought you told me she had a beau," he then said.

"All I know is that she wrote me a while back that she'd become close friends with a girl from Austria, a Hapsburg, no less. Her family had moved to Zurich to escape the war. Marilee met the girl's brother and seemed quite taken with him, and I had the impression he was courting her, but she hasn't said anything else about him.''

"I'm surprised Valerie asked her to be maid of honor," Colt said. "They hardly know each other.''

"I asked her," Jade said, "to help her feel like part of the family.''

"The truth is," Colt said, "I love Marilee. So does Kit and Travis. But she has no spunk, no spirit, no personality. If she can find a man to marry her and take care of her, that'd be the best thing for her.''

Jade pondered that, then reluctantly, sadly, nodded.

Within the bedroom, about to step onto the balcony to invite herself to join them for morning coffee, Marilee froze.

They had not heard her knock on the outer door, and Carasia, whom she'd just passed in the hall, had told her they were on the balcony, so she had let herself in and wished she had not.

Chapter Two

WHEN she could trust her rubbery legs to move, Marilee fled back to her room.

She didn't belong and never had, but she was going to see this wedding through, and then, by God, the Coltranes would not be bothered with her again.

She rolled over onto her back, stared up at the lace canopy, taking deep breaths to try and quell the turmoil within. The more she thought about what she'd just overheard, the more depressed she became.

It bothered her that she had never in her whole life made a decision concerning her own welfare. It had not been necessary. Kitty had pampered her. Then she'd gone off to school, where teachers and counselors made the rules. So here she was, grown, educated, and everyone thought she was so weak and helpless that her only hope for survival was to get married and have a man take care of her and make all the decisions.

She had to admit she had been thinking seriously of accepting Rudolf's proposal, and now she found herself worrying whether the temptation had been due to her own subconscious telling her she could not face life on her own. After all, she could not truthfully say she loved him, but then how was she supposed to know what it would feel like if she did? His kisses gave her no particular thrill, but, again, no other man had ever kissed her, so how could she know?

Boyishly handsome with curly dark hair and brown eyes, he was also charming and intelligent, and she certainly admired his great talent and ambition to be a concert pianist. They had spent many pleasant evenings in the dormitory parlor, she sitting beside him on the piano bench as his slender fingers danced on the ivory keys to bring his music to life.

She had also enjoyed the company of Rudolf's sister, and when Elenore had left school months ago, she'd stayed in touch, urging Marilee to accept her brother's proposal.

When school ended, Rudolf and Elenore insisted she visit them for as long as she liked. Sympathetically, they pointed out that since she hadn't heard from her father in so long, she really had nowhere to go except to the Coltranes.

Marilee had hesitated, wanting time away from Rudolf to search within herself and decide if she wanted to marry him. Now, she bitterly mused, it seemed she had no other choice, since everyone around her apparently considered her a moron.

If only she could get in touch with her father, she thought desperately. She would not let herself believe he was dead. When his letters had abruptly stopped, she'd written in desperation to Czar Nicholas, only to learn a few days later of the revolution and his forced abdication . . . and she knew there would be no reply. Fear for her father's safety grew with each passing day.

When Rudolf had gently pointed out that she really had no home of her own, she had proudly reminded him of Daniberry. He was horrified that she could even consider going there, with Germany at war with France. Still, she knew if she had a home, it was the palatial estate just outside Paris that her father had so lovingly built for her mother. Forever would she treasure the memories of that Christmas she'd spent there with her father, the year after Kitty died. They had been so happy, so close, sharing ten beautiful days together. When, sadly, it had to end, he had promised that when her schooling was finished, he would leave Russia and, at long last, they would be together as father and daughter, and make Daniberry the home it was meant to be.

But now, standing at a crossroads in her life, she was determined that she would, ultimately, make the decision on which road to take, and no matter what anyone thought, said, or did, it was going to be *her* choice.

With a sigh of resignation, she got up, bathed, and dressed for the wedding breakfast. Staring at her reflection in the full-length mirror, she frowned. She had chosen a simple gray dress with a square neckline, short sleeves, a wide waist belt, and pleated skirt. Her shoes were black leather, with pointed toes and a silver buckle. She wore her chestnut hair parted in the middle, then wound in rolls above her ears. Rudolf liked it that way, just as he approved of conservative colors and styles. She'd never really cared much for fashion, feeling that since she was tall and slender, demure and alluring designs would only look ridiculous on her. Tiny, petite girls like Elenore were meant to wear them. Now, however, she wondered what it would be like to try something new. Her gown for the wedding was certainly different—peach chiffon with a slightly plunging neckline, pouf sleeves, a wide satin belt, and a gently billowing skirt that daintily touched her ankles above silver shoes with the highest heels she'd ever worn. Yet she knew that despite everything, she would still look dull, colorless.

There was a knock, and she heard Jade calling to her. When she opened the door, she could not help thinking that the look of disappointment in her aunt's eyes matched her own in the mirror.

With a forced smile, Jade said, "Well, I see you're up and ready for the breakfast, and since we've got a few minutes, I'd like to talk to you, if I may."

Marilee shrugged, gestured to the chairs in front of the fireplace. They sat down, and Jade got straight to the point.

"We're worried about you, dear," she began gently. "All of us. You seem so unhappy."

"I'm sorry if I'm making everyone uncomfortable," Marilee coolly said, not looking at her but staring down at her folded hands.

"Oh, no, dear. It's not that. We care. We really do. I just wanted to know if there's anything I can do, if there's anything you want to talk about. Heavens, I know you're worried about your father. We all are, but for the moment, there's nothing we can do but pray for his safety."

"I wish I could go look for him," Marilee said miserably. "I feel so helpless."

"If I thought it would help, I'd encourage you to do just that."

Jade absently gave her hand a flutter, as though to wave away unpleasant thoughts on a day that was supposed to be a celebration. "Back to you, my dear." What about that young man you wrote to me about? The Austrian lad? You haven't said anything about him since you got here, and I had a feeling you might be getting serious about him."

Marilee told her about Rudolf's invitation to visit his family and was not surprised that Jade urged her to go.

"There's no need for you to just sit around here worrying about your father. There's nothing you can do. Go to Switzerland, dear. It's safe there, and it might just lead to a proposal."

Marilee swallowed against the bitterness, the hurt. Jade had not even asked if a proposal was what Marilee wanted. As far as the Coltranes were concerned, it didn't matter. They just wanted her married and out of their way. "You *did* say you'd go, didn't you?" Jade prodded.

"I haven't decided exactly what I want to do." Marilee saw Jade's look of disappointment and quickly added, "But I won't be staying on here after the wedding. I'll travel, do something . . ."

"Nonsense! I'm going to be worried enough about Travis and Colt without having to worry about you, too. You'll either go and visit this young man or you'll stay here with me."

"Wait a minute. What are you talking about? What about Travis and Uncle Colt?"

"It seems," Jade began, "that my son and my hus-

band think that after all these years they can keep
something from me. They forget that I love them so
much, know them so well, that I can feel instinctively
their every emotion. Travis is going to the front in
France, because he feels called upon to do his duty
to his country. Colt is doing the same in his own way,
by serving in the diplomatic corps.''

"Oh, I'm so sorry," Marilee said, touched that
despite her own worries, her aunt found time to care
about Marilee's.

"Enough gloomy conversation," Jade said too
brightly. "I came here to talk to you about your future. I think you should accept Rudolf's invitation.
It'd be good for you."

Jade then left, and Marilee stared after her, knowing she would quickly spread the word to the rest of
the family that they should also encourage her to go.
Now she wished she hadn't told her aunt.

She went to the mirror once more to stare dismally
at her reflection.

Would it have made any difference in her life, she
wondered with abject misery, had she been born
beautiful? Would she have had a different outlook on
things had she been blessed with that certain flair
some girls had that just made them glow—like her
aunt? Like Kit and Valerie? They always knew how
to dress and seemed to sparkle on every occasion.
She, on the other hand, felt like a dusty statue in the
corner of someone's dark and gloomy library, seldom
noticed or seen.

It doesn't have to be that way, a little voice within
needled.

Suddenly, as though someone else had taken over

and was in control, Marilee reached up and began to yank the pins and combs from her hair. She had always hated the slight natural curl, but no more.

With hands that seemed not her own, she picked up a pair of scissors and began to snip at her hair.

And when she was finished, she stared in a mixture of horror and delight, for she had just copied the new style that was sweeping Britain and America—the *Irene Castle bob!*

With her natural curl, the effect was pixie-like, and she grinned at herself, genuinely *grinned*, for the first time in so long she could not remember.

She liked the effect! No, *loved* it, for it made her look young, fresh, and, miracle of miracles—glowing!

Taking a deep breath, she turned from the mirror and made ready to face the reaction of the rest of the family.

Chapter Three

THE wedding festivities were set to begin at two o'clock in the Tanners' splendorous gardens. High-ranking government officials and nobility from all over Spain were expected to be in attendance. Anyone of social status in all of Europe had been invited.

The ceremony would start when the wedding party rode in carriages up the gently rising ridge from the sea, all the way to the crest where Kurt had built the palatial stone palace for Kit.

Afterward there would be a champagne luncheon; then, to entertain guests until the formal dinner later, many activities would be offered—an orchestra playing constantly in the gardens for those who wished to dance, horseback riding, and even bullfights in the huge arena on the castle grounds. Kurt had also made sure his crew was standing by at his docks to offer short cruises along the Mediterranean coastline aboard his lavish yacht, the *Lady Kit*.

In order to give the family one last intimate gathering before the horde of guests began arriving, Jade had arranged for the wedding breakfast to be held at the Coltrane Casita. Valerie would not, of course, be in attendance, in keeping with the tradition that Travis should not see his bride until the wedding.

Carasia, proud of her succession from maid to head housekeeper, carefully checked the breakfast room. Satisfied that all was in order, she opened the double doors to the front hallway, promptly saw Marilee—and screamed!

"Oh, come now, Carasia, is it that bad?" Marilee patted her curly bob, sounding more confident than she felt. "It's the latest style. It's called the Irene Castle bob, after the famous American dancer. She and her husband practically invented the fox-trot." She did a few steps, whirled around, and curtsied.

Carasia's black eyes rounded with wonder as she took a really good look. *"Dios mio,* señorita, I have never seen a woman with the haircut of a man."

"It's the rage of Europe." Head held high, Marilee walked on into the room, found her place, stood behind her chair . . . and waited.

"Well, I like it," Carasia declared, "but I think you should have waited for another time to give everyone such a shock."

"I don't."

They turned to see Kit crossing the marble foyer, lavender eyes shining with happiness, coppery red hair glistening. Holding her arms open to Marilee, she cried, "I didn't recognize you at first. You look absolutely stunning, and I love it! Really!"

They embraced, and Marilee couldn't help thinking that if her new bob made such a difference, she must have been a lot frumpier than she'd thought.

Kurt was right behind his wife to agree the change

was for the better, and, as always, Marilee experienced a little shudder of delight at the sight of him. She had to admit to having had a crush on him from the first moment they met, more than four years ago. Tall, well-built, with broad shoulders and sinewy muscles, he presented an admirable figure in his white suit this morning. His hair was the color of the raven's wing, and he had rich brown eyes. He was, she determined once more, the most handsome man she'd ever met.

"I can't believe what a difference it makes." Kit shook her head in wonder. "Amazing. I've been tempted to do the same thing, but I'm afraid Kurt would divorce me."

Kurt laughed, "No, but I have to admit I like your hair as it is. The thing that's so fascinating about Marilee, though, is that she did this on her own."

His attention turned to Joseph and Natasia, who were running through the front door ahead of their harried nanny. Kurt scolded them for being so boisterous, but then they spotted their grandparents making their way down the circular stairway and the squealing began once more as they ran to meet them.

Marilee was stung by Kurt's offhanded remark, then realized with shock that he was right—cutting her hair had probably been the first decision she'd ever made about herself in her whole life. That realization made her feel strange . . . but wonderful.

Kit gave her an encouraging wink as they waited while Jade and the children came toward the breakfast room.

Marilee tensed, but needn't have, because Jade took one look at her and cried, "I don't believe it! I just don't believe it!'' She clapped her hands in delight, then rushed to circle her, all the while marveling at the effect. ''Now if we could just get you into some glamorous clothes instead of those matronly costumes they taught you to wear at that mausoleum of a school . . .''

Colt joined in to agree, and Marilee found herself the center of attention and loved every minute of it.

Travis arrived and at once marveled over his cousin's new and welcome look.

Marilee was so happy, she almost felt like part of the family, but a casual remark from her uncle brought her sharply back to reality.

''Yes, I'd say with the right clothes and a bit of makeup, we won't have an old maid on our hands after all.''

Everyone laughed, and Marilee managed a stiff smile which she did not feel. Then Kurt wanted to know her plans since she had finished school, whether she would be staying on in Spain.

Jade replied before Marilee had a chance to speak. ''She may be going to Switzerland. Her young man has invited her to visit him and his family.''

Marilee felt her cheeks blazing and could not resist snapping, ''Please don't worry about me. I promise I won't be a burden to this family, no matter what the future holds.''

An awkward silence descended like a giant, invisible shroud. Everyone exchanged uncomfortable glances, then Jade quickly changed the subject. ''I think it's time we got back to matters at hand, like proposing a few little intimate toasts together, before half of Spain arrives for the wedding.'' Her trailing laugh was forced, tense.

"Here, here!" Colt boomed his approval, got to his feet, and lifted his glass of champagne to Travis. "A toast to my son on his wedding day, with the good wish that he will forever be as happy in his marriage as his father and grandfather before him."

The toasting passed to Jade, Kit, Kurt, finally to Marilee; by then she was feeling as bubbly as the champagne. "To Travis," she said boldly, tipsily, "whom I've loved like family, even though he wasn't . . ."

Jade decided it was time to end the breakfast. Everyone began to file out of the room, but she called to Marilee just as she got to the door. "I'll be leaving for Kit's house in half an hour, and I'd like for you to ride with me. Can you be ready?"

Marilee glanced at her watch and asked, "Why so early? We've lots of time."

Jade gave her a secret smile. "You'll see. Just be ready."

Marilee nodded, continued on her way.

"What is wrong with her?" Colt demanded, exasperated. "I have to admit I'm getting a little bit sick of feeling like I'm walking on eggs every time she's around."

"Well, I'm going to see if I can talk her into going to Switzerland. She really needs to go," Jade said.

"Maybe you'd like to go with her, get away for a while," Colt suggested.

"I've thought about it. It might take my mind off worrying about Travis going into the war and you getting involved."

He swore under his breath. "How did you find out? Did Valerie tell you?"

She touched his cheek with her fingertips. "I didn't

know for a fact, but I could feel it, so please, let's not pretend any longer.''

"I just wanted to get through the wedding. This is supposed to be a happy time, and I didn't want to have any more shadows than we've already got.''

Quietly, lovingly, she said, "Coltranes have always used shadows as a shield against the painful glare of reality. I intend to remember that.''

He kissed her gratefully and whispered, "Thanks for reminding me of the family philosophy.''

"You taught me, remember?" She smiled. "Now let's go see our son properly married, and then maybe we can sneak away from yet another reception and take a second honeymoon.''

He grinned. "Honey, that sounds great, but I don't think the first one ever ended.''

Chapter Four

MARILEE sat next to Kit on the plush leather seats in the rear of the new Rolls-Royce Silver Ghost. They wore fashionable ankle-length dust coats, with wide-brimmed hats and veils covering their faces. As Jade settled behind the steering wheel in front, they exchanged uncomfortable glances.

Jade sensed their apprehension. "You needn't be so nervous. I've had driving lessons."

"The car was only delivered last week," Kit reminded her. "How many lessons have you had?"

"It's a simple car to drive. Really. It has a four-speed gearbox with direct third and overdrive on fourth."

"I know. I know. I've heard Daddy go on and on about this model." She rolled her eyes at Marilee and whispered, "And with a horsepower of forty-eight giving it a top speed of over a hundred kilometers, I'd prefer to have the horses pulling me!"

Jade pretended to be angry. "Much more talk like that and you'll walk home, young lady." Suddenly they were thrown forward, then backward, as she made a quick, jerking start, finally easing out into the driveway and heading for the open road.

Kit said to Marilee, "When Mother drives, Kurt and I don't ride together with her. We're afraid of leaving the children orphans."

They burst into laughter, but Jade ignored them.

Marilee settled back to enjoy the ride. It was a gorgeous day for a wedding, with a peacock-blue sky shared by billowing clouds that would periodically offer relief from a brazen sun.

Marveling at the landscape, she became lost in her own imagination. How easy it was to think of Spain as Europe's lady of mystery, dressed in black velvet and holding a red rose . . . eager suitors crossing her courtyard. Yes, she mused dreamily, Lady Spain was the eternal enchantress.

Suddenly Kit urged, "Tell me about Rudolf!"

Marilee shrugged. "I guess you could say he's handsome, charming, polite, well-bred. Very talented. He's studying to be a concert pianist. His family lived in Vienna before the war but fled to Switzerland."

"Do you love him?"

Jade was aghast. "Kit! Don't be so nosy!"

Kit ignored her and pressed on. "Well, do you?"

Marilee stared at her for a few seconds, then, with candor and honesty, asked, "How am I supposed to know?"

Kit started to laughed but realized Marilee was quite serious. "A girl just knows," she said. "Like when you're saving a rare and special bottle of wine, and you wonder when the occasion will come when you want to open it, and when it does, somehow you just know it and realize that was why you were saving it.

"It's the same with love. You just *know,*" she repeated emphatically.

Marilee laughed. "That sounds very romantic, but I don't think you were quite that sure about Kurt. I remember when you first met him, you couldn't stand him."

"That's right. You loathed him, as I recall," Jade teased.

"We had personal problems," Kit said defensively. "I won his precious horse in a race and didn't know he was stolen, remember? Kurt wanted him back, but I felt like he was mine. Of course, now I'm happier than I ever thought I could be, and so will you be when you meet the right man."

"Maybe she already has," Jade was quick to suggest.

"He's Austrian, and you're half Russian. Does that ever cause any dissent?" Kit asked. "After all, when the Russians attacked in Galicia last year, they killed over a million Austrians and took nearly half a million prisoners. Your father is an officer in the Czar's brigade, or was, before Nicholas abdicated, and he was also a top-ranking adviser. Does Rudolf know all that?"

Marilee nodded. "It's never caused any problems. Actually, he seems fascinated with my Russian heritage and asks a lot of questions, but there's not much I can tell him—only things Daddy has told me through the years."

"I wish we knew where he was," Kit murmured. "It's been a while, hasn't it?"

"Since Christmas. I think he's either with Nicholas or working underground. Either way, I keep telling myself he's all right. He *has* to be," she added vehemently.

Determined that the day was not to be shadowed, Jade cheerily agreed. "Of course he's fine. Drakar is brave, courageous, and resourceful, and no matter why he's out of touch, he can take care of himself."

They reached a fork in the road. The curve to the left went to the rear of the Tanner property, where the servants' compound was located, as well as service buildings and barns. Jade started to turn toward the right, where the road disappeared within a grove of orange trees.

"No!" Kit cried, leaning forward to point to the service road. "That way! I have a surprise you can't see till time for the wedding procession. I had to make Valerie promise not to go on the front lawn, and I'm determined you all aren't going to see it, either."

Jade nodded, willing to cooperate.

They passed the cattle pens and barns, then came to the elaborate stables and training rings for the prize Hispanos. "There's Pegasus," Kit said proudly, pointing to a magnificent horse lazily grazing in the distance. "He's sired four beautiful colts so far."

Passing through the servants' compound, Marilee was once again dazzled by it all and wanted to know, "Just how many people does it take to keep this place running?"

Kit thought a moment, then replied, "I think around fifty altogether. Kurt has a secretary who keeps all the records, so I'm not sure, exactly. I know I have about twenty servants in the house, but not all at once, of course. They work in shifts. Then there are the stablehands and the horse trainers.''

"And that doesn't even include the vaqueros, who live on a different section of the ranch,'' Jade put in. "They've got their own little village a few miles away.''

"Well, it's necessary,'' Kit explained. "After all, Kurt has enlarged his operations. He has about fifty thousand head of cattle, plus he's raising bulls for three major arenas, and now we have the Hispanos. The vineyard is also growing, and he said we'll probably need to build some cottages for those workers in the next few years.''

Marilee laughed. "And I thought Daniberry was a palace. Compared to your castle, it's hardly a cottage.''

Jade slowed as they approached the massive structure, and Kit said thoughtfully, "You know, I never wanted anything this colossal, but it seemed so important to Kurt to build it for us that I went along. I was amazed how fast he did it, too, but then he kept the construction workers going twenty-four hours a day.''

"Four stories.'' Jade shook her head in wonder. "Sixty rooms. An indoor swimming pool. A solarium that goes through all the floors. And *I* thought the Czar's Winter Palace was sumptuous!''

The outer yards were splendid to behold, with gardens of wisteria and roses and jasmine and honeysuckle, and exotic plants from the Orient and Central America. There was even a pagoda with charming tinkling bells, and a magnificent statuary.

"It was Kurt's dream,'' Kit said almost wistfully.

"I was content with my little farmhouse, but if it makes him happy, it makes me happy."

"And me, too, dear," Jade was quick to declare, "even though I do think he went a little overboard."

Marilee agreed but did not say so. After all, her father had done the same for her mother, built her a dream palace. Would Rudolf do the same for her? She doubted it . . . doubted his family had that kind of money, did not think she would ever want something so grandiose, anyway.

Admitting that, even if only to herself, was always surprising, because she had never known anything except wealth. Yet she had never felt it a prerequisite to happiness. Once, she'd said as much to Jade and was promptly told that should she find herself poor, she would surely change her mind.

Jade drove into the courtyard and stopped before the back entrance, a canopy-covered breezeway, where a footman was waiting to open the doors for them and park the car in one of the nearby garages.

Kit led the way up the marble steps. A uniformed butler greeted them. Marilee smiled to herself, thinking how the back entrance was as grand as the front entrance of most fine homes.

"This is new," Marilee marveled as Kit ushered them onto a small elevator. "When did you add this?"

"We have two. One in the foyer for us, and this one for servants. Kurt had them installed a few months ago in preparation for the wedding, because tonight we're going to have to use not only the ballroom on the main floor but the one up on the third, as well, and he felt it would just be too much for the guests to climb up and down so many stairs, not to mention the servants with all the food and wine.''

They got off the elevator on the second floor, where Kit said she'd prepared dressing rooms for them. Carasia had seen to it that all the clothes they would need had been brought, as well as accessories. They would be changing several times during the festivities. First there would be the wedding, then attire for whatever activity they chose for the afternoon, and finally, elaborate dress for the dinner and reception that night.

The room given to Jade was like a jewelry box, all gilt paneling and beveled mirrors, with an electrified chandelier of ruby and gilt. Fresh flowers had been placed in vases everywhere, the air perfumed with their sweetness.

"If you need anything, just ring." Kit pointed to the velvet bell cord by the door, then motioned Marilee to go with her.

"Don't forget to ask Valerie to come here for tea in about a half hour," Jade said, reminding Kit of an earlier request, then nodded to Marilee. "I'd like you to be here, too. This is why I asked you to drive over early with me."

Marilee did not have time to wonder why her aunt wanted to take time for tea with so much going on, because Kit grabbed her arm and laughingly urged her to hurry along, and she was smiling as though she knew a wonderful secret.

Finally Kit paused before a closed door and said, lavender eyes twinkling with mischief, "I've got a surprise for you. I worried for a while that maybe you'd be angry, but after seeing how you were so daring as to cut your hair this morning, I feel better about it and think maybe you're ready for a real change in your life.''

Taking a deep breath, she opened the door and stepped aside.

Hesitantly, but curiously, Marilee looked into the room and was astonished at the sight before her.

Everywhere she looked there were gowns and dresses of all colors and fabrics and designs. Why, she had never seen so many outfits at one time, not even in a dress shop.

Slowly, she walked around to stare at the wardrobe laid out on the bed, across the chairs, hanging from drapery rods and picture frames—everywhere!

"I don't understand . . ." she gasped, shaking her head in wonder. "Is all this supposed to be for me? And if so, why?"

Kit giggled with little-girl delight, pleased and relieved that Marilee did not seem offended. "Of course it's for you. I just thought this was a good time for you to stop looking like a birthday cake and start dressing like the glamorous *femme fatale* you really are!''

Marilee could not help laughing at that declaration, but then began to blink back tears of happiness as she paused to admiringly and lovingly touch the hem of a stunning gold lamé evening dress. The neckline was low, edged in tiny diamonds and pearls, the waist high, with the skirt draped to ankle length. She did not have to try it on to know it would fit perfectly, for she knew Kit would have somehow managed to have everything designed and made to size.

"I just don't know what to say," she softly cried,

overcome with emotion. "I can't believe you went to this much trouble for me."

"It's something I've wanted to do for quite a while now, and this was the perfect opportunity. Besides," Kit gently pointed out, "I was afraid you wouldn't have nerve enough to do it for yourself. I always thought you were a little mouse, remember?"

They giggled together as they rushed around the room trying to decide which gown would be worn that night, but could not make up their minds before it was time for Marilee to meet with Jade.

"We'll do it later," Kit promised, then left.

Feeling better than she had in a long time, Marilee hurried to Jade's room and found Valerie already there and absolutely trembling with the ecstatic joy of her wedding day. She had always reminded Marilee of what an angel would be like if one floated down to earth—soft golden hair, eyes the color of a summer sky, a sweet smile and disposition to match. Fragile. An almost ethereal air about her. Everyone loved her, and Marilee had never heard Valerie say an unkind word about anyone.

"Marilee! Your hair!" Valerie cried, rushing to give her a hug of greeting. "I love it. You look so . . . so sophisticated!"

"No longer a birthday cake?" Marilee laughed.

Valerie blinked, not understanding, but then Jade said, "Girls, time is short, and I want to talk to you. It won't be long before the guests start arriving, so come sit down, please."

They positioned themselves on the divan, with Jade in a chair opposite. From a pocket she brought forth a small pouch of red velvet, tied with a gold cord, and laid it on the table between them. She looked at each young woman in turn, then began to speak in a voice that was tremulous with emotion. "This is a very special day for me, and I wanted to celebrate it by giving each of you something to remember it by. On Kit's wedding day I gave her the diamond and emerald earrings her father gave to me on our wedding day.

"On *your* wedding day, Valerie"—she paused to give her a loving gaze—"I want you to have this." She reached into the pouch, then held something out to her.

Curious, Valerie took it; then her fingers began to tremble as she saw what it was, and she nearly dropped it as she stammered, "This—this is the ring Travis's grandmother gave to you on your wedding day. Travis told me about it. He said his grandfather gave it to her on their tenth wedding anniversary."

Jade nodded as she looked fondly at the pearl and emerald ring. "I want you to have it, with the wish that the love Travis Coltrane had for Kitty, that Colt has for me, is carried on with my son's love for you."

Marilee felt awkward and she started to rise, but her aunt held up a hand for her to remain seated. "I could come back later, Aunt Jade," she suggested.

"Don't go, please."

Marilee sank back onto the divan.

"The truth is, this is a very emotional time for me," Jade admitted. "With the world in such turmoil, there's no telling when, or if, we'll all ever be together again. So I wanted to give each of you something meaningful, as a symbol of my love for you."

She reached into the pouch once more, then held her hand out to Marilee.

"Oh, my God!" For a moment, Marilee could only stare at the stunning gold, garnet, and ruby pendant, for it was the most exquisite piece she had ever seen. Then she touched it ever so cautiously, as though it might burn her flesh. Incredulous, she whispered, "You're actually giving this . . . to *me?*"

"Yes. It was a special gift to me from Nicholas on my wedding day. He had it fashioned by the Imperial Court jeweler, Peter Carl Fabergé. Now it's yours, as a token of my affection for you, Marilee."

Marilee stood to walk around the table and embrace her aunt. She felt deep, abiding gratitude . . . and guilt for the way she had been regarding the Coltranes.

"I'll treasure this forever," she fervently vowed.

Suddenly, there was a sharp knock on the door, and Jade frowned, for she'd left word they not be disturbed. "Yes, what is it?" she called irritably.

The door opened with an apologetic hesitancy. Kit's head housekeeper, Lowinda, appeared, looking quite agitated herself. "I am sorry, señora," she cried, wringing her hands. "I know you requested not to be disturbed, but there is an early guest downstairs who demands to see the señorita at once." She nodded almost accusingly at Marilee, as though it were *her* fault this was all happening.

Marilee blinked, bewildered. "But I'm not expecting anyone. Who—"

Lowinda sniffed with disdain, still blaming her for the chastisement she was surely to get from her mistress. She walked to where Marilee was sitting, held out a small white card with stiff fingers.

Marilee, completely baffled, took it, then gasped as the name leaped out at her: *Herr Rudolf of Hapsburg.*

Chapter Five

IN her efforts to give her brother and his bride a wedding that they would never forget, Kit Coltrane Tanner's imagination had soared to superb heights.

Kurt Tanner had lovingly gone along with his wife's every whim and wish, surprising even himself by consenting to her most astonishing request. Large spiders were brought in from China and set free in the trees lining the driveway to the castle. For weeks great webs had been spun, and on the morning of the wedding, workers had been given bags of gold and silver dust and, with bellows, coated the webs. This created a fantastic canopy, aerial and metallic, that billowed in the moving air, quivering and glinting in the morning light.

Gallons of imported and expensive French perfume had been sprayed into the air so that the entire area was fogged in sweet fragrance.

The wedding party was taken by carriage from the rear of the castle so they would have full benefit of the startling view that awaited them when they reached the great webbed canopy.

Travis and Colt, his best man, led the procession, both awed by the wonderland that had been created.

Then came Jade, riding with Kit, little Joseph, and Natasia in a gold-and-white horse-drawn carriage.

Jade could only stare in astonishment, while Joseph clapped his hands in delight. Natasia did not understand the beauty nature had created, and merely looked around with wide, almost frightened eyes as she sucked her thumb.

Marilee rode alone in a small blue carriage, the skirt of her peach-colored silk gown billowing about her on the leather seat. She was only dimly aware of the gold- and silver-dusted webs, did not even notice the overwhelming sweetness of the air, and smiled vaguely, absently, at the strange faces of the guests mingling along the driveway for a better view of the bridal parade. She was still dazed by Rudolf's unexpected arrival. There had not been much time for conversation, only a few moments of greeting. He had laughed with delight to have taken her so totally by surprise, roguishly warning he'd come to abduct her and carry her away by force, if need be, to his own castle in Zurich.

A footman was waiting now to take the reins of the horse from her driver; another stood by to help her alight.

She smiled demurely at Travis, Uncle Colt, and could not help glancing about till she met Rudolf's gaze. He was standing close to one side, looking at her with open adoration. A few of the unmarried girls in attendance hovered nearby and, seeing the way he was looking at Marilee, began to glower with disappointment.

She took her place, then turned to await Valerie's arrival.

Everyone was excited, whispering among themselves as the orchestra began to play the wedding procession, and they strained to see the arrival of the bride.

And then it came into view—the pink-and-white carriage, drawn by six stunning white horses, all wearing pink velvet coats, with pink harnesses adorned with little golden bells. They strutted and high-stepped, but with gentle precision, the way they had been carefully trained, so as not to cause the princess they carried to be jostled from her throne.

Valerie was radiant in her wedding gown of white satin and lace. A fortune in diamonds studded the billowing skirt, and her tiara was fashioned of emeralds and pearls, her veil brushed with thousands of tiny diamond chips.

When her carriage reached the pagoda, where the ceremony would take place, Travis could restrain himself no longer. A footman moved to help her alight, but he stepped out of place to brush him aside and set her gently on the ground. An approving ripple went through the two thousand or more guests in attendance, crowded there on the lawn, as he went one step further. Unable to resist, he lifted her veil and whispered, "God, you're beautiful, and I love you so," and he kissed her tenderly before taking her hand to lead her to her place before the altar.

Colt and Jade exchanged loving, amused glances for their son's impromptu behavior.

Kit and Kurt also looked at each other and smiled,

for they knew what it meant to be so dazzlingly in love.

Marilee saw what went on, then lowered her eyes to stare at her satin shoes, not about to glance at Rudolf, for she knew, somehow, that she just couldn't look at him that way, knew he was expecting her to, and she didn't want to hurt him.

The music faded, ended, and a hush fell over the crowd. The minister began to speak, asking everyone to bow their heads in an opening prayer. Then Travis and Valerie exchanged their vows, and finally Travis was lifting her veil, kissing her as his wife. Everyone cheered.

Colt had his turn to kiss the bride; then other men playfully joined in, brushing their lips against Valerie's glowing, upturned cheek. And Travis turned to kiss the ladies, first his mother, then Kit, finally Marilee.

She felt a possessive hand on her arm and found herself looking up into Rudolf's adoring gaze. "You're more beautiful than the bride," he said, his voice a soft caress as he slipped his arm around her, slowly guiding her away from the crowd. "I'm living for the day when you're *my* bride, you know."

"Rudolf, not here," she protested. "We can talk later about—"

"About so many things." He laughed. "Like when I can expect you in Zurich, and when we can announce our engagement. Oh, Marilee, my mother is so anxious to meet you. In fact, you can blame her for my showing up like this. She and Elenore both insisted that I come here and persuade you to go back with me."

"I can't do that. Not now. I've got so much on my mind right now, Rudolf."

"Like what?" he challenged, then softly intoned, "I know you're worried about your father, Marilee, but there's nothing you can do. Worrying isn't going to help. Russia is in such a turmoil now that it's no wonder he can't get a letter out, if . . ." His voice trailed pointedly.

"*If* he's still alive," she finished tightly. "I won't let myself believe he's dead, Rudolf."

"I know, I know." He gave her a gentle squeeze. "But you must face reality. It's just a matter of time till the Bolsheviks succeed in overthrowing Kerensky and his Provisional Government. There's going to be even more bloodshed. If your father *is* still alive, and dear God, I pray he is, he'd be wise to leave Russia.

"Tell me," he suddenly urged, "what do you think happened to your father when the Czar was arrested shortly after he abdicated? You've told me they were close friends and confidants. Don't you suppose he's also being held as a political prisoner?"

"No. I told you my uncle Colt has a lot of influential friends in high places, and the American Embassy in Russia told him they had no evidence he was arrested, but they don't have any idea where he is, either." She shut her eyes, attempting to close out the misery Rudolf's probing questions provoked. "If you don't mind, I really don't want to talk about any of this just now. This is supposed to be a happy day, and—"

"I'm sorry," he quickly apologized. "Forgive me. I didn't mean to cause you any distress."

"I know, Rudolf. And I don't mean to be difficult,

and I'm certainly not trifling with you. It's just that I have to make a few decisions on my own . . ."

"Like changing your hairstyle." He smiled, nodding at her new bob.

"Do you like it?"

He pursed his lips. "Frankly, I like long hair on women. It will grow out."

She felt like telling him she had no intention of letting it grow out, but decided there was enough tension between them for the moment. "I really need to be getting back to the guests, and I'd like some champagne, too."

They had reached the statuary with its surrounding hedges. Suddenly he pulled her out of sight of anyone and crushed her against him, his lips pressing down on hers in an almost bruising kiss. Then, just as abruptly, he released her and brazenly said, "I'd rather stay here and taste your lips than champagne."

Feeling terribly awkward and self-conscious, she quickly pulled away from his embrace. His kiss had not moved her at all!

"I really have to get back to the guests, Rudolf," she nervously babbled, "and then I have to change, because I'm going riding this afternoon. I promise to meet you later, and we'll talk, about Zurich . . . about everything . . ." And she turned and ran, back toward the tents and the people and the champagne and caviar, feeling like a little girl once more, and not feeling very good about herself at all.

His amused laughter rang out behind her. "You can't run from me forever, my darling. I know you love me, and you know it, too, and soon you're going to have to face the truth."

Marilee slowed to a walk, struggling for composure.

The *truth,* she grimly reflected, was that she doubted if she'd ever know when to open that special bottle of wine Kit had compared to realizing true love.

Her wine, she feared, would turn to vinegar before she ever knew such splendor. . . .

Chapter Six

JADE was wearing a floor-length gown of emerald satin for the reception dinner. Her hair was fashioned in a chignon, dozens of tiny diamonds shimmering, the net holding them so wispy as to not be noticeable. The sleeves were capulet, the neckline squared, and crusted with sequins. Her jewelry was her favorite opal and emerald earbobs, with matching choker.

She reached for her elbow-length gloves of white silk just as Colt came out of his dressing alcove, dashingly handsome in a formal black tuxedo with ruffled shirt and bold red satin tie.

"My God," she said without exaggeration, "if I weren't already married to you, I'd pursue you like the most wanton of Jezebels!" She rose from the dressing table to eagerly receive his embrace.

"You always were the most ravishing woman I ever knew," he murmured huskily, mouth brushing hers.

He'd had a bottle of cognac, their preferred aperitif, sent up earlier and poured them each a glass. "To us, our children, our grandchildren, and the future."

Their eyes met over the rims of their glasses, and

suddenly, in that strange way that lovers have, when their souls are somehow laid naked before each other, Colt lowered his drink and whispered, "You aren't going to stop worrying, are you?"

Jade shook her head, shuddering from head to toe, and he set aside his glass, did the same with hers, then wrapped his arms around her.

"Travis will be fine. He's a trained soldier, an officer, and he'll serve proudly, and bravely."

"I know." She managed to sound confident, but inside she felt stark, cold dread. Then, struggling to reach out for any solace, she forced a smile and said, "At least you won't be on the front. You'll be in Paris, and the embassy should be reasonably safe, and . . ." Her voice trailed off as she saw his expression, new fear rising.

He turned away, unable to face her.

"Colt, what is it?"

"I'm not going to Paris," he wretchedly confessed, forcing himself to face her, wincing as he saw the emerald eyes he adored now inflamed by terror. "I'm being sent to Russia."

Her hand flew to her mouth, and her gasp was barely audible. "Oh, God, no . . ."

He gathered her against him once more. "Jade, Jade, my darling, you've got to understand. Our government is worried that the July uprising of the Bolsheviks was only a forerunner of their ultimately overthrowing the provisional government, and if they succeed, in all probability they'll make peace with Germany."

In a rare burst of rage, Jade cried, "I don't give a goddamn about the war, or patriotism, or any of that.

All I know is my son's going to the front, and you're going into the middle of a bloody revolution, and it's not fair!''

He grabbed her by her shoulders. "Listen to me, Jade Coltrane. Get hold of yourself. One of the reasons I've always loved you is because of your spirit, and you aren't going to wilt on me now. I need to know you're strong. And so does Travis.''

Jade closed her eyes, but only momentarily. He was right. They had been through so many trials and tribulations in their life together, and she was not going to bend now, not when strength was needed the most. "I'm sorry.'' She mustered a brave little smile, lower lip trembling only slightly.

He grinned, holding her gently once more. "God, I shudder to think what the outcome would've been if you'd gone all to pieces way back when! Let's not talk about it anymore. I'll come back, and so will Travis, and we'll all grow old together. Now hold your head high, and remember I love you.'' He cupped her chin in his hand and kissed her lips. "And later tonight, I'll show you how much.''

They shared one last glass of cognac to brace for the arduous evening, then Colt said he wanted to go downstairs.

Jade glanced at her wristwatch. "It's only six-thirty. Kit set seven as the cocktail hour.''

"Yes, I know, but I sent a courier into Valencia with a message for young Hapsburg that I'd like to have a private meeting with him.''

Jade was pleased. "I think it's time we found out his intentions.''

He laughed. "Oh, I think his intentions are quite

clear, and Marilee would probably do well to marry him.''

"She's so worried about Drakar. At least when you get to Russia you'll stand a better chance of finding out what happened to him.''

"I doubt it, but I'll try. I thought at first that, as close as he was to Nicholas, it was likely he was on the Imperial train with him in Pskov when the decision was made to abdicate, but from what I've been able to find out from the embassy, he wasn't on the train when it arrived in Mogilev.''

"Maybe he was never on that train.''

"You don't honestly believe that.''

Soberly, Jade shook her head. "No. Drakar would've been with him at such a time.''

"Frankly, since Drakar was nowhere around when Nicholas was arrested, I think he and some other trusted advisers just slipped away to plan a counter-revolution. It he were dead, or a prisoner himself, we'd have heard. And if he's working underground, he won't dare contact anyone,'' Colt pointed out. "But I promise I'll do everything I can while I'm there to try and find him.''

Rudolf had arrived early and been shown to Kurt's private smoking salon, situated on the ground floor of the castle in a quiet, almost isolated wing. He walked about, admiring the room. The walls were covered in leather, and there were many paintings of the famed Tanner Hispanos and prize bulls. The carpet was thick, red wool, and the furniture was of caramel-covered leather, with luxurious sheepskin throws for added comfort. There was a huge stone fireplace that took up one wall, and a mirrored bar opposite.

Very nice, he concluded with a sneer, but when he and Marilee got married, they would live just as luxuriously. Not only did she have the Coltrane inheritance, but her father had set up a tidy trust. He knew, because he had made it his business to find out.

Rudolf had experienced both wealth and poverty and found he much preferred the former, despite his pretense of adhering to the Bolshevik doctrine.

After Rudolf's father had died when he and his sister, Elenore, were still children, their mother, Amalia, had married a distant cousin of Francis Joseph and delighted in claiming kinship to the revered House of Hapsburg-Lorraine. No matter that there was no blood relation. The necessary doors to acceptance and high society were opened, and by the time Rudolf and Elenore reached puberty, they were accepted in court.

It was not until his stepfather died that Rudolf and his family found themselves in dire straits.

Amalia never knew her husband, Fritz, was so deeply in debt until he died of a heart attack three years ago. The ghouls had descended to claim everything owed them.

Consequently, the family saw no choice but to go to Zurich and seek refuge with Rudolf and Elenore's paternal grandmother, Ilsa Gutten.

Ilsa, however, was actually not wealthy. When she died shortly after they moved in with her, about all she left was her drafty old castle, small by European standards, and some valuable objets d'art that Amalia promptly sold.

Amalia had almost fanatical goals for her children.

Elenore would go to an exclusive finishing school to be groomed to attract a wealthy husband, and Rudolf would be a piano virtuoso. Amalia had been glad for the excuse to leave Austria, lest her son be made to join the fighting and perhaps injure his precious hands.

Yes, Rudolf mused bitterly now, his mother was a driving force, and her nagging and harping, even worse when she was drinking, drove him and Elenore away from her. That was when they had begun frequenting an out-of-the way coffeehouse, where they'd met other young Austrian refugees who were also bored and disillusioned with life. And gradually, more to be accepted by their new friends than anything else, they had become involved with the Bolshevik supporters.

It had given Rudolf a particular thrill, never to be forgotten, to have met the great man himself—Lenin. And there had been many occasions when Rudolf had been tempted to leap to the defense of his mentor's doctrines when in the company of others, but the particular group he and Elenore affiliated themselves with adhered to absolute secrecy. That way, they could be used in many ways, for no one considered they would ever turn their backs on Austria in support of the enemy, Russia.

When certain leaders learned that Elenore had become friends with the daughter of one of the Czar's closest confidants, Rudolf had been ordered to court her in hopes of learning more about Drakar Mikhailonov's activities. At first he had been reluctant, but when he met her, realized just how beautiful she was, he no longer considered his assignment a chore! And he had managed to keep hidden his enthusiasm over discovering how wealthy she was. *That* would certainly not go over so well with socialist-minded comrades, but no matter.

Rudolf turned at the sound of the door opening, then graciously held out his hand to Colt Coltrane.

"Did I keep you waiting long?"

"No, no," Rudolf assured him. "I was early. I've been enjoying just looking around. It's a beautiful salon."

A white-coated butler brought a tray with snifters and a decanter of brandy, then left.

They sat down, and Colt poured them each a drink. "When we met earlier today," he began, "there was so much going on we didn't have time to talk. That's why I asked you to come early so we'd have some time together before dinner."

Rudolf nodded. "I'm glad you did, sir."

Colt opened a fruitwood box, offered Rudolf a cigar, which he took. Then he sat back, crossed his legs, and regarded Rudolf thoughtfully for a moment before asking candidly, "Tell me, why did you and your family leave Austria? It would seem a young man like you would be fighting for his country."

Rudolf assumed a sad expression. "It would seem so, wouldn't it? But the truth is, family obligations have taken precedence over patriotism. My stepfather died of a heart attack two years ago, at the same time my paternal grandmother became ill in Zurich. My mother wanted to go care for her, which she did until her death, and we stayed because, frankly . . ." He set the brandy snifter down and raised his hands, spreading his fingers. "I'm bent on protecting these.

Forgive me if I brag, but I've been called a piano prodigy by many in a position to know. I protect my hands, and I care for my mother and my sister. If there are those who would condemn me for that, so be it,'' he finished with a shrug.

Politely, Colt said, ''Well, it's not for me to judge,'' but inside he was thinking the young man somewhat of a coward, even though he acknowledged that Rudolf had the right to freedom of choice. ''And I suppose you wouldn't be here if you were politically inclined. Our countries are enemies, too, you know. Tell me, are you studying your music now?''

''Yes, but not as much as I'd like. I'm not privy to the same quality of conservatories we had in Austria. They were nonpareil to anywhere in Europe, in my opinion, except for Russia, of course.''

Colt nodded. ''I've heard that, but Russia isn't a very good place to be right now,'' he sardonically pointed out, then could not help probing. ''Doesn't it ever bother you that Marilee is part Russian?''

Rudolf's eyes widened, reflecting his surprise at such a question. ''Of course not. If it did, the relationship certainly wouldn't have progressed this far.''

It was the opening Colt had been waiting for. ''And just how far is that, Rudolf?''

He did not hesitate to declare, ''I love her, and I've asked her to marry me.''

Colt raised an eyebrow. It was his turn to be surprised. ''And has she said yes?''

Rudolf sighed. ''She says she's not sure, but I know that's just an excuse. She's so worried about her father she can't think about anything else right now. I'm trying to be patient, but frankly, I think he's dead, and while I don't mean to sound coldhearted, the fact is—life is for the living, and I wish she'd get on with hers—*and* ours—and set a wedding date.''

"You make it all sound so simple."

"I wish it were. Maybe you can help me. That is, if you approve of me, sir."

Colt could not find any reason, on first impression, to feel anything negative. Rudolf was obviously intelligent, of good breeding, ambitious, and, most of all, seemed genuinely fond of Marilee. "So far, you have my endorsement," he said, then quickly pointed out, "But I don't want to get involved in Marilee's personal life to the point of persuading her to do something she's unsure about."

"All I'm asking is that you use your influence to get her to accept my invitation to visit my family in Zurich. That will take her mind off her father and give me time to make her see she does love me."

"Well, I think I can agree that's a good idea, but, as you're probably well aware, she's somewhat of a loner, and the only person she was ever close to was my mother. But I'll see what I can do, and I'll let her know you have my blessings."

Relieved, Rudolf grabbed Colt's hand and shook it with exaggerated gratitude. "Thank you, sir. I'm sure she respects you and your opinion. And I promise I'll take good care of her."

Colt, likewise, felt relief. Maybe, he mused guiltily, he shouldn't be so eager to see Marilee married off, but the truth was, grim though the thought might be, if something did happen to him, she would just be another responsibility for Jade to cope with after he was gone.

They smoked their cigars, sipped their brandy, and made small talk, and then Jade and Marilee arrived.

After exchanged greetings, Jade said, "Colt, we need to get in line with Travis and Valerie to receive the guests. They're starting to arrive now." To Rudolf, she said, "You'll have to excuse Marilee for a little while, but I did ask Kit to seat you next to her at dinner."

Everyone moved to the door—except Rudolf.

He had politely stood when the ladies entered the room, but his eyes had locked upon Marilee, and he stood frozen, unable to tear away his gaze.

The object of his fixation was not her gown, a stunning gold lamé that made her look more glamorous and beautiful than he'd ever seen her before.

It was the pendant.

Hanging on a gold chain, the gold and garnet and ruby pendant at her throat mesmerized him.

"Rudolf?" She laughed a bit nervously, for she'd never seen him behave so strangely. "What is it?"

He swallowed hard, licked his dry lips, struggled for composure, then managed to ask, "Where did you get that stunning piece?"

"I gave it to her," Jade told him. "It was a present to me on my wedding day from Czar Nicholas."

"You *knew* the Czar *personally,* madame?"

Marilee was quick to proudly inform him, "Of course. They're related to each other, and he named her a princess the night before she married my uncle. Didn't you know? My aunt is a *Romanov!*"

Rudolf's eyes narrowed, ever so slightly, but no one noticed, and he was barely able to conceal the excited tremor that was going through him at this stunning news.

Chapter Seven

THE wedding dinner was lovely, and everyone was in a mellow mood. Rudolf continued to charm and captivate the Coltranes, but all the while his brain was whirling with the exciting revelation and what it could mean.

He could not believe his good fortune at being seated on the other side of Jade. During the course of the evening, he managed to delicately ask questions about her Romanov heritage, careful to appear only respectfully in awe of such elite company.

At first she was reluctant to talk about it, then eventually divulged that her mother was Russian and a cousin of Czar Alexander II, while her father was Irish. When she became orphaned at an early age, she was unofficially adopted by Marie Pavlovna, sister-in-law of the new Czar, Alexander III, and subsequently raised in the Imperial Court.

Jade then launched into an enthusiastic recount of her career as a prima ballerina with the Imperial Ballet, and as she talked, Irish eyes shining with pride and fond remembrance, it was only with great effort that Rudolf was able to appear properly impressed, nodding at appropriate moments, smiling now and then. He was having difficulty swallowing against the bile that rose in his throat when she had mentioned the name of Alexander III, for he knew only too well of the sorrow suffered by his idol, Lenin, over his eldest brother, Aleksandr, having been convicted and hanged for conspiring with a revolutionary terrorist group that had plotted to assassinate him.

I should be an actor, he told himself fiercely, taking a gulp of wine to ease the burning within, *instead of a pianist . . . because only a great actor could pretend to enjoy the company of such capitalistic swine!*

And it was good, he thought with a mechanical smile of adoration at Marilee, that she did not feel a part of this family, for he'd be damned if they'd ever fraternize with the Coltranes once they were married.

Rudolf was relieved when dinner finally ended. A full orchestra began to play, and hundreds applauded as Travis Coltrane led his bride, Valerie, to the center of the room for the traditional first dance. Then they parted—Travis dancing with his mother, Valerie with her new father-in-law. At last the other guests could join in, and Rudolf led Marilee onto the floor for a spirited waltz.

He gave her the adoring gaze he'd practiced before his mirror and huskily murmured, "I can't wait for our time, my darling, when we lead the wedding waltz."

Dizzy and giddily happy as the result of too many glasses of champagne, Marilee felt a warm glow . . . but not in particular over Rudolf's intimate flirting. She was caught up in the glittering atmosphere of the romantic evening. "Maybe . . ." she said coquettishly, "One day. Who knows?"

He squeezed her hand, pressed harder against her waist. "At least say you'll visit my family in Zurich and give me a chance to win your heart."

The dance ended, another began, and suddenly Kurt was there to take Marilee into his arms. It was what Rudolf had been waiting for. Quickly, he went in search of Jade and found her standing to one side, talking to some ladies. He nearly tripped in his haste to get to her before someone else did. "Princess Jade." He bowed with a flourish. "May I have the pleasure of this dance?"

The other women exchanged envious glances, and Jade, flattered, allowed him to lead her onto the floor.

"I've never danced with a princess before," he said.

She laughed softly. "Is it any different?"

"Oh, yes. It's the aura, the enchantment. Of course, it also helps that you're quite beautiful."

"All right, Rudolf, you can stop now," she pretended to scold, emerald eyes shining. "You've won me over completely, and I assure you I'll give Marilee my wholehearted endorsement. Colt and I both agree she should accept your invitation to visit Zurich. It will do her good."

"Why don't you accompany Marilee to Zurich?" he glibly suggested. "My mother would love to have you as our guest, and I'd feel better about Marilee traveling if you were with her."

"How nice of you! I think I'd like that very much, and you're very kind to include me," Jade agreed enthusiastically.

Marilee had finished her dance with Kurt and was on her way to the terrace herself to get some fresh air in hopes of clearing away too many champagne bubbles from her head. She was surprised to see Rudolf and Jade coming in, did not have time to speculate as to the reason, or a need, for Jade quickly, and excitedly, told her of Rudolf's invitation.

". . . So," she finished, "if you decide you'd like to go, you'll have a traveling companion, and I think it would be a wonderful trip for both of us."

Marilee looked from one to the other and decided perhaps it was the only way she would ever find out whether Rudolf was the man for her.

"All right," she said quietly, without enthusiasm. "I guess I might as well."

Jade was distressed to hear such defeat in her voice and said, "We'll have a lovely time, and I'm looking forward to *our* being together, too."

Rudolf was bristling inside to see Marilee's reluctance. He could name dozens of women who'd leap at such an invitation. Just who did she think she was?

It was only with great effort that he was able to muster a tight smile and say, "Yes, my darling, we'll *all* have a lovely time."

But the smile was genuine when he added, "And I promise it will be a visit neither of you will *ever* forget!"

Chapter Eight

AMALIA was livid.

There had not been a day since Rudolf had
sneaked off that she had not reread the terse note he
had left on his pillow, crying and cursing all the while
she did so.

> Mother, dear,
>
> I have gone to Spain to attend the wedding of a
> special friend's cousin. I did not tell you of my
> plans in advance because I knew you would worry.
> I should be back in a few weeks.
>
> > Love,
> > Rudolf

The note was worn, tattered—and so were her
nerves.

"Elenore!" she screamed in the quiet gloom of her
bedroom suite. "Elenore! I want you to come in here.
Now!"

She did not stop to think that her daughter might be
out. Elenore knew better than to be like her disobedient
brother and leave without asking permission.

How Amalia wished it had never been necessary to leave Vienna. There, she'd had control over the children. Here, it was different. The city was filled with refugees from the war—all kinds and classes—and she had not wanted them exposed to such. If only Elenore were still in school and she could persuade Rudolf to go away to a conservatory and get on with his music, she would not have to worry about their being exposed to undesirable company.

Both of them had been acting mysteriously lately, but Rudolf was worse . . . and his leaving for so long without permission was the final blow.

"Elenore! I want you in here now!" she bellowed again.

Amalia wanted to interrogate her once more about Rudolf's "special friend." Oh, Elenore pretended not to know anything and swore Rudolf had confided nothing to her about his plans and that she had no idea whom he had gone to visit. But Amalia was sure she was lying. She had always prided herself on being one step ahead of her children and was now furious with herself for not having sensed that Rudolf was up to something.

Once again she read the note, straining to see in the dim light. She had ordered the thick velvet drapes closed against the sunshine. When Amalia was unhappy, she detested sunshine and blue skies, preferring stormy weather to match her dismal mood.

In ultimate frustration, she wadded the note and threw it furiously into the empty grate of the fireplace.

She began to pace aimlessly about the cheerless room. It was so dreary, with its dark, heavy furniture,

faded wallpaper, and worn carpets. But it was the
nicest room in the decaying old castle, so she had
moved Ilsa out, even before she died. The old lady
was so crazy in the head she never said a word when
she was locked away in a small room in the basement
to wait to die. Amalia could still remember the feeling of relief that morning when Ulda, the housekeeper, came running up the stairs, nearly stumbling
and falling in her haste and terror, to report she had
found her mistress dead in bed when she'd taken down
her breakfast tray.

Ilsa, Amalia felt, had only been in the way, and
once she was gone, the castle legally became the children's. Oh, not that it was worth all that much in its
present state of deterioration, but it was a place to
live, and there were still boxes in the basement to go
through in hopes of finding more valuables to sell to
pay for Rudolf's studies at a conservatory.

"If he ever recovers from his temporary state of
insanity!" Amalia said aloud.

"Oh, Mother, he's not insane!"

Elenore's exasperated voice startled her. "How
dare you sneak up on me this way? My nerves are
shattered enough as it is, thanks to your thoughtless
brother, without you scaring me half to death."

"Are you sure you aren't just afraid Grandmother's
ghost will come back to haunt you . . . again?" Elenore boldly taunted as she walked over to pull the
drapery cord, flooding the room with light. "God,
how do you stand it in the dark all the time?"

"I like it! It's my room. I'll do as I wish, and I
won't put up with your insolence." Amalia hurried to
close the drapes, cursing herself for what must be the

thousandth time for ever having confided to Elenore about those horrible nightmares in which she thought she saw Ilsa standing at the foot of her bed. Elenore had just laughed and said it was her conscience bothering her because of the way she'd treated her. Amalia had not been able to make her or Rudolf understand that their grandmother had to be locked away for her own protection, because her mind was gone.

"Where have you been?" Amalia demanded. "I've been calling you for hours."

"Walking."

"Indeed."

Elenore threw up her hands. "Oh, why do I even bother answering your questions, Mother? You never believe me, anyway."

"That's your own fault. I can tell when you're lying, and you're lying when you say you don't know anything about this 'special friend' of Rudolf's. I want to know who she is and what makes her so 'special,' " she added with a sneer.

"Who says it's a 'she'?"

Amalia glared at her incredulously. "Do you take me for a fool? Rudolf would never make such a long journey for one of his new, fanatical men friends." She nodded smugly when she saw the look of surprise on Elenore's face. "Oh, yes, I've heard the rumors about you two keeping company with political zealots. The servants hear gossip and they pass it all along to me.

"But that's not the point for the moment," she went on, waving her hand to dismiss that particular subject. "Believe me, I'll take all that up with you and your brother later, because we're going to start cultivating a normal life around here. You're going to make some kind of social debut, no matter how difficult, what with the war going on. It's time to present you as an eligible young lady, because the sooner I find a husband for you, the better. And Rudolf is going to continue his studies.''

She walked over to shake her finger beneath Elenore's nose as she glared at her menacingly. ''You are going to tell me where Rudolf has gone, and you are also going to tell me everything you know about the little bitch he has gone to see, or so help me, I'll call Vincent and have you locked in the same room where your crazy grandmother died till you feel like talking. I'm not bluffing, Elenore. I mean what I say.''

Elenore realized her mother was, indeed, serious. If her mother ordered the big, hulking gardener to drag her off to the basement, there would be no way she could stop him, and she would be kept there till Rudolf returned. He was due back any day, according to his original plans, but there was always a chance he might be delayed.

''I'm waiting!'' Amalia snapped.

Elenore knew confinement would mean not being able to sneak out to be with Cord—an unbearable thought. No matter that she had sworn not to tell, since Rudolf wanted to be the one to break the news about Marilee. She was not about to be held prisoner just to keep a promise.

With a ragged sigh of defeat, she declared, ''She's not a bitch, Mother.''

''Aha!'' Amalia cried in gleeful triumph. ''So I was right. Rudolf sneaked away because he was too ashamed to be breaking his promise that he would never get involved with a woman. He knows as well as I do there's no room in in his life for anything except his music, not for a long, long time. Now, tell me everything.''

Elenore flashed a venomous glare, and Amalia responded by slapping her.

"Talk, damn you, or you'll live to regret it!''

Elenore's cheek stung, but she was too proud to cry. Biting back the tears of humiliation and pain, she hoarsely whispered, "What is it you want to know? I'm not privy to what goes on inside Rudolf's head, or his heart. I only know he went to Spain to see her and to attend her cousin's wedding. It was supposed to be quite lavish, and—"

"Who is she?'' Amalia sharply cut her off to demand. "Who is this little fortune hunter that her family stages such 'lavish' affairs?'' she asked with a sneer.

Elenore dared to snicker, "I'd hardly call her a fortune hunter. If anything, it could be the other way around.''

"What do you mean by that?''

Elenore's smile was gloating. "I mean, Mother, dear, that Rudolf's 'special friend' is actually *quite* special.'' She paused, enjoying the moment. "She's a Coltrane. Her grandfather was *Travis* Coltrane.''

Amalia was properly impressed. She knew about Travis Coltrane and the respect accorded him in government circles, just as she knew his son, Colt Coltrane, was equally revered. The family was said to be extremely wealthy and considered the crème de la crème of society in both Europe and the United States.

"It doesn't matter!" Amalia suddenly screeched out loud, startling Elenore with the unexpected outburst. "I will not have it! Rudolf is going to be one of the greatest piano virtuosos that ever lived. He has the gift, and he's not going to throw it away! Whether he wants to or not, I'm going to do what I should have done when we first moved here—send him to the Conservatory of Music in Geneva!"

Tiptoeing till she reached the door, Elenore made her escape as her mother began to rant and rave. Behind her, she could hear her mother screaming for her to return, but she kept on going, not about to be a substitute for Rudolf, and she was going to hide till either he came back or her mother calmed down.

Rudolf was already back in Zurich, had arrived that very morning but had other things on his mind besides facing his mother's wrath. He went straight to the Wolfa coffeehouse on Schulleslgasse, in the oldest part of the city. It was situated at the end of the cobblestone street, with a boarded-up building on one side and a private residence on the other, so there was little traffic, making it an ideal place for private gatherings.

He was glad the coffeehouse tradition had carried over from Vienna. It was like a private club, a large and well-furnished establishment where customers always felt at home. There were billiard tables, chess sets, cards, as well as writing materials. One of the most popular amenities was the choice of newspapers from all over the world, ringing the walls on cane holders.

Rudolf's friends at the Wolfa had one day jokingly

referred to themselves as the "Zurich Zealots." Then, as their casual conversations became serious, and goals and philosophies united, they adopted the name, as well as the Bolshevik slogan: "Peace, Land, All Power to the Soviet."

Rudolf did not like it when Elenore became involved, and he'd accused her of merely looking for a man. That had infuriated her, and she'd said she had as much right to pursue ideals as he did.

When Rudolf walked in that morning, he was glad to see that the Zealots' declared leader, Hanisch Lutzstein, was already there.

Rudolf was trembling with excitement over his news but had to restrain himself because Lutzstein was not alone. He sat at the favored table in a rear corner, surrounded by a dozen or so comrades, and they were engaged in deep conversation.

Rudolf went to join them, his presence acknowledged, for no one just "walked up" without being noticed—and identified. They could take no chances on spies in their midst.

They were talking, as usual, about the July uprising in Petrograd that Lenin and the Bolsheviks had been unprepared for. Half a million people had marched carrying banners of protest to the war and the PG— the Provisional Government—and the PG had crushed it. They had also circulated among the regiments documents that were supposed to prove Lenin was a German agent and the uprising had actually been planned to betray Russia from the rear while Germany advanced at the front. Bolshevik strongholds had been stormed, and while Trotsky, to Rudolf's personal dismay, had surrendered to the police, Lenin had escaped over the border into Finland.

The Zealots had just heard that Lenin had sent word from Finland that he was not at all concerned over the failure of the uprising. He called it more "demonstration" than "revolution."

But Rudolf quickly learned that his friends were concerned with other news from Russia. It was reported that Prime Minister Kerensky, who was also Minister of War, had decided since the July uprising that it was dangerous to leave the Czar and his family where they were being held at Petrograd. Everyone was wondering where they would be taken.

"If we had gold, we could buy the information," Lutzstein gruffly proclaimed, banging his fist on the table. "We have manpower, brain power, and by Lenin, we've got the will and the courage. We just don't have the gold to buy information that disillusioned soldiers are willing to sell. All we can do is sit here all day and all night and drink and protest. I think the time has come to stop complaining and do something to help our Bolshevik comrades."

A round of cheers went up.

At the next table, Cord Brandt sat quietly, sipping now and then from a stein of beer.

Rudolf saw him, started to join him but hesitated because he looked so preoccupied, his thoughts far, far away. Yet Rudolf could sense the man was very much aware of everything going on around him.

When Cord had first appeared at the coffeehouse last winter, he was regarded with suspicion. He would divulge nothing about who he was or where he came from, and he kept to himself. So they ignored him and minded what was said when he was about.

Then came the night he saved Hanisch Lutzstein's life by deliberately taking a bullet intended for him. It happened during the Zealots' celebration of the news of the Czar's abdication. A stranger came in, did not share their joy, and subsequently got into a heated debate with Hanisch. When he became abusive, then threatening, Hanisch had him thrown out. It was Cord Brandt, however, who happened to see the stranger sneaking in the back door, gun in hand, and leaped to his feet in defense just in time to keep Hanisch from being shot in the back. Fortunately, Cord had only been grazed, but from then on, his loyalty was never questioned, and Hanisch proclaimed him a friend for life. The would-be killer got away and was dismissed as a wandering drunk, and the attempted assassination was considered merely the result of the previous altercation.

Cord Brandt became a hero and a respected comrade, and Rudolf was somewhat impressed when Elenore caught his eye. And he really was not concerned over their mother being outraged that they could both be involved with people who were half Russian. She was going to learn sooner or later that he was now the head of the family. Besides, if her drinking got worse, Amalia was going to find herself tucked away in a sanitarium. He was getting tired of her tantrums.

Rudolf decided to intrude, walked over, sat down, then signaled the barmaid to bring a fresh pitcher of beer before cheerily greeting him. "Well, it's good to be back. How've you've been, comrade?"

Cord nodded absently.

Rudolf was bursting to tell someone his news, so he paid no attention to Cord's lack of enthusiasm over his company. He waited till the barmaid brought the beer, then excitedly whispered, "Did you hear what Hanisch was just saying about gold being needed to buy information? Well . . ." He grinned smugly. "*I* have it!"

Cord poured himself a beer, then asked with a slight sneer, "Which? The gold or the information?"

Rudolf stiffened. He did not like his sarcasm but then saw that Hanisch was disengaging himself from the others. He frantically waved to get his attention, then motioned him over.

Hanisch pulled up a chair to sit between them before asking Rudolf, "So, when did you get back from Spain?"

Rudolf told him, then repeated what he'd said to Cord, how he had what was needed.

"What are you talking about?" Hanisch said.

Rudolf glanced from one to the other, enjoying his moment of rapt attention, even though Cord did not seem interested. Taking a deep breath, he announced proudly, "A *Romanov* is going to be a guest in my home!"

For an instant, Hanisch did not react; then he shook his head, bewildered. "Surely you don't mean the girl you were told to court? Her father is important, but he's not a Romanov."

Cord said nothing, just sipped his beer and looked bored.

"No, no, not Marilee." Rudolf clutched Hanisch's arm, drawing him closer to reveal what still made him dizzy to contemplate.

When he'd finished, Rudolf leaned back in his chair, folded his arms across his chest, and beamed. "Don't you see? We've got a real prize. Can you imagine the ransom we can collect? The Coltranes would pay a fortune to get her out of the hands of the revolutionaries screaming for Romanov blood."

Hanisch scratched his chin thoughtfully, dark eyes beginning to glow with shared enthusiasm. "Yes, I think you've got something," he said finally, mind whirling. "The Zealots can take care of kidnapping her, and you won't be suspect. It won't keep you from your pursuit of Mikhailonov's daughter."

Neither noticed the way Cord suddenly frowned, how the nerves in his jaw tensed.

"This calls for a real celebration," Hanisch proclaimed. Then he slapped Cord on the back. "Ah, was it not a good day when our leaders ordered Rudolf to court Drakar Mikhailonov's daughter? Never did they dream what it would ultimately mean—gold!"

Cord forced himself to appear enthused. Rudolf's news was an unexpected, and *important,* development.

Dammit, when it was first learned that Rudolf had been ordered by the subversives operating out of Zurich to court Drakar Mikhailonov's daughter, Cord had not really worried about him actually succeeding. After all, from what he'd been told about how she looked, she could have her pick of men. Still, his orders had been to keep an eye on things, and it had concerned him when he learned from Elenore that Marilee might be coming to Switzerland; he knew that could indicate the relationship was getting serious. And now, to hear of a suddenly planned kidnapping, well, he would have to get to his own headquarters soon and make a report.

He stood up to leave.

"Don't go," Hanisch protested. "Stay and drink to our good news!"

"I think I'll just leave the celebrating to you two till it's determined whether you can pull it off."

Hanisch threw back his head and laughed. "Well, maybe we'll just see that *you* get the assignment, Brandt, since you're so worried we can't succeed!"

"Fine. I'd like that very much." He hoped his enthusiasm did not show, because, oh, how he *did* want that assignment!

"He's going to see my sister," Rudolf cracked, merry with drink. "But once he sees my fiancée, how beautiful she is, he'll have an eye for her, I'll bet."

Cord continued on his way, thinking to himself, *I already do, you fool, but for a very different reason!*

Chapter Nine

"THIS is madness!"

Rudolf watched his sister as she sat, furiously ranting, on an old, battered, mold-covered trunk in the corner of the basement chamber where their grandmother had died. She was holding a tin cup, fingers clutching it tightly. Every so often she would raise it absently, nervously, to her lips, to sip the whiskey he had given her . . . only to shudder, and grimace. She was not used to drinking hard liquor, but he had insisted she take it, because she had become so upset when he had told her about the plan to abduct Jade Coltrane and hold her for ransom. He hoped the whiskey would get her mellow so he could reason with her, make her see what a good plan it was—an *important* plan. "No, Elenore," he said gently, standing over her, ready to pour more whiskey into her cup. "It's not madness. It's sheer genius, and I'm sure even Lenin himself has heard by now of my wonderful idea."

"Wonderful idea!" she scoffed. "It's mad! You are mad. We'll go to prison if we're caught! Kidnapping is a crime, you fool!"

"Don't call me a fool!" he warned, then turned away, cursing himself for having had to tell her. It had damn well not been *his* idea to do so, but Hanisch said she had a right to know what was going on, especially since Cord Brandt had been placed in charge of the actual abduction.

Elenore drunkenly whimpered, "I don't want Cordell to go to jail!" She liked to refer to him by his proper name because it seemed more possessive somehow, more like he was *hers.* "And he will if you're caught. We *all* will! The Coltranes are important people. Do you really think they'll just pay the ransom and forget about it? They'll track all of us down, hire however many people it takes to do it. I won't do it! I will not be a part of this insanity."

Rudolf, disgusted, pointed out, "You don't have to do anything, you stupid girl. Just keep your mouth shut when it happens. And who's to know *we* were involved? That's the beauty of the plan. We are not implicated in any way. It will all appear to be part of the Bolsheviks' hatred of the Romanovs. And . . ." he added in an ominous tone, "Cord will be very disappointed in you if you don't cooperate."

Slowly, she raised her head to look at him with fearful eyes.

"Yes, he'll be *very* disappointed, and angry, too," he repeated, seeing that he'd hit on his only weapon. "You, of all people, should know how dedicated he is to the cause, and if you don't help us—and help *him*—no doubt he'll decide you aren't his kind. After all, a man needs a woman who shares his ideals . . . believes in the same things he does."

She pondered that for a moment, then derisively

challenged, "Oh, is that so? Well, what about you, brother, dear? If you succeed in getting Marilee to marry you, I don't think you can expect her to share *your* ideals."

"Once she's my wife, she'll think like I tell her to think, and you know it."

Yes, Elenore knew Rudolf would expect that in a wife. Whether Marilee acquiesced remained to be seen.

"And we aren't talking about me," Rudolf reminded her. "We are talking about you and whether or not you will cooperate. You know," he continued, pointing an accusing finger, "this is one of the reasons I objected to your getting involved with the Zealots, because all you were ever interested in was finding a man. You think you've found one in Cord, but you just might get fooled when he finds out what a little coward you are."

He walked toward the door but then hesitated and turned slowly, tapping his finger to his chin thoughtfully, the play of a smile on his lips. "You know, of course, that if you betray us, if you do anything to jeopardize the plan, I can't guarantee your safety. The Zealots will want to rip your heart out, and I won't be able to do a thing to stop them.

"I wouldn't even try," he added, no longer suppressing his grin.

Elenore's lower lip began to tremble. "Damn you," she whispered. "Damn you to hell, Rudolf. You know I have to go along with what you want."

"I really don't see why you're so upset. No one is asking you to do anything except stay out of the way."

"All right, but not because I'm afraid of you, or *them*. I just don't want to lose Cord."

Rudolf was not about to say so, but he had doubts as to whether she even had Brandt to lose him. As far as he knew, no commitment had ever been made, and the enigmatic German never mentioned his sister around him.

"Just how soon will it happen after they get here?" she wanted to know.

"I'm not sure."

"Well," she asked impatiently, "what happens when it does?"

Rudolf was losing patience. "Oh, for heaven's sake! Stop asking so many questions. The less you know, the better."

But Elenore was not to be put off. "If I'm to be involved in something that could get me sent to prison, I'm going to know everything that's going on."

"Will you just stop worrying about it till the time comes?" Rudolf emitted a weary sigh, reached to open the thick iron door. "We've got several weeks to finalize the plans. Stop worrying."

"Have you told Mother?"

Another sigh. "Told her what? That one of our houseguests is going to be kidnapped by the Bolsheviks? No, you little fool. Ye gods, I wish I could have convinced them to keep you out of this. You're such a little nitwit."

"You're the nitwit around here if you think I'm that naive, Rudolf. I'm asking if you've told Mother that Marilee's aunt is a Romanov."

He shook his head. "No, and I'm not going to. We've got to keep the conversation away from that subject. She got so upset when I told her Marilee was coming that I don't dare mention anything that will really send her into a rage.''

"Is she going to be nice to them?''

"Of course. She can't afford not to, because she now thinks I'm so much in love with Marilee that if she doesn't accept her as my future wife, she'll alienate me forever." He winked. "I'm not like *you*, Elenore. *I* can think for myself.''

"Oh, really?'' She laughed derisively. "And what will happen when Marilee finds out her aunt has been kidnapped? Are you a good enough actor to pretend you had nothing to do with it?''

"That's the least of my worries,'' he retorted with a laugh of his own, "because if all goes according to plan, we'll be on our honeymoon when it happens, and she'll have no reason to think I had anything to do with it.''

"Honeymoon? She hasn't even said she'd marry you.''

"I have to leave now. I've wasted enough time with you.'' He took out his pocket watch, checked the time. "The train arrives in an hour. I have to pick up flowers, a few gifts. Make sure tea is ready when we get back, and make sure Mother is dressed—and *sober*.''

She started to call after him, knew it was no use.

Rudolf hurried on his way, down the narrow, dimly lit corridor with its damp, sour smell and dusty cobwebs draped everywhere. A rat scurried in the shadows. He paid no attention, lost in his thoughts.

Stupid, stupid Elenore!

Was she actually so ignorant as to think he would

be anywhere around when Jade Coltrane was abducted?

He smiled to himself in triumph. Marilee would be quite anxious to marry him—after he seduced her!

Oh, yes, he silently gloated, the prim and virginal Marilee Mikhailonov would race to the altar in an attempt to restore her virtue.

Of course, it would be a small, informal ceremony, what with the war and all. No one would question it. Afterward, they would leave on their wedding trip, and that very night the kidnapping would take place. By the time they returned, matters would be settled, and no one would ever suspect he had anything to do with it.

Back upstairs, he took one last look at the rooms that had been prepared.

Jade Coltrane's was on the first floor, conveniently near the door to the cellar. She would be told it was the nicest accommodation available due to the castle being refurbished, which activity, of course, had been temporarily stopped during their visit so as not to cause unnecessary noise and inconvenience.

Their rooms were nice, he mused proudly, thanks to the wife of one of the Zealots. She worked in a fine antiques shop and had arranged for the loan of splendid furniture.

Marilee would be in the suite near his, convenient for his planned seduction.

He went to his room to check his appearance, and was about to leave when his mother called out to him.

"I suppose you're going to meet them."

He took a deep breath, turned to look at her standing in the doorway of her eternally shadowed room.

"Yes, Mother. As I told you earlier, they arrive today, and we'll be back in time for tea this afternoon."

His gaze swept over her scornfully. She was still wearing her robe, a wretched, faded piece. "I thought you promised you would get dressed, let Elenore do your hair, air your room out, for God's sake . . ." His voice rose irritably.

"So help me, if I bring my fiancée back here to this . . ." His voice trailed off, and he waved his arms in a gesture of disgust.

He could tell she had been drinking again, and he thought once more how her weakness and inability to face life only served to reaffirm his belief in socialism. Like so many others, his mother had to have the status of imperialism, and when it was lost, her life no longer had meaning.

God help him if *he* should ever be so inferior.

Amalia swayed slightly as she whined, "There are strangers in and out of my home all day. Who are they? They won't talk to me when I ask them."

He smiled. "What strangers, Mother? The new maid? The new cook? The new butler? I've told you, but your memory isn't so good these days. They're friends of mine, doing me a favor so we can make a good impression on Marilee and her aunt, and you aren't to bother them. They have their orders. They know what they're to do. Just stay out of their way."

She lifted her chin indignantly. "It doesn't seem right. You even ran Vincent off."

Because he was big and could prove formidable, Rudolf grimly reflected.

Breezily, he said, "Oh, Vincent was ready to move

on to another job. And you have Ulda,'' he reminded her. Ulda had been Ilsa's housekeeper, and she was old and harmless.

He crossed to give his mother a patronizing kiss on her cheek, not wanting her riled today of all days. "Now remember what I told you, Mother. I love Marilee, and I want to marry her. I'm depending on you to help me make a good impression.''

Amalia bit back the resentment and anger that were like raw bile burning in her throat, but could not resist the usual harsh reminder. "You promised your music would always come first. You take a wife, you can forget your dream . . . and mine.''

"Mother, Mother, Mother! How many times do I have to tell you? Marilee will complement my career. With *two* good women behind me—my wife *and* my mother—how can I fail?''

He hurried on his way, and Amalia grudgingly stared after him. She had already made up her mind she did not like this husband-hungry girl who was chasing her son, but she had no intention of losing Rudolf's love, alienating him for all time. If Marilee Mikhailonov was what he wanted, then she would have to accept it, like it or not.

She turned and went back into her room to pour herself another cup of vodka, which could help to ease the frustrations that seemed to consume her every waking hour these days.

Chapter Ten

RUDOLF took one last polishing swipe with his handkerchief across the gleaming red hood of the Fiat Zero. With a white top, lots of brass trim, and red spoke wheels, he decided it was impressive enough. No matter that it was probably stolen and also nearly three years old. He had neither asked questions nor criticized when Hanisch Lutzstein and the others had so proudly presented him with the Italian roadster. It was expected that he meet his guests at the train station in, supposedly, his own automobile. But he could not help wondering if his comrades would have gone to so much trouble if only Marilee were expected.

He picked up the two bouquets of flowers lying on the black leather front seat. Red roses for Marilee, white for Frau Coltrane, provided by one of the Zealots who worked in a floral shop. There was also an expensive bottle of French perfume and a dainty gold bracelet—deftly shoplifted by Hanish's wife, Gerda.

"The train from Zug just pulled in," Hanisch called as he came down the marble steps of the hauptbahnhof—the Central Station. Dressed in a red-and-

81

gold chauffeur's uniform, he looked quite professional. "I'll wait at the baggage area for you to bring them to claim their trunks."

Rudolf spotted a conductor helping Jade down to the platform. Marilee was behind her. He waved, called to them, hurriedly pushed his way through the crowd.

Marilee, stunning in a gold velvet traveling suit trimmed in mink, greeted him with a cordial smile. She lifted her cheek for his kiss, reached to accept his offered bouquet.

He caressed her fingertips, his gaze adoring, devouring, as he fervently murmured in recitation, " 'If love where what the rose is . . . and I were like the leaf . . . our lives would grow together . . . in sad or singing weather . . .' "

Marilee's smile remained fixed. "You've been reading Swinburne, Rudolf. That was lovely, thank you."

Jade looked on approvingly, reaffirming her opinion that Rudolf was the epitome of good breeding, background, class. Her eyes met Marilee's, and she could not help giving a nod of consent.

Rudolf presented the white roses to Jade, then began to lead the way back toward the terminal building.

Jade held up a hand. "We have to wait for Carasia and Manuel. They were traveling in a coach car."

Rudolf felt a sudden stab of foreboding. "Carasia and Manuel?" he echoed. "Who—"

"Oh, I'm sorry. Didn't Marilee tell you? Carasia is my maid. She goes everywhere with me. And Colt insisted a bodyguard come along."

Rudolf felt the nerves in his jaw tighten. No, Marilee had not told him, he thought angrily. A maid and a bodyguard were the last things he needed around.

Jade noticed the strange way he was reacting and gently asked, "Is there a problem?"

Trying not to let his frustration show, he replied, "Yes, I'm afraid there is. You see, the castle is being refurbished, and while I've managed to have rooms ready for the two of you, I just don't have anywhere comfortable for your servants. Can they stay at a hotel for a few days?"

"I suppose," she said uncertainly, quick to add, "I'm sorry, really. We should have made it understood we weren't traveling alone."

Just then Carasia and Manuel approached.

"I'm really embarrassed by this." Rudolf displayed his most innocent expression. But if we bring in two more people, I'm afraid my mother will be upset, and she hasn't been feeling too well."

"Oh, it's all right, really," Jade assured him, then turned to Manuel and Carasia to explain the situation. She took money from her bag, gave it to them for their hotel and meals, and said she would be in touch.

Rudolf was thinking that he could put them in the old servants' quarters above the garage, where they would be out of the way, but the truth was, he needed a few days to make arrangements. Also, he would need to let the Zealots know of unexpected strangers being present.

Anxious to be on the way, he steered the women toward the luggage claim area, asking how they enjoyed their trip.

"It was wonderful, just wonderful," Marilee exulted. "We had time in Zug to get off the train and take a taxi to the Fischmarkt for dinner last night, and the Bernese Alps seemed to be glowing in the moonlight."

Rudolf laughed. "You are glowing, my darling, as always. I've never seen you look so happy." He leaned to give her an intimate wink. "I hope it's because you're so glad to see me."

"Well, of course I'm glad to see you, Rudolf," she assured him, then, not to falsely encourage him, was quick to add, "And I'm glad to see Switzerland again and looking forward to seeing Elenore. How is she, by the way?"

He was momentarily taken aback by how she'd steered the conversation away from a personal note. It was not like Marilee to be so talkative, anyway. Usually, she nodded, shook her head, or murmured, seldom taking the initiative, but he'd first noticed the change at the wedding. He was not sure he liked it. "She's fine," he said crisply, "and looking forward to seeing you, too."

They reached the baggage claim area, and when Marilee and Jade pointed to only one wardrobe trunk apiece, Rudolf frowned. He knew how women traveled, and these two were not planning to stay very long if they had packed so lightly. Mustering a cheery tone, he said, "I can see I'm going to have to introduce you ladies to the wonderful shops of Zurich, because it looks like you haven't brought enough clothes for all I've planned for you."

Jade said, "I can't speak for Marilee, but I've brought enough clothes for my stay. I'll be wanting to get back in case there's word from Travis or Colt, and I don't like leaving Kit and the grandchildren all alone, either."

Rudolf was barely able to mask his annoyance as he lightly warned, "I'm just going to have to make sure you have such a wonderful time, Princess, that I can change your mind. The snows will come soon, and then you'll see what a wonderland Switzerland really is."

"She's seen Switzerland in the winter, Rudolf," Marilee interjected, noticing his irritation. "Besides, neither of us can stay very long, so let's not ruin our trip by arguing about it, all right?"

Rudolf really did have to bite his tongue then to hold back an angry retort, because he did not like Marilee's arrogance. Soon enough, she would learn who was in control.

"And please," Jade said, gently touching his arm, "don't call me princess where others might hear." She smiled to let him know she was not angry.

He nodded to her, then signaled to Hanisch, who had been standing to one side and took care of the trunks.

"If you aren't planning to be here very long, what do you propose to do with yourself when you leave?" Rudolf asked Marilee.

"I haven't decided," she replied absently, glancing about with interest as they left the station. Northwest was the beautifully flowing Sihl canal, a greenish-blue ribbon snaking its way through the city. She could also see the Platzpromenande, the public garden on the triangular spit of land between the Sihl and its tributary, the Limmat, and, beyond, the outline of the city's large industrial zone.

Things were not going as Rudolf had hoped. Finding out from the first moment that their stay was not to be indefinite had taken the glow off the day. Dully, he handed Marilee her satin-wrapped gift of the gold bracelet. "This was to welcome you. It might as well be a good-bye gift given the duration of your stay."

She sighed, exasperated. Jade probably regarded his behavior as that of a disappointed paramour, but Marilee had come to know it for what it was—pouting when something did not go his way.

"Rudolf, I appreciate all this," Marilee said. "The flowers, the gift, but I didn't promise to spend the entire winter with you. Can't we just enjoy ourselves the time I am here, and not let the visit be ruined because we aren't able to stay as long as you'd like us to?"

"Of course we can," he said tightly, his smile forced. "Forgive a man who merely loves you, my dear."

Rudolf checked the time. He wanted to postpone their meeting his mother. "We can take the scenic way if you aren't tired," he suggested.

"Actually, I am," Jade admitted. "We can sightsee another time, if that's all right."

"Elenore told me all about the delicious teas your mother has," Marilee said. "I'm looking forward to it this afternoon—and meeting her, too."

Rudolf nodded to Hanisch and murmured they should take a direct route home.

Marilee knew that the concept of "castles" covered a wide range in Switzerland and France. The German *Schloss*, like the French château, could be either a medieval castle, a Renaissance palace, or even

a large country house. When Rudolf's home came
into view, she termed it the latter. Regal, three stories
tall, of neat, square-cut stone, it was, she decided at
once, delightful. A wrought-iron fence surrounded the
property, which, being not too far from the city
proper, probably consisted of an acre or so.

It was impressive, but not opulent, and Marilee
thought how it could be made into a warm, cozy
place. Now, however, it somehow appeared austere,
cold . . . and neglected.

Hanisch turned into a side gate, drove on across a
brick courtyard to stop at the back doors.

"Here we are!" Rudolf announced proudly, opening the car door and bounding out to help them alight.

Just then Elenore came out onto the portico and
called a greeting. "So wonderful to see my future
sister-in-law!"

Marilee winced.

Jade laughed.

Rudolf wanted to strangle her.

The two girls embraced, happy to be reunited; then
Rudolf introduced Jade.

Elenore curtsied. "We are so honored to have a
Russian princess grace our home."

Rudolf shot her an angry look. It would take only
one slip like that around their mother and all hell
would break loose. "I told you she doesn't like to be
called a princess."

He spoke so sharply that both Jade and Marilee
stared at him.

"You asked me at the station not to address you as
a princess, remember?" Rudolf quickly said.

"But there's no need to be upset with your sister,"

Jade said, seeing Elenore's discomfort. "How is she supposed to know that I don't consider myself royalty anymore, since I've been away from court so long?

"But the main reason," she confided to Elenore, putting her arm around her shoulder in a gesture of friendship, "is that it's necessary to be cautious these days about who knows I'm a Romanov. You never know who might be listening. I'm afraid my Russian family is not too popular with certain people right now."

Maybe not popular, Rudolf thought wickedly, but certainly *valuable!*

They went on inside, and though the rear hallway was dark, Marilee could appreciate the architecture and asked how old the castle was.

"Maybe a couple of hundred years," Rudolf told her nonchalantly. "I don't know how long it's belonged to my father's side of the family."

He motioned them to follow as he led the way. "As I told you earlier, we're in the process of refurbishing. My grandmother had let the place run down, and it will take a while to get things as we want them, but eventually we will."

Pausing to slip a possessive arm around Marilee's waist, he whispered intimately, "I'll be happy to have suggestions from the lady I hope will be mistress of my castle one day soon."

Marilee stiffened, made no comment.

"Well?" Rudolf prodded anxiously, seeking some sign of enthusiasm . . . or affection.

She could only murmur, "You have a lovely home, Rudolf."

"That's not what I'm talking about, and you know it."

"And I've asked you," she reminded him, "to give me time."

He drew a ragged breath of exasperation and dropped his arm from around her.

Elenore took Jade to her quarters, and Rudolf led Marilee up to the second floor.

They walked in silence, and when Rudolf opened her door for her, he stepped back and said quietly, "If you don't find everything you need, there's a bell cord by the door, and a maid will assist you. When you've finished freshening up, I'll be in the parlor on the main floor."

He turned to go, but Marilee suddenly reached out to touch his arm. "Wait, please." She felt compelled to explain. "I'm sorry if I disappoint you, Rudolf, but please understand that I won't be rushed into anything. Maybe I was wrong to even come here."

"No, you weren't," he quickly assured her, his gaze once more devouring as he reached out with firm fingers to clutch her shoulders and give her a gentle shake. She had brought up the subject, so he decided to take advantage of it, since he felt there was no time to waste. "Listen to me. You know I love you. And I swear I'm going to make you love me. If only you knew how I've counted the minutes till I could hold you in my arms . . . for this . . ."

His lips pressed down on hers hungrily, possessively, as he drew her almost roughly against him, his hands moving up and down her back.

She felt nothing but pretended to respond so as not to hurt his feelings—again.

And Rudolf could tell.

He tensed with anger. Dammit, he knew it was not his fault. He had enough experience to know women found him desirable. He had yet to bed a woman who had not seemed adequately satisfied afterward. He suspected Marilee was just one of those women he'd heard the famous Sigmund Freud lecture about— women who had mental problems that kept them from responding. Accordingly, seduction would be difficult, if not impossible, unless, of course, she were drugged, and he could certainly take care of that little detail.

He released her to save her further embarrassment. With a tender touch, he brushed back a wisp of hair that had fallen onto her cheek. Her "bob" was starting to grow out, and he was glad. He much preferred long, flowing tresses.

"I'll see you downstairs, my love," he said, and left. He was anxious to find Hanisch and discuss the possibility of moving faster than originally planned. Too many things could go wrong—Elenore's nervousness might cause her to make a slip at the wrong time, his mother's drinking could cause tense situations, but most of all, he was worried that Marilee and Jade would leave too soon for the Zealots to carry out their plan.

Marilee stared after him and knew that as long as she felt no emotion, she would never marry him, or any man. If it meant having to endure the humiliation of pretense when kissed or caressed, then, by God, she would live her life void of love.

And let the wine turn to vinegar!

Chapter Eleven

RUDOLF hurried to the kitchen, where Gerda, Hanisch's wife, was busy preparing to serve tea. "Where's Hanisch?" Rudolf asked.

She nodded to the door leading to the courtyard. "Getting ready to leave. He said to tell you he was taking the car—urgent business."

"What kind of business?" he demanded.

"I'm not sure. There was a telephone call for him. A voice I didn't recognize. When he rang off, he said to tell you he was leaving. I don't know anything else."

Rudolf dashed for the door, flung it open in time to see Hanisch turning the Fiat around. Waving frantically, he called out for him to wait as he ran toward him. Hanisch frowned but stopped the automobile. "I have no time to talk just now," he said when Rudolf reached him. "I've been summoned to headquarters. Don't ask me why. I wasn't told anything except to get there as soon as possible. You go back to your guests. We'll talk later."

He started to ease away, but Rudolf slammed his hands down on the car door. "While you're there, you better let it be known we may have to act sooner than we'd planned, with very little notice. They're not staying as long as I thought.

"Another thing—a bodyguard came with them. And a maid. I've stalled bringing them here, saying due to refurbishing, accommodations weren't available. I persuaded the princess to send them to a hotel for a few days."

"Princess!" Hanisch sneered, then said, "I'm glad you caught up with me. We needed to know all this. I'll talk with you as soon as I get back. But don't worry about the bodyguard. He'll come in handy to deliver the ransom note to the Coltrane family."

Rudolf returned to the kitchen and told Gerda the news.

"The sooner the better as far as I'm concerned," she said. "Hanisch wants us to move to Russia as soon as the Bolsheviks take power, which everyone says won't be long the way Kerensky is crumbling. I've things to do to get ready, and I don't need to be spending my time preparing tea," she added with a disgusted sniff.

Rudolf could not care less about her inconvenience. "How is my mother?"

"Your mother!" She gave him an angry look. "Your mother can be quite unpleasant, comrade. Elenore and I had difficulty getting her out of that frowsy robe and into a decent dress. She wouldn't let us wash her hair, but she did let Elenore braid it. Then she got angry because she said she couldn't find her 'tonic.' Of course, she was talking about her vodka, which I found and hid. We heard her tearing around in her room for nearly an hour, and then she got quiet.''

''And?'' he flared, annoyed. ''What happened then? Have you been up to see her? Is she ready to join us for tea?''

Gerda lost her patience. She found Rudolf arrogant and unappreciative. She wiped her hands on her apron and looked at him with cold, angry eyes. ''You listen to me,'' she said evenly, ''and get down off your high horse. You seem to forget I'm not really your hired help, that I'm only doing this to help the cause—not you. And having to bow and scrape and play nurse-maid to your sot of a mother was not part of what I agreed to do. If you don't like the way things are being done, go and do them yourself!''

Rudolf reeled with fury but was determined not to lower himself to argue with her. Hanisch, however, would hear about his insolent wife, and the task of chastising her would fall on him.

He turned on his heel and strode out of the kitchen, was about to go see about his mother when he heard Marilee and Jade coming down the stairs. Quickly, he returned to tell Gerda, ''Find Elenore. Tell her to go see about my mother!''

Pasting on an amiable smile and assuming his most genial air, he met his guests and escorted them to the parlor. He was relieved that they seemed properly impressed with the borrowed furniture. Jade marveled over a Vienna porcelain mantel clock, and he knew he'd have to keep an eye on that, lest his mother sell it. He'd asked Hanisch and the others not to bring in small decorator pieces for that very reason, but they'd felt it necessary for effect.

"Your rooms are comfortable, I hope?" he asked.

"Lovely," Jade said, and Marilee agreed.

Gerda came in, carrying a silver tea service Rudolf had never seen before. She set it on the table in front of the divan, then hurried out to return with a tray of delectable-looking Swiss treats. Along with rosebud cake squares, there was a plate of *Basler Leckerli*, a kind of gingerbread; *Zuger Kirschtorte*, cream-filled meringues; and *rissoles*, pear tarts.

"Fräulein Elenore tells me your mother fell asleep," Gerda carefully said, "and she's had to awaken her and get her ready to come down for tea. She sends her apologies to your guests for being late."

Rudolf winced, sucked in his breath between clenched teeth. There was no mistaking the hidden message: his mother had no doubt found her "tonic" and fallen asleep after taking a few nips. All he could hope for was that she'd napped long enough for most of the effects to wear off.

Looking directly at Gerda, who was waiting for his reaction, he instructed, "Tell my sister that if Mother isn't feeling well, she should just let her rest." He then turned to Jade and Marilee. "I'm sorry. I'm afraid she hasn't been herself since my stepfather died."

"You're very close to your mother, aren't you?" Jade asked.

"Oh, yes, very!" Holding up his hands, he wriggled his fingers. "These are the reason she was willing to leave the home she loved. She was afraid I'd be called to fight and my hands might be injured. She lives to see me achieve greatness as a pianist. She was willing to give up family, friends, anything.

"I just hope I can live up to her expectations," he added with an exaggerated laugh of humility.

Jade smiled. "I'm sure you've nothing to worry about. Marilee has told me how wonderfully you play. But tell me," she suddenly urged, "how does she feel about your interest in Marilee? Does she worry you might be putting your career aside for her?"

Marilee promptly cried, "Aunt Jade, I don't think that's something we should discuss!"

"Oh, you're too sensitive!" Jade laughed. "Rudolf has serious intentions, and we both know it, or he wouldn't have invited you here. And you've got some feelings of your own, or you wouldn't have come. So why pretend otherwise?"

Marilee felt her cheeks grow warm. She did not want to make a scene but could not help resenting that her aunt would broach such a personal subject. "Can we talk about this another time?" she curtly suggested.

"If it bothers you, I'm sorry." Jade looked at her thoughtfully. "I meant no harm."

Rudolf felt the tension and quickly said, "Oh, there's no need for you to apologize, Jade." Then he turned to Marilee. "Because she's right, you know. You *are* too sensitive. Haven't you told her I proposed to you a long time ago?"

Jade looked from Rudolf to Marilee, eyes wide with pretended surprise. "No. As a matter of fact, she hasn't." She was not about to let on that Colt had recounted his conversation with Rudolf, but had wanted Marilee to give her the news herself.

Rudolf shrugged to indicate he was not surprised. "She hasn't given me an answer. I don't think she realizes just yet that she loves me, but she does." He turned to Marilee, hoping he conjured a look of absolute love and devotion. "Because," he went on, making his voice soft, tender, "when you love someone as much as I love her, they just have to love you back."

"Rudolf, please!" Marilee shifted uncomfortably.

Jade thought she was just pretending to be embarrassed and teased, "I'm afraid your coquettishness is only making this young man miserable, dear."

Rudolf readily played along. "Terribly! The truth is, she's driving me mad, and I think she knows it."

They both laughed, which only served to infuriate Marilee, and suddenly she took them both by surprise by doing something she'd never been known to do— she lost her temper. "Just stop it, both of you!" She set her teacup down with a clatter, cinnamon eyes sparkling. "Stop talking about me as if I'm not even here, for heaven's sake.

"Rudolf!" She turned on him furiously. "How many times do I have to tell you that you're rushing me? I've been here only a few hours and you're badgering me, and if it keeps up, I swear I'll leave."

Rudolf ground his teeth together, and it was only with a great effort that he was able to bite back his own fury. Oh, one day she was going to pay for being such an arrogant little bitch, making him look like a lovesick fool.

She then whirled on Jade. "And please, Aunt Jade, I must respectfully remind you that some things are personal!"

She stood, heart pounding. Moving around the coffee table, she headed for the door, calling over her shoulder, "Excuse me, but I'm tired. I think I'll rest till dinner."

When she had gone, Jade shook her head and mused aloud. "I guess I can't blame her. We've both been pressuring her, haven't we?"

Rudolf did not immediately respond. He was giving his furiously pounding blood pressure time to slow down, lest his anger show. Finally, he was able to take a deep breath, a sip of tea, paste a doleful smile on his lips, and effectively offer a forlorn sigh. "I can't help it. If I'm guilty of badgering her, so be it. I'm merely a man, completely, helplessly, hopelessly in love."

Jade covered his hand with hers. "I know you are, but maybe Marilee is just more worried about her father than we realize. Maybe now isn't the right time for her to be thinking about marriage."

Rudolf could tell she was on his side, and he was about to confide his appreciation when suddenly there were sounds from the hallway, and they turned expectantly. He felt a momentary flash of hope that Marilee was returning, embarrassed over her outburst and wanting to smooth things over.

That hope, however, quickly gave way to despair, then melted into sheer panic as his mother appeared.

And she was reeling.

Elenore, holding onto her arm, looked at Rudolf fearfully in a silent plea for him to understand she had tried to keep her from joining them but lost the battle.

Seeing Jade, Amalia stiffened with embarrassment and shrugged off Elenore's hand with an indignant cry. "Stop treating me like an old lady, for heaven's sake!'' With head held high, she walked right over to Jade, extended her hand, and introduced herself. ''Welcome to my home.''

Jade warmly responded, ''Thank you. It's nice of you to have invited us here. I apologize for my niece not being here, but she was tired from our trip and went to lie down. She's looking forward to meeting you at dinner.''

''That's nice,'' Amalia murmured absently, not really caring. She sat down in the seat Marilee had vacated, waved away Elenore's offer to pour tea, and, pointedly ignoring Rudolf's angry stare, brusquely demanded, ''Tell me, what does your family think of my son courting your niece?''

Rudolf moaned under his breath, exchanged an anxious look with Elenore, signaling with his eyes to get their mother out of there.

Elenore shrugged helplessly. There was nothing she could do.

Before Jade had a chance to respond to such candor, he quickly admonished, ''Mother, your question is a bit premature, don't you think? Now, have some tea—''

''I hate tea, and you know it!'' Amalia snapped, then, seeing the assortment of goodies on the table, wanted to know, ''Did that new cook you hired make those? I must say Ulda never was much when it came to pastries, but then I didn't hire her. She came with the castle.''

She gave Jade a probing look. ''Where do you live? Spain, I think Rudolf told me. He sneaked away to go to that fancy wedding, you know.'' She paused to glare at him and wagged a finger as though he were a naughty child. "Worried me to death, he did."

Elenore rolled her eyes.

Rudolf, however, saw the way his mother swayed ever so slightly as she reached for a tart; he knew she was not just tipsy—she was very, very intoxicated—and a potentially disastrous situation was at hand. But he also took note of Jade's expression—compassion for his mother, embarrassment for him. Quickly he decided there was no more need for pretense; sympathy could be very useful.

He stood, clasped his mother's shoulders, and solicitously declared, "You're in no condition to socialize with our guest, Mother. I'm taking you to your room, and Elenore will stay with you till dinner to make sure you get your rest—and no more tonic!" he added meaningfully to Elenore, then shook his head pathetically in Jade's direction, sending her a silent plea for understanding.

Jade reacted as he'd hoped, giving him a concerned nod to excuse himself, do whatever needed to be done. She understood.

Amalia protested as he pulled her to her feet. "What is wrong with you? I'm fine. I—" The tart fell from her hand, making a gooey mess on the expensive, and borrowed, Veramin rug.

She screeched, "Now look what you made me do!"

"We'll clean it up. Come along, Mother. You're very tired." He half carried her, half dragged her from the room, Elenore following.

When he returned to the parlor, Jade was not there.

He cursed, began to pace furiously, till he suddenly

realized all of his problems were actually working to his advantage. He calmed then, smiling to himself to think that Jade would tell Marilee his mother was an alcoholic; they would both feel sorry for him. Perhaps Marilee would be a bit more tender.

Just then he heard the sound of Hanisch returning, and he rushed out into the courtyard to meet him. Hanisch drove the Fiat all the way into the garage, and Rudolf followed.

"It's good that we need to move faster than planned," Hanisch said.

"I don't understand," Rudolf said.

"That's why I was called to headquarters—because we have to move fast in all directions."

Rudolf felt a shiver of excitement.

Reaffirming what they had finally been able to learn—that the destination for the Czar and his family had been Tobolsk—Hanisch confided that agents were already hard at work attempting to infiltrate the guards there to gain information.

"But things are starting to explode," Hanisch explained. "Kerensky and the PG are crumbling. The word is—Lenin is ready to make his next move.

"Comrade . . ." He paused to flash a grin that seemed to split his rugged face wide open with its ebullience. "The revolution we've been waiting for is right around the corner. I'm heading for Russia, because I want to be a part of it."

Fearfully, because he did not want to be involved in actual combat, Rudolf asked, "What, then, are my orders?"

"The abduction will take place as soon as you decide the time is right. Agents are waiting for word from you. Cord Brandt will be in charge after I leave.''

"When is that?"

"I'm not sure, but soon!" He pounded his chest in triumph. "No more dreams and fantasies about what might happen! I will be there to help make it happen!"

"Then Brandt will take care of the ransom for our Romanov princess," Rudolf mused out loud.

"Right. He has his orders and knows what is to be done."

Rudolf felt annoyed. The abduction and ransom had been *his* idea, and now it appeared he was being pushed aside. With barely contained bitterness, he asked, "After it's over, what will the Zealots and Bolsheviks want from me then?"

"Your orders are to proceed to marry Marilee Mikhailonov as quickly as possible to keep her here. Let nothing stand in your way. She cannot leave Switzerland."

Rudolf's laugh was mocking. "That's easier said than done, Hanisch. It may come as a shock to you and everyone else, but the young lady is not willing to marry me for the moment. I have a plan, however, and—"

"Make it work, dammit!" Hanisch growled, grabbing the front of his shirt and giving him a shake. His eyes were stormy, narrowed, as he hoarsely whispered, "You haven't heard the rest of why I was summoned! Word has just come that Drakar Mikhailonov has escaped with a large portion of the Czar's personal wealth. It was smuggled to him by a cousin of the Czar, a woman, said to be in love with him. She was captured but refused to tell where he was going, but we do know the money was to be used to try and buy freedom for the Imperial family.''

He released Rudolf, who instinctively stepped back out of his reach.

"Mikhailonov, we have been told by one of our informants, was seen on the Imperial train at Pskov, where the Czar signed the formal papers of abdication. He was *not* on that train when it left for Mogilev. He has not been seen since, but it stands to reason that sooner or later he will get in touch with his daughter. That's why you will marry her and keep her where she will be under surveillance. When Mikhailonov contacts her, our people will be ready to grab him—and the gold.''

Suddenly a voice came from the shadows: "A very good plan . . . if it works."

Hanisch drew a knife from his boot so fast Rudolf did not see the lightning-quick movement, only the glint of steel as he turned in the direction of the intruder.

Cord Brandt stepped into the light. "You should make sure you're alone before you start telling secrets, comrade.''

Hanisch bristled but laughed nervously to cover up his error. Brandt was right. "I thought we were alone. What business have you here, anyway?" He returned the knife to its hiding place with an equally swift motion.

"I came to look the place over, make sure I know my way around when the time comes so I won't stumble in the dark.''

To Rudolf, he said, "I'll need a diagram of the castle."

"I have one ready for you," Rudolf informed him.

"Good. It's nearly dark. I'm going inside to look around."

When he was gone, Rudolf felt compelled to admit, "There are times he makes me uncomfortable."

"Why? Because he's German?" Hanisch ridiculed. "Contrary to what they want the world to believe, the Germans are on the Bolsheviks' side, Rudolf. They know revolution and the overthrow of Kerensky and the PG are the fastest roads to peace with Russia. Maybe Brandt *is* a German agent. I've thought of the possibility, and if he is, so what? He's on our side, he saved my life. Don't worry about it. You've got more important things to do—like getting married!"

Hanisch was right. He did have important things to do . . . and tonight might be the time to start.

Chapter Twelve

RUDOLF knocked hesitantly, afraid of what terrible situation might wait on the other side of the door.

Almost at once, it opened. Elenore, looking extremely harried and agitated, motioned impatiently for him to enter.

"How is she?" He was relieved to see his mother lying quite still, her eyes closed. "Is she asleep—or drunk?" he scornfully inquired.

Elenore irritably countered, "What difference does it make? I'm not going to try and get her up for dinner. You can say she's sick . . . whatever. I don't care." She walked over to the faded velvet chaise and threw herself on it. Drawing her knees up to her chin, she folded her arms about her legs and stared solemnly at nothing in particular.

"Well, what the hell is wrong with you?"

She gave her long dark hair a toss, met the challenge of her brother's angry stare. "How long is this going to continue? I've got my own life to live, you know. I'm sick of having to play nursemaid to her. I had no idea she was drinking so much."

The fury left him for the moment. He lowered himself into a chair next to the chaise. "We were too busy to notice how bad she was getting. No doubt it's been going on for a long time. I fired Ulda, by the way."

Elenore was surprised. "Why? Mother will have a fit, you know. Ulda is intimidated by her tantrums, waits on her hand and foot. No other servant has ever taken so much off her. She likes that."

"Ulda has been smuggling in her vodka for her."

"How did you find that out?"

"I pretended I already knew, told her Mother had said it was her. She started crying and admitted it, said she needed the extra money she got to do it. We'll just tell Mother she quit."

Elenore gestured toward Amalia. "Just what do you intend to do about her drinking? She'll find a way to get it herself. This is a fine time to discover she's an alcoholic," she added with a sigh of disgust.

He explained how it was actually working to his advantage.

She listened, shaking her head. "I'll just be glad when it's over. I've done nothing but tend to her all day. When am I supposed to have time to be with Cordell?"

Rudolf had toyed with the idea of not telling her Brandt was on the premises, afraid she'd create an awkward situation that might raise questions. Then he decided it was best to let her know, lest she see him and react the wrong way due to surprise.

"You may see him tonight, here. Don't act like a fool if you do."

At once she swung her legs around, sat up to face him, but he waved her to silence before she could start arguing. "He is here to observe, to find his way around the castle, in preparation for the abduction. He may have already left for all I know, but he said he wanted to go over every inch of the castle just to be safe, so if you run into him, don't make a fool of yourself. Besides," he finished, "you've got work to do."

She clenched her fists, gritted her teeth. There had been men in her life before, but never one who drove her mad with passion like Cord Brandt. Being in his arms, tasting his kisses, was an experience nonpareil to any other. Thinking about his lovemaking made her want him fiercely, and the realization he was somewhere close only made it worse.

Rudolf suspected she was dying to jump up that very minute to go look for Brandt. "Listen to me, Elenore," he said tightly. "Things are happening faster than we thought. There's a lot going on, and I can't have you getting in the way. Just do as you're told, because the abduction is going to take place very soon. We've received word the PG will fall any day, and Hanisch and the others want to leave for Russia to help the Bolsheviks take power. We have to hurry and take care of things here."

Elenore had known that Cord might be leaving. She sensed he would not want to take her with him, and she really did not want to go, anyway. After all, while she pretended to believe in the Zealots' philosophies, the truth was she enjoyed the comforts of the well-to-do, comforts the Zealots found so abhorrent. But as long as Cord was around, she wanted to be with him as much as possible.

"So just remember he won't like it if you mess things up," Rudolf reminded her.

She knew that was true. With a defeated sigh, she conceded, "What is it you want me to do?"

Rudolf glanced at Amalia. She was out, but he could take no chances of her waking up and stumbling downstairs in the middle of dinner and causing another scene. "We'll just lock her in here. Her room is far enough away from Marilee's that she won't be heard if she starts yelling."

"What about Marilee? How can you have her aunt spirited away if she hasn't agreed to marry you?"

"Let me worry about that. You just go get ready for dinner."

"What will happen if you leave Zurich?" She certainly had no intention of taking care of their mother the rest of her life.

Matter-of-factly, he declared, "We'll put her in a sanitarium. That will be best for everyone." He got up to leave, then paused. "By the way, I don't want you lingering after dinner. Just say you're worried about Mother and go check on her and then don't come back. Maybe our Romanov princess will take a hint I want to be alone with her niece and retire early. Since we're going to have to move faster than planned, I've got to have some time for seduction, don't I?"

Elenore's expression was piteous. "I'm afraid that's a part of your plan you'd better be prepared to see fail, dear brother. Frankly, I think the only reason she agreed to this visit was because she doesn't have anything else to do for the moment, not because she's in love with you."

Harshly, hotly, he informed her, "It doesn't matter

whether she loves me or not. She's going to marry me—and soon. Who knows?'' He gave a wicked wink. ''By tomorrow morning, she may be begging me to marry her.''

Elenore did not have to figure out what he meant. ''It won't work, Rudolf. She's not the type. Marilee is too shy to be seduced. She'll run like a scared rabbit.''

He threw back his head and laughed jeeringly. ''Do you really think I would be sporting enough to give her a chance to run?'' He headed on out, then flippantly called from the doorway, ''Just make yourself scarce after dinner, little sister, and leave the hunting to the fox!''

He stopped by the kitchen to make sure Gerda had prepared the special after-dinner cordials for his guests—*Zwetsch*, a plum brandy.

And it was to be a very special brandy, indeed.

Jade's drink would contain a drug made from the snakeroot plant, which would make her sleepy.

Marilee's cordial would have a smaller dose, just enough to make her weak . . . and vulnerable.

And later—Rudolf smiled to himself—she would also sleep . . . but in his arms.

The shabbiness of the dining room was camouflaged by the use of mellow candlelight. Rudolf had Gerda inform Marilee and Jade that his mother would not be at dinner, and when they came down to the dining room, they both expressed concern.

Jade said they had no idea Amalia was so ill. ''Perhaps we should make arrangements to leave, Rudolf. We don't wish to impose,'' she offered.

"I was afraid you'd feel that way," he murmured, eyes doleful. "That's why I hoped I could keep her problem hidden."

Elenore breezed into the room. "She's asleep," she said to no one in particular and sat down.

Marilee could not resist asking, "Just what kind of problem are you talking about, Rudolf?"

He hesitated for effect, then, with a practiced look of humiliation, whispered, "Drinking."

Jade and Marilee exchanged sympathetic glances, and Marilee said, "I'm so sorry, Rudolf. I had no idea, really."

"Of course you didn't," Elenore cut in, wanting to be a part of her brother's sham. "Few people do. We hope you will be tolerant and understand it's a sickness."

Rudolf concluded, "Yes, that's what it is, but please, let's not discuss it now, and no more talk about your leaving!" He wagged his finger teasingly at Marilee, who was seated on his right. "Haven't you realized by now you're my prisoner . . . of love?"

They all laughed, though Marilee's was forced. She felt more and more uncomfortable around Rudolf, because she had about reached the conclusion they could never be more than friends and knew he would settle for nothing less than marriage.

"Don't you agree, my dear?"

She looked up sharply. She had been so lost in the desolation of her musings that she had not heard a word he said.

He frowned, wondering what was on her mind that was so distracting. "I said tomorrow is a good day to go sight-seeing in Zurich. You should be rested from your trip by then.''

"Yes, I suppose so," she responded vaguely, as though she could not care less.

With a curt nod, he signaled Elenore to ring the little silver bell beside her plate that would alert Gerda they were ready for the first course to be served. He wanted to get on with the meal, get to the plum brandy—and the ensuing effects.

Though Gerda struggled to conceal her dislike for her assigned task, she was an accomplished cook, and Jade and Marilee were impressed by the sumptuous meal. Rudolf was counting the minutes till the cordials. But when Gerda finally set the little crystal glasses of brandy in front of Jade and Marilee, he felt a sinking sensation as Jade declared, "Oh, no, nothing more for me, please," and Marilee also declined.

Nevertheless, he succeeded in keeping his voice less than hysterical as he urged, "But it's a custom in our family to serve our guests this special brandy the first night. If you refuse, Elenore and I will both be disappointed.''

Elenore's eyes widened, for she knew he was lying and quickly figured out why.

Good-naturedly, Jade shrugged and said, "Oh, very well, what's a few more sips?''

Marilee followed suit.

Rudolf felt a flush of relief.

Elenore decided it was time for her to leave and excused herself, saying she needed to see about Amalia. Actually, she was anxious to meet Cord. She had finally spotted him slipping across the courtyard and into the garage, and had persuaded Gerda to take a note to him. She'd told him she would meet him in the basement that night.

Rudolf watched her go, laughing inside to think of how disappointed she was going to be. Gerda had, indeed, given the note to Cord Brandt—but not before reading it herself. She had then divulged the contents to Hanisch, who, in turn, told Rudolf. Rudolf had then ordered Gerda to lock the door behind Elenore when she went to check on Amalia, confining her till morning. Cord would eventually give up waiting for her, thinking she had been detained by social obligations.

Rudolf felt no remorse in thwarting the lovers' rendezvous. He wanted Elenore with Amalia, should she awake and become too loud and abrasive over discovering she was locked in her room with no vodka, and Ulda nowhere around to fetch it for her.

The brandy worked effectively—and quickly. Jade began to yawn even before coffee was served. "I'm sorry," she said, motioning for Gerda not to pour for her. "I'm really more tired than I thought." She looked at Rudolf and Marilee and teased, "You two won't be too angry with me if I retire early, will you?"

"Of course not" Rudolf graciously stood to pull out her chair for her. "We want you feeling good for our sight-seeing tomorrow. I've got a full day planned."

Marilee was also feeling a little sleepy but was actually relieved to have another chance to be alone with Rudolf to try and explain the way she felt. "Go on, Aunt Jade," she urged. "I'm not going to be up much longer myself."

No, you aren't. Rudolf wickedly smiled to himself as he escorted Jade as far as the arched doorway. *You're going to be in bed a lot sooner than you think, my dear . . . but not to sleep.*

He watched as Jade made her way down the dimly lit hall, then turned to go back into the dining room. He nearly ran right into Marilee who was on her way out. With fingertips to her forehead, she apologized, "I think I'll say good night, too, Rudolf. I'm more tired than I thought—" A yawn consumed her voice.

"No!" he objected, sharper, louder, than he intended. Firmly grasping her arm, he urged her down the hall and into the parlor. Hanisch had obligingly made a cozy fire, and Gerda had turned out all the lamps and lit candles to provide overall ambience conducive to seduction.

The burgundy velvet settee glowed like a giant waiting and caressing hand in the soft light from the crackling flames. Rudolf drew Marilee down beside him, slipping his arm about her shoulders to pull her close.

Marilee felt more relaxed than sleepy. At first she enjoyed the crackle of the fire, the warm atmosphere. Another glass of the delicious plum brandy magically appeared, and she sipped it, liking the delicate fruity taste. But then Rudolf drew her even closer, and she could feel the warmth of his breath on her cheek and was suddenly repelled. Stiffening, she moved out of his embrace and whispered, "Please, Rudolf, not now—"

Rudolf did not miss the lack of resolution in her voice, knew the drug was doing its job. He nuzzled her neck, hands moving up and down her back as he whispered, "Enjoy, my darling . . . enjoy the kisses of the man who loves you . . . wants to marry you . . . enjoy and let me take you to paradise."

Gently he maneuvered her down until she was lying on her back.

It was so easy, Marilee dreamily, dizzily, thought, to let his hands move over her body, to succumb to his kisses, to feel wanted, needed, and, perhaps most of all, desired. But then she felt his hand inside the scooped neckline of her gown, heard the way he gasped, deep in his throat; then, almost fiercely, he manipulated his body on top of hers. She could feel his hardness pushing against her, and he began to shove up her gown, attempting to render her exposed and vulnerable.

Struggling with all her might, she pushed against his shoulders, tried to scream in protest, but he had covered her mouth with his in a hungrily bruising kiss. She then began to beat on his back with her fists, writhing and twisting beneath him as he pressed her down.

He lifted his lips just enough to taunt, "You know you want me, darling. Stop pretending you don't. It's all right. We're going to be married soon—"

"No!" she managed to cry before he clamped a hand over her mouth.

In the firelight, his brown eyes burned like embers with his lust and fury. "Listen to me," he said between clenched teeth, words pouring forth in a torrent. "It's mental, believe me, a sickness of the mind. I heard the famous psychiatrist, Sigmund Freud, lecture about it once when I was in Vienna. He says women like you are what is known as frigid. You are not capable of enjoying lovemaking, but I'm going to change all that you for, I promise.''

Her eyes were wide with terror as she stared up at him, struggling to breathe against his pressing hand.

Rudolf realized the drug had not worked as quickly as he'd thought. She was nearly hysterical, and there was no way he was going to be able to get her to submit. He decided there was only one thing to do: let her go. Later, when she was asleep in her own bed, he'd carry her to his, let her wake up there and think they'd made love, whether they had or not. Hopefully, the drug would continue to be effective.

He released her, turning to sit with face lowered to his hands in a pretense of shame and embarrassment. ''Forgive me, my darling, forgive me,'' he whispered in anguish. ''I just love you so much, need you so much. You don't know what it's like—I'm so lonely. My father is dead, my mother's an alcoholic, I was driven from my homeland. I need you, need your love . . . please don't hate me . . .''

Marilee struggled to stand, felt a wave of revulsion as she stared down at him. ''What you said . . .'' she hoarsely cried, ''it's not true. I'm not what you said.''

He gave her a piteous look and made his voice thick with patronizing regret. ''Yes, it is, my darling. You are what is known as a frigid woman. You can't help it. And your only hope is a patient, understanding man. You have that in me. We'll work together to make you normal, and—''

''Stop it!'' she hissed, covering her ears as she backed out of the room. Everything was whirling around her, and though she had not fully grasped the meaning of his words, did not understand everything that was happening, she was filled with a sense of desperation to escape.

"Marilee, wait—"

She turned, began to run down the hall, but instinct for survival took over, propelling her almost unconsciously into an empty statue nook in the stone wall of the corridor. Pressing herself back as far as possible, she held her breath as Rudolf rushed by in pursuit.

Too much to drink, both of them, she fiercely told herself. Rudolf was to be pitied, not censored. He had called her—what? Frigid? She shook her head to dispel such a ridiculous thought. Tomorrow, she thought giddily, she would set him straight on many things, but tonight, she was too weary to attempt to cope with him. But, as tired as she was, she did not dare go to her room lest he look for her there. Surely there was some other room in the castle where she could hide and sleep till morning.

She stepped into the hall. She had heard Rudolf's footsteps as he went up to the second floor in search of her, so she decided not to go there. Instead, she moved along, trying each door, only to find them all locked.

She reached Jade's room, was not about to waken her and let her know how ridiculous Rudolf was behaving, but knew she had no other choice except to go upstairs, where he was, no doubt, waiting.

Then she saw the door leading down to the basement. Ordinarily, the thought of going down into an unknown region would have been terrifying, but Marilee's senses were dulled by the drugged brandy. Slowly, cautiously, she made her way down the narrow steps. The sound of something unseen skittering in the darkness made her flesh crawl as she imagined all kinds of repulsive creatures . . . but she kept going.

When she reached the bottom, an antiquated lantern hanging from a hook on the stone wall illumined the cobblestone floor—but not well. She could make out an open door and moved hesitantly in that direction.

It was a small chamber with a cot. It was so inviting, with its carefully folded blankets and soft white pillow. Her eyelids felt heavy, her head was spinning. She could not resist; she made ready to lie down, then hesitated. If Rudolf came in search, she wanted no light for him. Let him stumble about in the dark so she could hear him and be forewarned. She went back and extinguished the lantern, then made her way in the darkness and lay down.

Later she would not even remember laying her head on the pillow, for sleep was waiting like a giant, invisible cloak to descend and wrap around her and take her away to blessed oblivion.

Warm.

Flowing.

Like a river of silk she felt the touch of his fingers upon her skin, causing great waves of delicious ecstasy to move over her body. With slow and tantalizing caresses, she felt the embryo of strange, unfamiliar emotions come alive, her senses raw, raging, crying out silently, desperately, for pleasures yet unknown.

It was a dream, for she saw nothing but black mist hovering over a never-ending sea of delicious, torturing bliss. It was not real, could never be real, for such delectation could only exist in her imagination, her fantasies.

Her body arched, endeavoring to get closer still, welcoming the assault, the violation of velvet recesses starving for yet unknown joy and fulfillment.

A kiss.

Oh, dear God, never had she known such a kiss existed. Warm—no, hot, very, very hot lips brushed across hers so lightly, like fairies tiptoeing on a dewy lawn, afraid to touch too hard . . . like the whisper of a spring breeze teasing her flesh.

Then, almost with brutal assault, the mouth claimed hers, and she welcomed the bruising sensation of such pressure, such hunger, and she parted her own lips to receive the probing tongue, the hungry tongue . . . the wonderful tongue that opened new tastes of wonder.

Instinctively, for the thought of resisting never occurred to her in her wonderful dream, Marilee reached out to wrap her arms about him. Such a broad back. Muscles. Sinewy. Tight. She reveled in just the man smell of him as she pulled him yet tighter, delighting in the taste and sensation of her own tongue exploring his sweet, hot mouth.

Then he moved his lips to her neck and began to suckle gently against her throat.

His hands were fondling her breasts . . . but suddenly froze.

She tensed.

What was happening?

Why had he stopped?

Was it morning?

Was her wonderful phantasm going to flee at dawn like a legendary vampire?

"Please, no . . ." she whispered through the fog that clung to her like a spider's confining web. She could sense his hesitancy to continue the magic. "Don't go . . . not yet . . ."

Quickly the hands explored, darting beneath her dress to almost roughly fondle her hips and buttocks, then boldly groped between her thighs.

Abruptly, the searching fingers moved up to trace her face.

A masculine voice, slightly accented, hoarsely uttered a curse.

His lips were no longer upon hers.

She could no longer feel his touch, could sense his sudden retreat back into that mysterious realm where dreams hide while being nurtured.

She sat up, groping about her, realized she was awake, and felt a wave of terror. Was there someone in the room? Did she actually hear the sound of ragged breathing, fading as someone retreated?

No.

A dream.

Nothing more.

Too much brandy.

She shook her head to clear it, then once again lay down, allowing the invisible cloak of sleep to claim her, carry her away.

Marilee was sure it could not have been real.

For such wonders, she sadly acknowledged, did not exist . . . for her.

Chapter Thirteen

THROUGHOUT the seemingly endless night, Marilee dozed fitfully on the cot. Every so often she would awake with a start, to stare dazedly into the dark abyss, wondering where she was, how she had come to be there . . . until, ultimately, it would all come rushing back in heated waves of passionate remembrance.

The stranger . . . the overwhelmingly sensuous stranger who had held her, kissed her, awakening alien senses and emotions.

Had it only been a dream?

Though she was exhausted, she was able to think more clearly as the hours wore on. It was difficult to recall much after the dinner hour, for her memory seemed shrouded by an impenetrable mist. Vaguely she recalled Aunt Jade retiring early, and then there was a flickering scene with Rudolf somewhere. Though the details were indistinct, she knew they had argued—no doubt about his persistence. So she had run away and somehow found her way to the cellar.

Where the stranger had been waiting.

Her phantom lover.

That part of the night seemed startling clear, for she still savored his scorching kisses . . . his burning caresses.

Dear God, she silently cried as a wondrous tremor swept her, who was he?

Certainly not Rudolf.

Rudolf might be charming, handsome, and he professed to love her, but never, ever had he ignited the feelings she had experienced. Oh, no, it had not been Rudolf.

She had not realized the room where she lay had a window till the first exploring fingers of dawn crept through the dirt-caked glass. As soon as there was light to see her way, she left the cold chamber to go upstairs.

As she rounded the corner on the second floor, where her room was located, she froze at the sight of Rudolf sitting right outside her door. He rested against the wall, head lolling to one side, eyes closed. His deep, even breathing told her he was asleep, so, moving quietly, stealthily around him, she was able to slip inside, locking the door behind her.

Rudolf awoke at the sound of the key grating in the lock. "Marilee?" he cried, leaping to his feet and knocking rapidly on the door. "Marilee? Are you there? I've been worried sick and—"

"I'm fine, Rudolf," she assured him coolly. Though she could not recall exactly why she should be angry, instinct told her aloofness was in order.

All of his frustrations poured forth as he cried, "Where have you been hiding? I know you're angry, and I'm sorry. I didn't mean what I said. It's just that

I love you so much you're driving me crazy. Let me in, please.''

"Let you in my bedroom?" Marilee demurely teased, smiling to herself as she began to undress. "Why, Rudolf, that would hardly be proper, now would it?"

"It could be," he said pointedly. "It could be very proper, indeed, if you'd admit you love me and marry me!"

The thought of a nice, hot bath and a few hours' nap was inviting, but she knew he'd never give her time for both. "I'll see you at breakfast, Rudolf. We'll talk then."

Damn her, he swore as he turned and stalked away. When they were married she would learn respect and discipline, or, by God, he'd show her the painful consequences of disobedience to her husband.

He headed down the hall to unlock his mother's door and, no doubt, face his sister's wrath.

Jade, lovely in a pale pink dress with matching knit shawl, looked up from her breakfast of poached eggs and salmon as Marilee entered the dining room. "Ah, there you are!" she cheerily greeted. "I thought I was the sleepyhead this morning, but you outdid me. You didn't let Rudolf talk you into another glass of that plum brandy last night, did you?"

Marilee sat down, waved away the platter of food Gerda offered, and said she wanted nothing but black coffee. Then she responded to Jade. "I'm afraid so. Never again. At least champagne just makes me bubbly. The *Zwetsch* really did me in."

"Are you sure that was the reason?" Jade teased,

"or did Rudolf keep you up till dawn trying to talk you into marrying him?"

Marilee said vaguely, "I'm not sure."

"What do you mean?"

Marilee shook her head, not wanting to talk about last night.

"Well, whatever happened shows on your face, because your eyes are shining, and I think you're even blushing."

Marilee forced a laugh. "Come now, Aunt Jade. I think you want to get me married off so badly you're letting your imagination run away with you."

Elenore walked in, and both Jade and Marilee were taken aback by her tight, angry expression. She mumbled a halfhearted greeting, sat down, and hungrily reached for the platter of eggs and salmon.

Jade exchanged a bewildered look with Marilee, then dared to ask, "How is your mother this morning?"

"Fine," Elenore replied curtly. "I hope you two will excuse me today, but I've got some personal plans." Did she ever, she mused furiously. She was going to find Cord, because, no doubt, he would be angry with her for not showing up last night, and she wanted to let him know her goddamn hateful brother was responsible.

Marilee had never seen Elenore in such a foul mood. "Of course, we understand, but if you change your mind, we'd love to have you join us for sightseeing."

Rudolf entered, wearing his most buoyant smile. "What's this? My dear sister isn't going with us today?" He knew why, of course, but did not care. He paused to kiss Marilee's cheek before taking his seat at the head of the table, then continued to goad Elenore. "My, my, that's a shame. I've got such a lovely day planned. What could be so important to rob us of your delightful company?"

Elenore's glare was one of barely contained rage. How she ached to scream at him to go to hell. "I'm sure you have a good idea," she said between clenched teeth.

Jade suddenly felt very uncomfortable and decided it was time to ease the tension that had descended. Brightly, she announced, "Elenore has just given me an idea. I think I'll pass on the sight-seeing, too."

"But you have to come, Aunt Jade," Marilee pleaded, desperation an undertone. "You heard what Rudolf said—he's got our day already planned. We'll both be disappointed if you don't join us."

Jade was not to be dissuaded. "Oh, I've got a feeling Rudolf wouldn't find it too great an imposition to have to spend the whole day alone with you."

"Not at all," Rudolf agreed, "but what will you do if you don't join us?"

"Have you prepared quarters for my servants?" she wanted to know, was not disappointed when he apologetically shook his head, because, although she did not want to say anything just yet, she doubted she would be staying much longer. "Well, then, I'll just pay them a visit and see how they're doing, maybe treat them to lunch."

Elenore was aghast. "You mean you take your servants to lunch?"

Rudolf shot her a warning look, which she ignored, too angry to care what he thought.

Jade was momentarily taken aback by such a question and stiffly defended herself. "Well, yes. Why wouldn't I? Even though they work for me, they can still be my friends."

"But they are servants." Elenore's laugh was haughty. "I mean, one hardly socializes with one's servants, does one?"

"One does what one wants to," Jade crisply informed her. "At least *I* do."

Elenore shook her head, still astonished. "But you—you're a Romanov, and everyone knows—"

"Everyone knows you have a big mouth sometimes," Rudolf quickly interjected, then apologized to Jade. "I'm sorry."

"Oh, there's no need for apology," Jade said with an airy wave of her hand, attempting once more to lighten the mood. "Some people have different ideas about things, that's all." Dear Lord, she wished for the hundredth time she had just stayed at home and let her niece take care of herself!

It was a perfect day—a warm majestic sun, framed by a flawless peacock-blue sky, and a gentle, cooling breeze. Except for one brief interlude when Rudolf again began to pressure Marilee and which she quickly put a stop to, the day was splendid.

When they returned home, Hanisch stopped the Fiat at the back entrance, then got out to perform the usual duties of a chauffeur. Opening the door on Rudolf's side so he could get out first and then assist Marilee, he glanced up to see Elenore running across the porch. She looked distraught, and he growled in Rudolf's ear, "What now?"

Rudolf followed his angry gaze, saw his sister, and tensed. She was waving her arms, motioning him to hurry. Dammit, if something was amiss, did she have to let it be known in front of Marilee?

Marilee saw, of course, and wanted to know what was wrong. He mumbled it was probably something to do with his mother, thinking how he wanted to wring Elenore's neck. He had no choice but to hold out his hand to Marilee so she could get out of the car to hear whatever ghastly news there was.

Hanisch deliberately hung back, not taking the car on to the garage, because he also wanted to know what was going on.

Elenore could contain herself no longer. "Oh, do hurry, Rudolf." She was near tears. "It's Mother and Frau Coltrane. There's been a terrible row!"

"Goddammit!" Rudolf did not try to control his fury. "How in the hell did you let that happen?" He ran up the steps, Marilee right behind him.

Elenore tried to explain as they hurried inside. "I went out, but only for a little while. I couldn't find the person I needed to see," she added pointedly.

Rudolf didn't care about that and said so. "Just tell me what happened here."

"I came back and Mother was screaming at Frau Coltrane to get out of the house, that she'd not have a *Romanov* under her roof."

Rudolf truly exploded then. They were inside the house, in the rear foyer. "Just tell me how the hell she found out Jade is a Romanov. I thought we agreed that we wouldn't say anything about it!"

Marilee felt her own indignant ire rising. "Wait a minute, Rudolf. What do you mean you agreed not to say anything about it? Is it something to be ashamed of around here? I mean, we were invited as guests to your home, and nothing was ever said about hiding the fact we have Russian blood! Aunt Jade isn't responsible for the war any more than I am, and it's not fair—''

He turned to grasp her shoulders. "No, no, darling, you don't understand. It has nothing to do with being ashamed of anything. It's just that when Mother drinks too much, she gets crazy. She probably started thinking about how my stepfather died of a heart attack when the Russians invaded Galicia. Who knows? The liquor poisons her mind. I can only apologize for her behavior.''

Marilee drew in her breath and let it out slowly. She did not like the situation but could understand why Amalia would be less than tolerant, especially when she'd had too much to drink. She asked of Elenore, "Where are they now?"

Rudolf didn't give his sister a chance to respond, curtly reminding her, "You didn't answer my question. How did Mother find out?"

Elenore shook her head, bewildered. "I honestly don't know. I walked in as Frau Coltrane was walking out, and Mother was ranting and raving.'' She looked at Marilee. "She's in her room and Mother is still in the parlor.''

Marilee started to go to Jade, while Rudolf could only run his fingers through his hair in agitation and say once again, "I don't understand how she found out—''

"Because she told me, you idiot!''

They all whirled to see Amalia coming down the

dimly lit hall, holding a glass in her hand and struggling to stay on her feet.

"The haughty little bitch told me! I asked her about her family, and one thing led to another, and the next thing I knew, I realized I had a goddamn *Romanov* in my house. I won't have it." She raised the hand holding the glass, pointed her index finger unsteadily at Marilee. "But *you* can stay, dear. My son loves you, and it doesn't matter your father is Russian. You can't help that. We'll get along fine, and—"

She slumped to one side, and Rudolf managed to grab her in time to keep her from falling.

Marilee felt tears sting her eyes, and her heart went out to Rudolf as she saw, felt, his misery and humiliation.

"Come along, Mother." He lifted her in his arms, and as he did, the glass fell to the floor and shattered.

He started walking down the hall, intent on carrying her to her room, and as they passed Marilee, Amalia's head lolled to one side, and she mustered a timorous smile and begged, "Please . . . don't be angry. If you leave him, he'll hate me forever . . ."

Marilee turned in the direction of Jade's room, hesitated as she felt Elenore's touch.

"She's right, you know."

Marilee stared at her, not understanding.

"If your aunt leaves and you go with her, Rudolf will never forgive Mother."

Marilee did not know what to say, knew only that she wanted to get to Jade and hear exactly what had happened. She hurried on her way with Elenore gazing miserably after her.

Rudolf did dump Amalia on the bed this time, teeth

grinding together in fury. It was all he could do in his
rage not to start pummeling her with the pillows . . .
or worse. *Damn her!*

He turned sharply at the sound of footsteps, was
relieved to see Hanisch.

Their eyes met in unspoken agreement.

It had to happen tonight.

Chapter Fourteen

MARILEE knocked, and when Jade did not respond, she opened the unlocked door and walked in to see that her aunt had already started packing.

"There's no need to say anything," Jade said without glancing up as she crammed clothes into a wardrobe trunk. "It's best I leave. The sooner the better. I shouldn't have come, anyway."

"Neither should I!"

At that, Jade straightened. "Please don't say that. Rudolf can't help what his mother says or does. She's a sick woman, and he has a pitiful situation on his hands. And now that she knows I'm a Romanov, it will only make things worse. It's best I go. Besides"—she managed to smile—"you two will have more time to get to know each other with me not around."

Marilee shook her head stubbornly. "If you leave, I'm leaving, too."

"Nonsense!" Jade turned back to her packing. "I'll call a taxi and get myself a room at Cavasia's hotel tonight so we can take the first train out in the morning. Frankly I wish we could leave on the midnight train. The sooner the better.''

Marilee could not bear the thoughts of her going. ''Wait till tomorrow, please. Maybe Rudolf can straighten things out with his mother. When she's herself again, she's going to feel awful about what happened, and even worse when she realizes you left before she could apologize and make things right.''

Jade shook her head adamantly. ''Don't you remember what Rudolf said about how his stepfather died of a heart attack when Russia invaded Galicia? His mother blames me for that because, to her, I'm representative of the Czar and the imperialism she blames for her husband's death. Drunk or sober, she'll hate me, too, now that she knows I'm a member of that family, and it can't help but put a strain on your relationship with Rudolf.

''No,'' she repeated, ''I'm leaving. She ordered me out of her house, and even though it's sad it turned out this way, I'd been thinking about going, anyway. I want to go home, to wait for Colt and Travis and be with my grandchildren. This is your future, Marilee. Not mine.''

My future, Marilee silently scoffed. Why was it everyone wanted to plan her life for her? Didn't what *she* wanted count . . . even if she didn't know what it was she did want? Last night something wonderful had happened, and if she never learned the identity of the man responsible, she would forever be in his debt for the awakening of a new self-awareness, for she had learned one important thing—there was nothing wrong with her! Rudolf just didn't make her feel like a woman—the way she so desperately wanted, and needed, to feel.

"I won't allow you to go with me," Jade went on to say. "Besides, if you left, too, Rudolf would blame his mother, and the poor soul has enough trouble without her son hating her forever."

That, Marilee dismally agreed, was true. Besides, she was not altogether sure she wanted to go back to Spain. She had her own money. She could stay till things were smoothed over between Rudolf and his mother, then find a small apartment in Zurich and live there till it was safe to return to Paris and Dani-berry. But, of course, she was not about to tell Jade of her plans, because she'd have a fit to think of her living alone.

"If you feel so sorry for her," Marilee suddenly pointed out, "why are you leaving? Rudolf will be angry with her over that, you know. What not stay a few more days just to smooth things over?"

"I'm sorry. It's best I leave now."

"But will you at least wait till morning?"

Jade sighed. "I guess so."

Marilee grinned, elated. "Good. Maybe by then I can change your mind."

Jade knew that was not going to happen but did not say so, and Lord, she hated to lie, but she had no intention of staying till morning. As soon as she could sneak away, she would. "I'm going to call a taxi to take these trunks on to the train station and get them checked."

Marilee then left to find Rudolf. He was in the parlor, sitting by the fireplace looking doleful and for-lorn as he sipped a brandy.

Marilee watched him from the doorway for a moment before entering. She revered him as a friend, could not bear to see him so distressed. Walking over, she knelt before him and gently said, "Don't feel bad, Rudolf. And don't be angry with your mother. Drinking is a sickness. She can't help herself."

He shook his head. "There's no excuse for what she did. How is Jade?" he asked worriedly.

"She's upset. She's in her room, packing, determined to leave. I got her to wait till morning, but she's having her trunks sent to the station tonight."

Rudolf suppressed a gasp of joy. Everything was falling into place. When Jade disappeared during the night, Marilee would merely think she'd not kept her promise to stay till morning.

Struggling to keep his voice even so his apprehension would not show, he pressed for reassurance. "You're sure she won't leave till morning? We have till then . . . to change her mind?" he hesitantly added.

Marilee nodded.

Reaching to lovingly caress her cheek with his fingertips, he whispered, "I'll make it all up to you, I swear. I want only sunshine for you, Marilee, the happiness of sunshine and the contentment of blue skies . . . and love."

Marilee tensed, then withdrew from his touch. "You don't owe me anything, Rudolf. And you mustn't think any of this is your fault. Now . . ." She got to her feet, escaping his attempted embrace. "It's time to dress for dinner."

He did not protest. He also had things to do, and it was difficult to keep from trembling in anticipation.

* * *

Dinner was uncomfortable for everyone, a meal eaten in silence. Jade and Elenore finished quickly and left the room as soon as they could.

"I think we should retire to the parlor for a sherry," Rudolf said when at last he and Marilee were alone.

Marilee agreed, wanting to speak her mind and get it over with.

When they were settled, once more before the fireplace, she did not give him a chance to embrace her or kiss her, for she maneuvered herself to the far end of the sofa and turned sideways to face him squarely as she firmly declared, once and for all: "I think it's time we understood each other, Rudolf."

He was momentarily taken aback but murmured, "Well, yes, I suppose—"

"I don't want to marry you," she rushed on to say. "Not now. Maybe not ever. There is nothing wrong with me. Nothing wrong with you. We just weren't meant for each other, that's all. I like you for a friend, and maybe once I thought I might be falling in love with you. But I'm not. Someday I might feel different, but for now, I won't consent to be your wife."

Rudolf listened, wide-eyed and astonished. Never had he heard her sound so—so *in control.* She was firm, resolute, and he could tell by the way she held herself, looked at him, that if he made one move toward her right then, she'd push him away. With a nervous little laugh, he said, "You don't mean this, Marilee, any of it. You're just angry about my mother causing your aunt to leave, and you won't admit it, but you're mad all the same and this is your way of punishing me. You love me, and you know it."

Staunchly, she disagreed and pointed out, "I never led you on. I never said I loved you. I only agreed to give us time to find out how we feel about each other, and you wouldn't give me that. You've pressured me, and that's not fair."

Infuriated, he could only tightly mumble, "I see!" and reach for the bottle of sherry on the coffee table.

"My aunt and your mother have nothing to do with it."

"That, I *don't* see!" he snapped irritably, then asked incredulously, "And you accuse *me* of being unfair? It's certainly not my fault your aunt hasn't got sense enough to keep her mouth shut about being a Romanov, for God's sake. Anyone with a grain of sense would know that's not something you brag about these days, especially to an Austrian!"

Marilee was struggling for control but could feel her temper rising. "Then you should have told us that before you invited us here."

He nodded, laughing cynically. "Oh, I should've known there would be a problem, all right. Imperialists are like that—bragging about who they are to make sure everybody else knows. And besides, we both know the only way I got you here was to invite *her,* too."

That did it.

And Rudolf knew it.

Marilee bolted up from the sofa, and he was right behind her to grab her arm and hold her back, instantly contrite. "Please, forgive me. I didn't mean it. It's just that I love you, and you're making me crazy."

Marilee sighed, sank back onto the sofa once more.

"Above all, I want us to be friends, and friends aren't supposed to hurt each other."

"Oh, God, Marilee . . ." He sat down beside her, tried to take her in his arms, but she struggled against him. "Don't you know I'd never intentionally hurt you? And you might think you don't love me, but you do. You've just got so much on your mind right now. Thanks to my mother, your aunt is leaving, and you're worried about that. And you've got your father to be concerned about, too. Don't you think I know all that?"

"I can take care of myself, Rudolf. Never, ever think that I can't."

His soft laugh was patronizing. "Oh, I know you think that, darling, but the truth is you need a man, and—"

"Wait a minute!" Marilee held up her hand for silence. Oh, dear Lord, enough had gone on this day, she thought furiously, and the last thing she wanted was another scene. "I need a man for one thing— love. *Not* to take care of me! And I'm getting a little sick and tired of you and my family thinking I'm some empty-headed piece of fluff who can't get by without one!"

"Every woman needs a husband to take care of her."

"Really?" She sniffed with disdain. "It might come as a shock to you, Rudolf, but a man has *never* taken care of me. My father, though I worship the ground he walks on, left me when I was an infant in the care of my grandmother, and it was she who took care of me. Not a man. And when I was placed in a finishing school, as my mother had wanted for me, I

was never taken care of by a man. There were ma-
trons, dear Rudolf. So believe me when I say that if
and when I do marry, it will be for one reason and
one reason only—that I can get something from a man
I can't get from myself!''

''Dear God!'' he breathed, awed and astonished to
hear such profundity from a lady.

''Now, good night!''

She hurried from the room before he could stop
her, not that he was about to try. He also had had
enough for one day.

He threw his glass into the fireplace, then turned
the sherry bottle up to his lips and drank it down in
great gulps. He needed something stronger, would
have something stronger, for this night he knew sleep
would not come easily. Oh, he didn't really care about
Marilee running out on him. Let her have a few hours'
sleep. Before morning, she would give him what he
wanted . . . or he would take it by force.

Marilee ran all the way to her room, threw herself
on her bed in a fit of turmoil. But she was exhausted,
and sleep came quickly.

Hours later she awoke with a start, and, though
groggy, she was instantly aware that she had to do
something. Things just could not go on as they were.
Spoiled and used to having his own way, Rudolf
would not stop trying to persuade her to marry him,
and they could never have a merely platonic relationship.

Her final, and perhaps most painfully sober realization, there in the middle of the night, was that
she really had no option except to go back to Spain

with Jade. After all, there was a war going on, and it was dangerous for her to remain alone even in Zurich. At least in Spain she would be safe, and her father would know where to contact her when he was ready.

She got up, realized she was still wearing what she had worn to dinner, and decided to change into a nightgown and robe before telling Jade her decision. No matter that her aunt had said she could not leave with her; Jade would soon realize she had no choice.

Opening the door of her room, Marilee stepped out into the hallway and frowned at the darkness. Usually there was a light, but tonight there was none. And she could not hear any sounds anywhere. Well, no matter. She knew her way—down the hall, down the steps, and Jade's room was at the bottom. She would not risk turning on lights and perhaps waking someone, particularly Rudolf.

Groping along, she reached the stairs, used the cold stone wall to feel her way along, moving as fast as she dared, anxious to reach Jade's room.

Finally she found her door and knocked softly.

There was no answer.

With trembling fingers she reached for the knob, turned it, was relieved when the door opened. Thank God, it wasn't locked or she'd have had to make noise to be heard, which might have brought Rudolf, and she certainly did not want that.

Stepping inside, she felt her heart constrict with dread, for she sensed, despite being eclipsed in total darkness, that Jade was not there.

She turned on a light, glanced about quickly to

realize her fears were confirmed, and, at the same instant, felt awash with sudden loneliness.

The bed was still neatly made, and she saw a note on the pillow. Stiffly, she walked over to pick it up and became incensed as she read what her aunt had written.

Jade said she felt it best to just slip away quietly, for fear Marilee might be swayed by family loyalty and insist on going with her if she stayed till morning. Again she urged Marilee to give Rudolf, and her heart, a chance, to put aside worries over her father for the time being, and to concentrate instead on her own life, her own happiness and future.

Marilee ground her teeth together to suppress a scream of rage, wadded the note into a tight ball, and threw it across the room.

Damn her, she fumed. Damn her, Jade had *lied!* Oh, it was so obvious now—how nervous she had been at dinner, how anxious to leave the table, intending the whole time to be on the midnight train out of Zurich.

Now what was she going to do?

She had no idea, knew only that she felt more alone than ever before in her life . . . and also very, very tired.

Turning out the light, she wearily crawled into Jade's bed, pulling the blankets up tightly around her.

At least Rudolf would never think to look for her there, and in the morning, she would feel better and could make plans.

She dozed off, falling into a deep slumber . . . a *vulnerable* slumber, for later, when her nostrils suddenly burned with a strange, penetrating odor, she could not react, could do nothing but succumb to the yet deeper sleep that took her down, down, down to murky depths of unconsciousness.

Chapter Fifteen

THE effects of the chloroform began to wear off.
Marilee opened her eyes to the grim sensation of being imprisoned in a sea of mud. She could not move any part of her body, and there was a great roaring in her ears, like a train chugging madly down a mountain, faster, faster—till it became a shrill scream.

She swallowed. Her throat was raw, burning.

She blinked but still could not see anything.

Then she felt something soft against her face, groggily realized it was a cloth of some kind. A stab of fright, her first real emotion, jolted her as she realized her head was encased in some sort of sack.

But why?

There was a sickening lump in her throat, and she felt a nauseous rumble in her stomach. Her head began to throb, and a grainy sensation assaulted her eyes.

Dear God, her benumbed brain struggled to scream, what was wrong with her? She felt so weak . . . so sick.

Yet, despite everything she was feeling, she was

strangely overwhelmed with the instinct to make no move, make no sound. With the primal perception of an animal of the wild, something told her that she was in danger, that whoever, or whatever, was responsible for her helpless state was nearby.

And slowly through the thick maze, it all came back to her.

She has fallen asleep in Jade's bed and could remember being awakened by the terrifying feeling of something being pressed over her face, suffocating her. Then there was nothing.

Till now.

She was aware of lying on her side, on some kind of bedding that was lumpy and uncomfortable. She could smell something like hay, heard a soft mooing sound, like that of a cow, from somewhere not too distant. Was she in a barn?

She was assailed by new terror to realize her wrists were bound, as well as her ankles. Oh, who would have done such a thing? she raged furiously within.

And *why?*

Certainly not Rudolf. If it were his idea of a prank, surely he would realize she'd never forgive him.

Then slowly, as insidiously as a spider stalking prey, the dread awareness came to her.

She had been in Jade's bed.

No doubt the kidnappers, if that was what they were, thought *she* was Jade, which assailed her with yet another needling question: if that were so, why would anyone want to abduct her aunt?

It hit her like a rock right between the eyes.

Ransom!

Of course.

So now Jade was on her way home to Spain, without a worry in the world, while *she* was trussed up like a calf in some dusty old barn somewhere, with a maniac who believed she was somebody else.

In a hysterical sort of way, Marilee thought it was funny, and looked forward to the time when her captor removed the bag over her head and realized he'd made a terrible mistake. True, he could probably hold her for ransom instead, and the Coltranes would, no doubt, pay it, but fear arose when she contemplated that whoever was responsible might decide she just wasn't worth it and dispose of her without even asking for ransom.

Though she had no idea how much time had elapsed since her disappearance, she was sure it had to have been hours, and when morning came, Rudolf would discover her missing. And wouldn't there have been a ransom note left somewhere? He would realize what had happened, how a mistake had been made, surely call the police and inform them of the entire nightmare. Perhaps her abductors would think it best to just let her go. After all, her face was covered, and she had seen nothing, heard nothing. With heart tremulously pounding, she knew it was up to her to save herself by protesting if they started to remove the bag, telling them she was keeping her eyes shut, because she did not want to be able to identify any of them, so they could just let her go and they could all pretend it never happened.

That was her only hope, and she clung to it tenaciously in the dark emptiness of her shrouded existence.

Finally, after what seemed an eternity, Marilee

heard the scrape of a door opening. She tensed, willed herself not to move, breathing slowly, evenly, pretending to still be sleeping—though every nerve in her body was raw with panic.

Someone was walking toward her with heavy footsteps, and she was aware of a presence leaning over her. Then a slightly guttural masculine voice declared, "She's still out," adding with a note of concern, "I hope you know what you were doing. Should the chloroform effect her so long?"

"She'll be fine. The longer she's out, the better."

Marilee noted the voice of the second man did not sound quite so crude as the first. He sounded younger, yet stronger somehow, and his German accent was quite pronounced.

"What about the ransom note?" the voice she preferred asked.

"Just like we planned," came the reply. "Gerda left it on the counter when the desk clerk's back was turned, just after midnight. He never saw her, but she said she peeked through the door after she ran out and saw him looking at it, so no doubt the princess' bodyguard got it when he came down for breakfast. By now he's probably on his way, unless he panicked and ran to the police with it."

"He won't. I made it clear what would happen if he did."

Marilee could not control the tremor that went through her, hoped they did not notice, then nearly choked in fright when she realized one of them had.

"Hey, she moved." The guttural voice spoke.

"She's cold. Get another blanket."

"Is this the best place to keep her? So close to

town? Hell, it's just a barn and cold and drafty. We don't want her getting sick on us.''

"We're fine for a while.''

"Well, just make sure you keep that pillowcase over her head, because I don't want her to ever be able to identify *my* face.''

"Don't worry.''

Marilee was gritting her teeth together so tightly her jaws ached, for she was trying to suppress the constant tremors within that threatened to erupt from head to toe. Then they would surely know she was awake, and listening, and scared out of her wits.

The buzzing and ringing in her ears had lessened as the chloroform continued to wear itself out of her system, and she was able to begin to clearly rationalize what had taken place. These . . . these fiends were not common criminals. They were spies of some sort. But how had they known Jade was even visiting in Zurich, much less who she was and how much she was worth?

The two men seemed to have busied themselves for the time being. When she could make out the sound of liquid pouring, the tinkle of glasses, she knew they were drinking something, and probably not *coffee,* she wryly mused. She only prayed they would stay sober, lest her plight become even more precarious. Surely it was early, she tried to comfort herself, and they would not be drinking so early in the day, and—

A loud roar permeated the silence at the same time she heard what sounded like angry fists pounding against a door. Hysterical shrieks followed the growling shouts: "You goddamn fools! You goddamn, stupid, blundering fools! Let me in, damn you all to hell—''

Chairs turned over, glass broke in the scramble of sounds to open the door.

Curses.

More yelling.

Marilee could no longer control her shivers, knew there was no need to even try.

She had recognized the voice, knew who it was beating on the door before they even let him in, and her cinnamon eyes glazed over with the burnt umber of raw, murderous rage as she glared into the face of the man who roughly yanked the pillowcase off her head.

''You got the wrong one, you bastards!'' Rudolf yelled, instinctively flinching when he met her fiery gaze. ''Dear God!''

Without saying a word, Hanisch walked over and hit Rudolf in the mouth with his fist, sending him reeling backward in a spurt of blood from a split lip.

Able to at last see her surroundings, Marilee whipped her head about to realize she was actually in a barn, and the cot on which she was lying was positioned in the middle, with crude wooden stalls surrounding it.

She watched, wide-eyed, as Rudolf fell back against one of the stall gates, then pitched forward, face-down, into the straw scattered about the floor.

She recognized the man who had hit Rudolf—the chauffeur! He was the one with the gravelly voice.

He walked over to grab Rudolf by his shift and roughly yank him to his feet. Then he jammed him back into the railing, holding his fist in front of his face, ready to strike him again. "Don't come in here cursing us for your mistakes, you son of a bitch! How the hell were we to know? She was in the Romanov bitch's bed! And if you hadn't shot off your goddamn mouth just now, she wouldn't have seen us, wouldn't know us!"

He had started to hit him again, and Marilee watched, mesmerized by all that was taking place, as the other man stepped forward to grab his arm and impassively say, "That's enough. Both of you."

Hanisch let him go, and Rudolf quickly moved out of his reach—but felt drawn to Merilee's fiery glare.

She could remain silent no longer. "You bastard!" she hissed. "You were behind it all, weren't you? You planned this the whole time, didn't you?"

He stood on uncertain legs, ignoring the blood that trickled down his chin. "That's right. I made a mistake, but you, Miss Mikhailonov, will be the one to pay for it, because we've no use for you now."

The man who had stopped him from being hit again sharply said, "Rudolf, don't be stupid. We're better off than we were before, if you stop and think about it."

Both Hanisch and Rudolf looked at him, puzzled, but then Hanisch snapped his fingers and happily bellowed, "By God, you're right! Who's got more gold to pay ransom with than Drakar Mikhailonov?"

Cord nodded. "Exactly."

Marilee screamed, "My father? You know something about my father? Oh, tell me, please . . ." She struggled against the ropes in her desperation to hear more. "What about him? Is he alive? Is he well?" Tears began to fill her eyes.

"He's alive!" Rudolf sneered, then decided to make her suffer for having fouled up the plan that would have reaped him such respect and accolades from his peers. "He's also a thief! A trader. All of Russia is after him for stealing gold from the Imperial treasury."

Marilee shook her head wildly and protested, "No! That's not true. My father would never steal. He doesn't have to! He has a fortune of his own, and besides that, he's loyal to the Czar—"

"The *deposed* Czar!" Hanisch was quick to say.

"It doesn't matter!" Marilee raged indignantly, "My father would never steal!"

"Oh, he stole, all right!" Rudolf taunted, grinning. "But you better hope he hasn't spent all that stolen gold, because that's the only way he'll ever see his daughter again—alive that is!"

"That's enough," Cord said.

Marilee looked at him then, *really* looked at him for the first time, and as she did, she experienced a strange sensation, like a soft velvet glove teasing her bare flesh.

He was tall, well over six feet. In the sunlight coming through the open window, his hair was a white-gold color, thick and shaggy, curling about his ears and the nape of his neck. His eyes were cornflower blue, with thick gold lashes. He had a perfect Grecian nose, and his lips were incredibly full, sensuous.

Her gaze moved to his broad, strong shoulders. He was wearing a tan suede shirt, open to the waist, exposing a thick mat of golden chest hairs that trailed down to a narrow waist set above perfectly molded hips and thighs in tight twill trousers.

He sensed her staring at him, turned, and their eyes met, held, in electrifying awareness.

In that instant, Marilee was swept with the awesome suspicion that this fiercely handsome man was the stranger in the basement!

She glanced away uneasily, nervously, afraid if it were so that he would read in her face the raw hunger he had ignited that night . . . and also now.

"For now, we'll keep her here," Cord said. "You get to headquarters and report what's happened, Hamisch. Ask them what to do. I'll stay here while Rudolf goes back to town."

Rudolf immediately whined, "Why do *I* have to go? Why don't you go? I'll stay with her—"

"The hell you will." Cord gave him a shove toward the door. "Now get back and see what's going on, then gather all her clothes and things and bring them here."

Rudolf did not like being ordered around, felt he had been humiliated enough for one day. "All right," he said finally, reluctantly. "But then what?"

"If anybody calls for her, just act like you think she left with her aunt. Meanwhile, we'll wait here till Hanisch reports from headquarters."

"Sounds good to me." Hanisch started out, motioned for Rudolf to come along.

He moved to follow, then gave in to the impulse to goad one more time. Looking back at Marilee, he declared with mock tenderness, "It's really a shame it had to turn out this way. We could have been happy together—once you learned how to be a *real woman!*"

Despite her misery, the futility of her plight, she was able to curl her lips back in a sneer of contempt as she laughed incredulously and informed him, "You stupid bastard! How could you expect to teach me anything? It takes a *real* man to make a woman *feel* like a woman!"

He started toward her, intending to do what he'd been aching to do—knock the hell out of her—but Cord was quicker, grabbed him by the nape of his neck, and slung him across the barn—and all the way out the door.

Hanisch chuckled his approval, walked out, and closed the door behind them.

When they were alone, Cord untied her ankles but left her wrists bound. "I don't trust you just yet." He flashed a confident smile. "But if you're hungry, I've got some cheese and milk. I can spoon-feed you till you get over your tantrum."

She hoped her anger would keep him from seeing how terrified she was. "Just leave me alone, damn you! When my father hears what you've done to me, he'll kill you!

"Who are you, anyway?" she raged on. "A spy for the Bolsheviks, no doubt."

"Just relax," he softly told her, brushing her hair back from her face. "You've nothing to fear from me."

She jerked her head back, away from his touch. "Leave me alone, damn you!"

Their eyes met, held, and despite her instant hatred for him, for he was the one, she was sure, who had carried her from Jade's room, there was an undeniable awareness between them.

She did not have to ask.

She knew.

He was her phantom lover.

Suddenly, impulsively, Cord Brandt leaned forward and pressed his lips against hers, his hand on the back of her neck to hold her. She struggled against him, then succumbed despite herself, but rage quickly returned and with one mighty jerk she was able to twist her mouth from his.

And despite the fires he so easily kindled, the passion aroused within, Marilee loathed him.

He was her abductor.

He was her enemy.

But most of all she hated him for the mocking look in his smoldering blue eyes—the look that said he knew she wanted him every bit as much as he wanted her.

She turned away, determined not to let him see into her soul. Instead, she would concentrate on the other fire burning in her now—no one was going to lie and call her father a traitor.

She would escape, somehow, some way.

Then she was going to find her father.

Chapter Sixteen

MARILEE regarded him warily. He untied her, then gave her a cup of water and a few crackers.

She did not want the crackers but sipped the water, for the chloroform had left her throat feeling dry.

They sat staring at each other.

Marilee hoped her eyes mirrored her loathing and fury, but she could not be sure of the message reflected in his. Arrogance or pity? She could not be sure. He was devastatingly handsome, but he also emanated mystery, and yes, danger, for she was all too aware of the predicament she was in.

It was he who finally broke the spell of silence. "Are you not eating because you aren't hungry, or are you just pouting?"

She lifted her chin in a gesture of defiance, wanting him to think her much braver than she felt. "I'm just particular about who I eat with."

He laughed. "Well, dear lady, the ransom your father pays will merely be for a sack of bones, because we're going to be constant companions."

She felt a tremor of both fright and anticipation, and silently chided herself for the latter. Suddenly she

155

felt compelled to ask stiffly "It was you, wasn't it? In the cellar of the castle."

His eyes twinkled even brighter with delighted mischief. "I don't think I know what you're talking about."

He did. And she knew he did. "You kissed me in the cellar the night before last."

"Did I?" He shrugged, pretending indifference.

She nodded. "You kissed me a little while ago, and I knew for sure." It was her turn to flash a mocking smile. "You knew who I was then, but what I'd like to know is who you thought I was that night in the cellar."

He remained quite composed. "I don't know. I happened to be there, and so did you." He chuckled. But then, with sudden seriousness, he murmured, "It was nice both times, Marilee."

She sat up stiffly and threw the tin cup away. "Well, I'm glad you enjoyed it, because it's not going to happen again."

"Unless you want it to."

"I won't."

"You can't deny you enjoyed it. Even in the dark, not knowing who it was."

"So what? I can like your kisses without liking you, but so help me, God"—she paused, wanting the full impact of her oath to sink in—"you touch me again, and I'll claw your eyes out."

He laughed softly. "I'll keep that in mind." The cloak of silence descended once more, but not for long.

Marilee lashed out abruptly, "You're all bastards

to lie about my father, and he'll kill you when he finds out what you've done.''

"Nothing has happened to you and nothing will, as long as you're with me. And believe me, I intend to keep you with me, Marilee.''

She was struck by the compassion of his tone and his expression—but not enough to let her guard down. "Who are you?'' she demanded. "And why are all of you lying about my father?''

He ignored her last question, speaking without emotion. "My name is Cord Brandt. I was born in Germany. I stand against imperialism. I support the ideals of the Bolsheviks. That's all you need to know . . . for now.

"But,'' he added sharply, getting up from the table to walk over and sit down on the floor in front of her, "I know you don't believe me, although I swear you can trust me when I say no harm will come to you.''

He reached out to brush back a tendril of ginger-colored hair that had fallen on her forehead. She slapped his hand away. "Don't touch me. Ever again.'' Then she dared to implore, "But if you care at all about my welfare, you'll let me go, now. Before that bastard Rudolf comes back.''

She was puzzled again by his amused demeanor as he laughingly tugged at her bathrobe and said, "What? Let you go? Dressed like this? And where would you go, little spitfire? No, no!'' He wagged a teasing finger in front of her nose. "Whether you realize it or not, you need me—in lots of ways,'' he added with a wink.

"Need you?'' she scoffed. "I don't need you for

anything. I can take care of myself. Just let me go, and I'll prove it.''

He started to caress her cheek, leaned slightly closer as though to kiss her once more, but then he saw the way her fingers were arched, ready to fulfill her vow.

He moved away but could not resist saying, "You need kissing, Marilee, among other things. I don't think I've ever sensed such hunger in a woman." He leaned back against the opposite post, and they were so close their knees were touching. She jerked her legs to the side, but he pretended not to notice. "When I heard Rudolf had orders to court you, I knew, even though we'd never met, that he wasn't the man for you."

She shot him a venomous look. "Oh, really? Well, just what do you know about me, Mr. Brandt?"

"Let's see . . . ." He feigned an expression of deep concentration. "Your father is Drakar Mikhailonov, lifelong friend and confidant of Nicholas. Your mother, Dani Coltrane Mikhailonov, died giving birth to you. You were raised by your grandmother, Kitty Coltrane, who really wasn't your grandmother but was actually your grandfather's only legal wife. When she died, you were sent to an exclusive finishing school here in Switzerland, and that's where you met Rudolf's sister, Elenore, and then Rudolf.

"And," he went on, enjoying her wide-eyed look of astonishment, "I was told you were quite beautiful, which you are, and vastly intelligent and perceptive, which is also true, but nobody"—he shook his head slowly from side to side, eyes twinkling mischievously—"could have told me how good it felt to hold you in my arms and kiss you."

Marilee surprised herself in that instant, for she was completely composed as she tartly informed him, "If you're the sort of man who has to take women by force, then that doesn't make you a *man* in my estimation."

His blue eyes narrowed. The nerve in his jaw tensed ever so slightly. But then his smugness returned. "Oh, I never have to use force, my dear, as you may be privileged to find out if you're fortunate enough to be in my company long enough."

She snickered and could not resist goading, "Oh? Do you resort to begging and wheedling like Rudolf?"

"No, *dushka. I* am never the one who begs."

How she loathed him in that moment. "Hold your breath till I do!" she hissed.

He gave her a confident grin, but it faded from his lips the moment he turned his back on her.

They heard the sound of a car approaching, and, quickly drawing a gun from his coat pocket, he darted to the window. Recognizing the Fiat, he sarcastically said to Marilee, "Your ex-fiancé has arrived with your things."

"He was never my fiancé," she retorted.

The door burst open with a loud bang, and Rudolf stormed into the barn.

Cord regarded him coolly. "Well, that was faster than I expected."

"I was in a hurry to get back and find out what's going on." Rudolf rushed over to Marilee, wincing slightly against her blazing glare. "Are you all right?"

Nodding to Cord, she said, "He seduced me. We fell in love. We plan to be married. Will you come to the wedding?"

"Bitch!" he cried.

Cord had had enough of the cocky little bastard. He strode angrily across the space between them to clamp a rough hand on his shoulder and yank him to his feet. Slamming him against the wall, he warned, "Get something straight, Rudolf, and get it straight now! No more! You got that? You aren't taking it out on her because everything got messed up. It's the way it is, so back off and leave her alone. I'm not putting up with the harassment and the name-calling. She doesn't deserve it."

Despite the fact that Cord Brandt was a head taller and, at the moment, angry, Rudolf dared to challenge him. "Who the hell are you to tell me what to do?"

Cord grabbed him by both shoulders and flung him across the room. Bouncing off a far wall, he slid to the floor to stare up stupidly as Cord casually informed him, "I'm a better man than you, that's who. Remember that if you want to live long."

The door swung open again, and by the time Cord recognized Elenore, his gun was pointed and ready. "What is going on here?" she cried, wide-eyed, looking from him to Marilee, and finally, to where her brother was picking himself up off the floor.

Cord put his weapon away. "That's a good way to get shot, Elenore. Don't come sneaking around like that again."

Marilee came to life, scrambling to her feet and rushing toward Elenore, but Cord grabbed her about the waist and spun her away, holding her tightly against him as she raged, "Let me go, damn you!" She struggled helplessly in his grasp, then beseeched Elenore, who was watching with narrowed eyes. "Go! Get help. They're both working for the Bolsheviks, and they thought they kidnapped Aunt Jade but got me instead, and—"

"Shut up!" Elenore stunned her by suddenly screaming, then she whirled on Rudolf. "You idiot! I knew something like this would happen, that you couldn't pull it off. Now look at what's happened. We'll all go to prison!"

Marilee reeled with the harsh realization that her best friend was actually a part of this madness. "Not you!" she gasped. "Oh, Elenore, not you, too!"

Cord felt her knees buckle and held her tight.

For the moment, Elenore ignored her as Rudolf shrieked, "How could you be so stupid to follow me here? You might have been followed yourself, you fool!"

"She wasn't." Hanisch stepped through the open doorway. "She was hiding in the car, under a pile of clothing, and you didn't even notice."

He added with a disgusted shake of his head, "You are really turning out to be a worthless clod, Rudolf."

His face red with fury and humiliation, Rudolf headed for the door, bellowing as he went, "Okay. Fine. You all handle it. I'm through. I'm getting out. Damned if I'm risking my neck when all I get is insults."

Hanisch made a move to block his path, but Cord ordered tersely, "Let him go. It's best this way. We don't need him anymore."

"But he's wanted at headquarters," Hanisch quickly explained. "I told them of his incompetence. They want him there at once. I advise you to report." He looked at Rudolf with a gloating smile.

"Gladly. I'd like to tell them a few things of my own." Rudolf stalked angrily out of the barn.

Elenore walked to the doorway to watch him for a moment. "He's throwing her things on the ground."

"Go pick them up." Cord ordered. He did not need her around to make things even more tense.

She hesitated, biting her lip thoughtfully as she pondered the situation.

"Elenore," Marilee pleaded one more time, "you have to help me—"

"And I told you to shut up." Elenore did not like the way Cord was holding her—more protective than restraining. "Let her go!" she commanded.

He held fast.

Marilee closed her eyes. Elenore, her dearest friend. One of *them*. Sadly, she declared, "I just don't believe it."

Then, warm against her ear, she heard Cord Brandt whisper, "Believe it, *dushka.*"

Her cinnamon eyes flashed open, and she attempted to twist about to stare at him in wonder. Why would he say such a thing? Call her a Russian pet name—"little soul," "darling"? It was the second time he had done so. But he was German!

But there was no time to ponder, for he gave her a sudden shake, tightening his grip as he tersely told Elenore, "I think it would be best if both you and your brother got out of here. You had no business coming." He dismissed her with a curt nod and turned to ask Hanisch whether he had their orders.

"Oh, yes," came the brusque reply. Hanisch also motioned for Elenore to go. "Hurry up, before he leaves. We'll pick everything up."

"No!" Elenore looked from him to Cord. "Not until we have a word in private."

Nodding toward the door, Hanisch growled, "Do it. Anything to get her out of here. Rudolf, too, till he gets hold of himself."

Cord released Marilee. Hanisch took a step forward, wary lest she needed further restraint. "She'll be all right," Cord said, giving her a gentle nudge back to where she'd been sitting, sending her a secret message with his eyes not to cause a fuss.

She obeyed. Not because she wanted to, but because something told her that he would not allow anyone else to harm her as long as she did what he told her to do. Whether or not she trusted him was beside the point. She could worry about that later. For the moment, she wanted nothing to do with the burly one called Hanisch, who stood glowering at her, obviously hoping she would give him an excuse to put his hands on her.

Elenore walked out, with Cord behind her.

Marilee reflected that the pieces of the puzzle were all starting to fit together, although there were still many unanswered questions.

In the beginning, when Rudolf had begun to court her, there could not have been a plan to kidnap Jade. That had to have come later, after he discovered she was a Romanov. Until then, his scheme had been to marry Marilee, no doubt having something to do with her father. But why? No matter what they said, she would never believe her father was either a thief or a traitor.

There was something going on she did not know about.

But for the present she could be sure of only one thing—the desperate need to escape . . . and not merely from the clutches of these radicals.

She knew, also, that she had to flee the man who could turn her blood to fire.

Long moments passed.

She could hear Elenore's angry voice, but not distinctly enough to make out what she was saying. Cord Brandt's response could not be heard.

She scowled at Hanisch. "You are all lying about my father."

"Don't worry about it," he told her. "Just keep your mouth shut and don't make trouble. He'll get word that you're being held for ransom—the same amount he stole from the Imperial treasury."

"He doesn't need to steal money. He'll pay my ransom with his own."

Hanisch snickered. "He doesn't have any. Not anymore."

She pondered his words for a moment, then forced a laugh. "That is also a lie."

He shrugged. "It doesn't matter what you believe. You'll find out for yourself soon enough."

She turned her back on him, forcing herself to ignore him. He was crazy. They were *all* crazy. Her father was very rich. He'd pay whatever they asked without blinking an eye—*if* they could find him. Evidently they had reason to think they could, and that thought gave her comfort.

As Cord came back into the barn, she heard the sound of a car driving away. "They're gone," he said to no one in particular; then he looked at Hanisch. "All right, let's hear the orders."

Hanisch told him, "I have a route planned for you, with help along the way should you need it."

They walked toward a far corner, and Marilee could not hear any more of their conversation. A few moments later Hanisch left, and she found herself alone again with Cord Brandt.

"Where are you taking me?"

He skirted her question with one of his own. "Do you want something to eat? Hanisch brought some food. Maybe a little wine would make you feel better."

"I asked," she repeated, "where are you taking me?"

He continued to ignore her questions. "We have your clothes, and you can change after you eat. Then take a nap. We'll go when it gets dark."

Marilee followed him to the table, where Hanisch had left a wicker basket. He began to remove a bottle of cognac, a loaf of bread, some cheese, boiled eggs, and fruit. "Why won't you answer me?"

He turned then. She saw the look in his eyes and knew there was something he dreaded telling her, and that realization chilled her with foreboding.

"Later," he said quietly, almost ominously, "we'll talk. For now, trust and obey me, and I'll do everything I can to see that no harm comes to you."

She took the cup of wine he held out to her and sat down at the table.

Neither spoke for several moments. Then Marilee asked candidly, "When you kissed me in the cellar, you thought you were kissing Elenore, didn't you?"

He grinned, that maddening crooked grin that made her feel so damn vulnerable.

"Are you jealous?"

"No. I—I don't care," she stammered. 'I was curious, and—"

He touched his finger to her lips for silence. The arrogant grin faded and was replaced by a somber expression as he told her, "There's a lot you don't understand yet, and for your sake, as well as mine, stop asking so many questions."

She bit her lip, feeling very foolish. Draining the cup of wine, she started to rise, but he reached out to grab her hand and declared huskily, "I didn't know who you were that night. If I had, maybe I wouldn't have left so suddenly."

She looked at him, astonished at his nerve. Snatching her hand away, she cried, "Well, what makes you think I would have let you stay?"

"Time will tell, *dushka*," he murmured, his blue eyes warm and caressing. "Time will tell."

Chapter Seventeen

MARILEE felt a hand on her shoulder, gently shaking her awake. She had not been sleeping soundly and was instantly aware of her desperate situation.

"It's time," Cord announced.

Dim light was provided by a lantern in a far corner. Marilee strained to see his face, curious because he sounded so tense. When she had curled up on burlap bags in one of the stalls to be alone with her worried musings, he had been reading the map Hanisch had brought. Certainly, he had not looked worried then. In fact, he seemed secretly pleased over something.

Then she saw the strange men sitting at the little table. After awakening her, Cord had walked over to talk to them. She could not make out what they were saying, yet she sensed the tension in the air.

Without turning, he called gruffly, "Hurry up. We're leaving now."

She got to her feet. She'd changed earlier into a soft wool traveling suit with a cape.

When she joined them, she could tell that Cord was annoyed. He grudgingly introduced the two men.

"Gretz. Ludwig. They have been ordered to go with us."

Marilee could not resist saying, "You mean you're afraid you can't handle me all by yourself?"

His retort was more a snarl. "It wasn't my idea. Now let's go."

She did not like Gretz and Ludwig. Both of them stared at her insolently, as though raping her with their eyes. The one called Gretz even ran his thick tongue across his lips as his gaze raked over her hungrily.

Cord held out his arm to her. She moved close to him without hesitation as they walked to the automobile. Gretz got behind the steering wheel. Ludwig started to crawl in the back seat but Cord clamped a rough hand on the back of his neck and steered him silently to the front beside Gretz. Then he helped Marilee in and climbed in behind her.

"Don't be frightened," he whispered in her ear as they settled back against the seat. "I won't let anyone hurt you, so just relax."

Somehow, she knew that, but she could not resist saying, "But who will protect me from *you*, Herr Brandt?"

She could not see his face as he murmured, "When that time comes, *I'm* the one who'll need protection from *you*, little one."

His soft laughter needled her and she moved as far from him as possible, overwhelmed by the desperation of her plight.

Gretz and Ludwig took turns driving, and they stopped only when necessary. Marilee fought against sleeping, for when she did succumb she would awaken cradled in Cord Brandt's arms. Despite the wonderful warm feeling, she chided herself for the pleasure. He smiled knowingly, and she loathed him all the more.

Marilee could tell they were heading toward France; however, she did not realize their destination was Paris until the night they stopped at the house of one of their confidants and she overheard a conversation among them.

After dinner, she drew Cord aside. "But why? My father isn't in Paris! He's still in Russia. Was a ransom note sent?"

"Let's go outside," he suggested tersely.

They were in a small farmhouse. Cord guided her toward the back door. Just as they were about to step outside, Ludwig came rushing after them. "Hey! Where do you think you are going?"

Cord whipped around. "I think you forget who's in charge here, Ludwig. I don't have to explain my actions to you."

Ludwig leered at Marilee. "I have orders to keep an eye on *you*, Brandt, and when you sneak off to walk in the moonlight, I'm going along to make sure you keep your pants on. Mikhailonov might not want his daughter back if she's soiled by our German seed," he added with a nasty sneer.

Cord moved so quickly that Marilee only saw his fist crash into Ludwig's face before Ludwig went sprawling to the floor.

She watched numbly as Cord yanked him to his feet and warned furiously, "Keep your dirty mouth shut, and don't try to spy on me, or so help me, I'll kill you. You got that?"

Ludwig nodded, blood streaming from his nose.

He turned on his heel and staggered back to where Gretz and their host stood watching from the dining room.

Marilee had backed away instinctively. Then she saw the vineyard beyond, shielding foliage that would provide cover while she ran—to where? She did not know, only that there was a glimpse of freedom. She started down the steps, about to bolt into what seemed like a long-sought sanctuary.

"Not thinking of leaving me, are you?"

She slowed, commanding her frantic brain not to panic. Gasping, pretending to be terrified, she whirled about to throw herself against Cord. "No, no, I was scared of that man. The way he looks at me—" She made herself tremble.

He put his arms around her. "I know. But I've told you before, I'm never going to let anything happen to you, Marilee. Now let's walk, and you get hold of yourself."

He took her hand and led her to the border of the vineyard. As they walked, he explained that they were, indeed, on their way to Paris, and soon she would understand why. Till then, there was nothing else he could tell her, except to remind her, "You've nothing to fear from me. All I want is to see you safe."

She could not help interjecting coldly, "For a price, of course."

He drew in his breath slowly, then admitted, "Yeah. That's the way it has to be."

She turned back toward the house. He did not call after her, and she kept on going, all the way to the room that had been assigned to her. There was no lock on the door, so she pushed a chair in front of it. Yet she knew that should he wish to enter, neither chair nor lock would stop him.

Instinctively, she knew that time would come, and she wondered whether she felt dread—or anticipation.

As they drove on the next day, Marilee pressed herself against the window, wanting to distance herself from Cord. If he noticed, he did not let on. Finally, she asked, "Why are you fighting the Bolsheviks' war? Germany is starving. Why aren't you concerned about your own country?"

He turned his head slowly, gazing at her absently. Then, in the front seat, Ludwig and Gretz snickered, snapping him out of his reverie. "What did you say?"

She repeated her question.

Ludwig and Gretz laughed again.

Cord frowned and turned to gaze out the window at the passing countryside. "Germany can't win without Russia. Russia will never help Germany under the PG. We need the Bolsheviks in power."

Realizing the futility of arguing, Marilee confided, "I have a cousin with the Allied forces somewhere in France."

"I know."

She blinked, surprised. "You do? How?"

"I know everything about you, *dushka*," he reminded her with a tender glance. "I know your cousin Travis Coltrane just got married. Rudolf went to the wedding. Your cousin is in the Army in France. His father and your uncle, Colt Coltrane, is in the diplomatic service. He was supposed to be sent to Russia, but things are too tense there now. The American government recalled him and sent him to London.''

Marilee was stunned. "How do you know all this?"

"It's my business to know. I'm a spy."

Marilee bristled, chiding herself for having warmed to him even a little. "That's right," she agreed. "A liar and scoundrel. God, I only pray my father hurries and pays my ransom so I can be rid of your company."

Marilee finally dozed. When she awoke she realized that they were just outside Versailles. "My God, we're near Daniberry!"

"Daniberry is our destination," he informed her.

Tears of relief flooded her eyes. "Oh, why didn't you tell me? Is my father here already? You sent the ransom note, and he told you to bring me to Daniberry, and . . ." Her voice faded away as she saw the way he was looking at her.

Cord reached to clasp her hand, but she yanked it away in horror. "You mean he isn't here? Then why are *we* here? What kind of cruel trick are you playing on me now?"

Ludwig yelled gleefully, "Tell her, Brandt!"

"Yeah," Gretz chimed in, "tell the haughty bitch the truth!"

"Stay out of this, both of you," Cord ordered, but he knew he had no choice. "When your father turned against the Czar and the Imperialists, he turned his home over to the Bolsheviks to use as a headquarters in France for their underground movements. And even though he betrayed us when he fled with our gold, we've got Daniberry and we intend to keep it.

"It's the perfect place for him to make contact."

For a moment, Marilee could only look at Cord in stunned silence. It had to be a lie. Her father would never turn his back on Nicholas, who was like a brother to him. And why would he have stolen the gold when he had a fortune of his own, unless—and the thought filled her with cold dread—it *was* true, and he had given away his wealth to the Bolsheviks, but then changed his mind and stolen the gold intended for the counterrevolution.

Dear God!

She leaned her head back and closed her eyes, trembling from head to toe as she fought back the bitter tears of denial.

"Marilee—"

Her eyes flashed open. She whirled furiously on him. "Damn you!" she screamed. "Damn you all to hell!"

The car turned into the driveway, and in the far distance, above the bare limbs of tall, magnificent trees, Daniberry came into view.

As the automobile approached the circular driveway lined with marble statues, Marilee knew there was no need to look for familiar faces. Platt, the gardener, would be nowhere around, for the huge fountain in the middle of the drive was dry, dirt and leaves scattered on the bottom. The windows of the three-story mansion were streaked with dirt. Ila, the housekeeper, had obviously been relieved of her duties.

Then she saw them—the strangers staring as Cord got out of the car, pulling her behind him. Her home, she realized with a sickening jolt, was hers no longer. It was a haven for spies!

"Inside," Cord whispered, grasping her arm and steering her forward. "I've been here. I know my way around. We'll take quarters on the top floor. I've got a few men who respect me and will follow my orders. I'll have the area sealed off. You'll be safe."

As though in a stupor, Marilee allowed him to lead her inside. She was shocked to see that the rare lapis lazuli table cabinet on a Charles II gilt wood stand was missing from the foyer, along with the Regency ormolu candelabra.

Cord released his hold on her, allowing her to wander sadly from room to room. He followed her to the back corner room, the glass sun porch that had been her mother's favorite place, and it was there she gave way to her tears.

"Come along," he urged.

She again allowed him to lead her like a little child. He had no way of knowing that inside she was burning with hatred. She would have her revenge—on him, and Rudolf, and all the others who had conspired in this fiendish deed.

Cord sighed with relief when they got to the top of the stairs and he saw Serge Kurakin on duty. Serge could be trusted. He was one of his own men, handpicked for this assignment.

They exchanged curt nods, but Cord did not pause as he steered Marilee along.

Suddenly she froze when she realized where he was taking her. "My father's room," she said thinly.

"It has the best vantage point, a corner room, large windows on two walls, and—" Cord attempted to explain.

"I'm not sleeping in here with you!" She turned

on him fiercely. "This is too much, Herr Brandt. First you abduct me, then you have the audacity to bring me to my own home to hold me prisoner, then you plan to seduce me in my father's bedroom. Have you no shame?"

He lost patience then and grabbed her wrists, giving her a shake. "Now listen to me, dammit!—" He maneuvered them both into the room, kicking the door shut behind him. He wrestled her to one of the beds and slung her down, holding onto her wrists as she glared up at him with raw hatred.

"How many times do I have to tell you—you've nothing to fear from me. It's *them* you've got to worry about." He nodded toward the door. "Men like Ludwig and Gretz. And the only way I can protect you is to keep you with me, at least until I make sure I've got absolute control over everyone here."

"You could sleep outside the door!" she shot back tartly.

"That's taking a chance. Barricaded in here, I'll feel safer."

"But what about me? Who's going to protect me from you? I know how you operate in the dark."

He released her, unable to resist laughing. "Well, the concern is shared, my dear. I seem to recall that you enjoyed what went on in the dark, and you'll probably dream about it one night and sleepwalk your way to *my* bed. I don't think I've ever experienced such hunger in a woman."

He ducked in time to miss being hit by the first thing she could get her hands on—a marble paperweight the scavengers had overlooked. It crashed against the wall as he slammed and locked the door after him.

Serge rushed across the landing at the top of the stairs to ask, "Is everything all right? She sounds really upset."

Cord sighed and rubbed the back of his neck. "It was a big shock to her, being brought here on top of everything else, and she's also very tired. It's been a long trip. I'll get her some tea and put something in it to make sure she gets the rest she needs."

Serge glanced about before whispering, "You are sure she suspects nothing?"

"Why should she?" Cord grinned wryly, giving Serge's shoulder a hearty pat. "I'm the enemy, remember? You will have to keep watch over her while I slip out tonight and see if I can make contact with headquarters."

Serge grabbed his arm, suddenly frightened. "That's taking a big chance, comrade. Where will you go? And how will you get there?"

"It has to be done. Don't worry about how, that's my problem. Just make sure nothing happens to Drakar's daughter."

Serge sighed and returned to his post as Cord went downstairs.

The huge mansion was secured by Zealots from Zurich and Bolshevik supporters from France. Cord had been told by Hanisch that there were only a dozen men guarding Daniberry. More than that might arouse the suspicion of the Allies. There was no reason to suspect that Daniberry was a holding point for the abduction and subsequent ransom of Mademoiselle

Mikhailonov, and Cord intended to keep it that way. The men were dressed as gardeners and some of their wives posed as maids.

Cord went through the entire house. Then, satisfied there was nothing else to be done for the moment, he went to the kitchen to make tea for Marilee. He wanted her to rest, yes, but most of all, he wanted her to sleep soundly all night.

One day, perhaps he could tell her that her father was actually his comrade, and that they were both working together with the counterrevolutionaries. Drakar, however, had been chosen to defect to the Bolsheviks in order to try to free the Czar and the Imperial family.

But for now, Cord could confide nothing. He could only continue his assignment to protect Marilee Mikhailonov with his own life, if need be.

However, he had not counted on wanting her so badly that it was like a knife in his loins.

Chapter Eighteen

DANIBERRY did not truly seem like home to Marilee. After all, she had never actually lived here, and the occasions when she had met her father here for a reunion could be counted on one hand. The room that was to have been hers held no memories. It did not matter where she was, she supposed. All she could hope for was imminent release and reunion with her father.

Cord Brandt tried to make things easier for her. Yet she masked her growing feelings with exaggerated resentment. No matter what he did for her, she complained.

The big four-poster bed was quite heavy and hard to slide across the floor, but she managed to shove it to the other end of the room. After a cup of tea, she fell so soundly asleep she did not awaken till the next morning—to see Cord sprawled across his bed. He had not attempted to move the four-poster back to its original place and, from all appearances, had not come near her all night long.

She awakened him, demanding to know how long

she could expect to be kept a prisoner. He looked at her groggily, then, without uttering a word, he got up and walked out, locking the door behind him. She was sure he went somewhere else in the house to go back to sleep. The thought that Elenore might be around made her bristle, and she hated herself for even caring.

When he returned later in the morning with a pot of coffee and a breakfast tray, he looked refreshed and wore clean clothes.

When she asked again how long she was going to be held prisoner, he looked at her for a long time before answering.

"Don't lie," she pleaded, her lower lip trembling. "If something has happened to my father, I want to know now."

He quickly allayed her fears. "Don't worry. As far as we know, he's alive."

"Was the ransom note delivered?"

He poured himself a cup of coffee and explained that he could not say for sure. "We won't know until we hear from him. And until then, we stay here."

"And I suppose I stay locked in this room?" Marilee sighed.

"For a few days," he told her, "till I get rid of the men I can't trust." He wasn't about to tell her of his own elation over receiving permission from the Bolsheviks to do just that. If he was in charge, he was going to do things his way. They had agreed, giving him permission to replace men he did not like, and he was doing just that.

* * *

So the time had passed. Days later Marilee awoke hoping that this would be the day she would be given some freedom.

Cord's bed was empty. She padded to the window to look out at the sprawling lawn but she could not see anyone about. Of late she had somehow sensed that there were less people in the house. Certainly, fewer automobiles came and went during the day.

She bathed and dressed, on guard should Cord walk in unexpectedly, although, so far, he politely knocked before opening the door.

She was standing before her father's mirror, one of the few personal items remaining, when she heard Cord's gentle knock, and she invited him to enter.

As usual, he was carrying a tray with coffee, juice, fruit. He set it down on the bedside table before saying quietly, "I have something to tell you."

"Tell me!" she begged, rushing over to him, forgetting, for the moment, to pretend that she loathed him. "Is it my father? Have you heard from him? Is he paying the ransom and coming for me—" She fell silent as she saw his expression change.

"I wish I could tell you that, but all we can be sure of is that the ransom note was sent and received."

She shook her head, bewildered. "But I don't understand. Received by whom—"

He turned away. "You were told, Marilee, that your father was one of those who deserted the Czar when he was forced to abdicate. He went with the Bolsheviks, then betrayed them for his personal gain, stealing all that gold . . ." He winced, hating to repeat the lies.

"But that's not true!" Marilee cried, maneuvering

herself to stand in front of him. "He loves Nicholas and the Empress, and he'd never steal. He'd—"

"He would, and he did!" Cord yelled at her.

"I don't believe you. I will never believe you." Marilee turned away from him, filled with cold hate.

He forced a steely laugh. "It doesn't make any difference what you believe. Sooner or later, you'll see that I'm telling the truth. Meanwhile I have orders to take you to a meeting with a French government official sympathetic to the Czar. It seems that your father, or whoever received the ransom note, wants proof that you are all right before the negotiations go any further."

"And you're going to allow me to go?" she asked dubiously.

He had no choice, as usual. During the night, he had managed to meet with both factions—the Bolsheviks and his people, the Whites. He had orders from both. "Yes," he said finally, "I'm going to allow you to go, and I'll be with you every minute. But it will be dangerous for both of us, especially you.

"I have orders to kill you if you say or do anything to make a scene, if you try to get word to anyone where you are being held," he said, looking at her soberly.

Marilee did not flinch. "And could you do that?" she challenged him icily. "Could you kill me?"

He was too good at his job to hesitate. "Oh, yes," he assured her, his blue eyes locking with her cinnamon ones. "I can . . . and I will, if I have to.

"Don't make me prove it," he added softly, "because I care about you, Marilee . . . more than you realize."

"Oh, I'm sure you do!" she snapped, unmoved. She stalked to the window, trembling with fury as she cried, "You're really just mad about me, aren't you? That's why you can threaten to kill me in one breath and vow that you care about me in the next."

"I don't expect you to understand," Cord said in a low voice.

He walked to the door, pausing to say, "You are free to move about the house for the rest of the day. Just be ready to leave at six tonight. Maybe once they see you're well, it won't be long till you're free."

She turned with her fists clenched, to lash out at him. "I do hope so, Cord Brandt—free of them and free of you!"

He walked out and closed the door behind him without saying a word.

On the drive to Paris, Cord sat in the back seat with Marilee while Serge drove.

"You are beautiful," he had murmured when she came down the stairs wearing an emerald velvet suit, the skirt brushing her ankles. Her hair curled provocatively about her lovely face.

She had thought him startlingly handsome in a dark blue suit, but was not about to tell him so.

They rode in silence for a while, then Marilee asked the question that had been needling her all day. "If my father is said to have betrayed the Czar, then why is a French government official, said to be sympathetic to the Czar, willing to help whoever received the ransom note make sure I'm all right?"

Cord had expected her questions and he was ready. He turned to face her, placing his arm across the back of the seat. "I'll try to explain. You see, Germany wants peace with Russia so Russia will pull out of the war. They helped Lenin get to Russia because they need a regime to make that peace, and Lenin promised he'd give it to them."

Cord went on to explain that with the Bolsheviks ready to seize power, the Allied forces were very nervous. The French government was more than willing to cooperate with any faction in Russia it could get along with.

"So," Cord finished, it doesn't matter to the man I'm taking you to whether your father is a traitor to the Czar or not. All he cares about is that your father is also said to be disloyal to the Bolsheviks, so he's willing to help out whoever it is who wants to make sure you're all right."

Marilee thought that made sense, but she could not help taunting, "Well, it's obvious your Bolshevik comrades have now let it be known I'm in France. Don't you think they'll start looking for me?"

"Not if they want to keep you alive. Believe me, every rule we've issued has been followed. Frankly, it wasn't even necessary to agree to this little tête-à-tête tonight, because we don't like to humor the enemy, but I thought an evening out might brighten your spirits," he teased.

"Oh, you're so kind!" she cried sarcastically, hating the way he was grinning at her. "It probably would have, had I been in different company," she added sharply.

He chuckled, and they rode the rest of the way in silence.

The château to which they went was on the out-

skirts of Paris. As Serge drove up the tree-lined driveway, he anxiously asked Cord, "Are you sure this
isn't going to be an ambush?"

Cord's reply was grim. "They know she'd get the
first bullet if it is."

Marilee shuddered. He reached to touch her in
compassion, but she shrank from him.

There were few cars parked outside, and Marilee
could see by the light of a half-moon that the château
was rundown. This was not the home of a wealthy
and revered French official any longer.

"I hope it's over quickly," she whispered.

Cord slipped a protective arm about her waist.
"Don't worry. This won't take long." He then instructed Serge to keep the motor running.

At the door, they were greeted stiffly by an austere-
looking man, who Marilee guessed was well into his
sixties. He anxiously looked her up and down, as
though searching for signs of abuse. Then he introduced himself as Monsieur Pomeroy Devane and motioned them inside.

He clasped Marilee's hand and asked solicitously,
"Are you all right, my dear? Are they treating you
well?"

Cord tightened his hold on her in warning.

"I'm fine," she said quickly. "Have you seen my
father? Is he well? Is there anything you can tell me—"

"You aren't to ask questions," Curt interrupted
brusquely. Then he said to Devane, "All right, you've
made sure she's well. Now get word to your people
that we're tired of waiting. We want the ransom paid.
No more stalling."

Devane nodded but kept hold of Marilee's hand.

"We've every reason to believe your father's well. You are not to worry. We're doing all we can to hasten your freedom from these madmen, and—"

"That's enough." Cord grabbed her hand from Devane and led her out the door and back to the waiting car.

As Serge careened out of the driveway onto the main road, Marilee was thrown against Cord. When she tried to jerk away from him, he held her tightly. She started to protest, but he snapped, "Shut up and keep your head down." Then he leaned forward. "You're sure you know exactly where the other car is parked?"

Serge nodded, intent on watching the road.

"I don't understand," Marilee said, no longer struggling in Cord's arms. "What are you afraid of? The whole thing was ridiculous, a sham. What did you accomplish?"

"They have the proof they need that you're all right. And while it might have seemed ridiculous to you, I don't think having a half-dozen men with guns all around me is ridiculous at all. I'd say it was pretty damn serious."

Serge swerved without warning, speeding down a bumpy, narrow path between thick shrubs and foliage, then screeching to a stop. Cord opened the door and quickly pulled Marilee out. As they hurried through the night she could see there was another automobile waiting. They got in and Serge took the wheel again.

"We took this precaution in case we were followed," Cord said, holding her closer than necessary. "But I still think you should keep your head down."

His voice was tender, and there, in the coziness of the back seat, wrapped in a velvet shroud of darkness, Marilee suddenly did not want to move away from him. After the stress she'd been under all evening, it felt good to be wrapped in his strong arms. Without realizing it, she snuggled even closer to him.

Long moments passed as Marilee pressed her head against his chest. He began to dance his fingers up and down her arm, gently caressing her.

Then, he suddenly gathered her close and kissed her—warmly, possessively, parting her lips with his tongue as he pulled her yet closer. She did not resist when he maneuvered her down onto the seat, his mouth moving hungrily to her throat as she stroked his hair with her fingertips. Strange but delicious tremors were running through her body. Her heart felt as though it were on fire, the flames igniting her with longing and desire.

She felt Cord's hand move to her breast and gently squeeze, and she gasped. He silenced her with a kiss that seared her lips and made her dizzy with delight.

He pressed his body on top of hers, there as they lay on the seat, and she could feel his hardness against her. She told herself to push him away, but her hands refused to obey. Instead she clutched him desperately, pulling him still closer.

Then she felt his hand slip beneath her skirt and something within told her not to yield. She knew instinctively that once she gave in to him, to her own gnawing, burning needs, there would be no turning back. Escape, revenge, finding her beloved father—none of those driving goals would exist anymore. She would succumb to him, his passion, and cease to think beyond. No matter that her whole body was alive and screaming for fulfillment—he was the enemy. She had to resist.

Mustering every ounce of will and courage she possessed, Marilee grabbed his seeking hand and tore her mouth from his. "No!" she whispered hoarsely. "Stop it! Get away from me. Now!"

He could have taken her then and there, and they both knew it. Yet Cord did not want her that way, and it was her awareness of this which gave her confidence.

He released her, and she moved away, straightening her hair and her skirt. Her heart was pounding in her chest, and her breath came in quick, hot gasps.

They were almost back at Daniberry.

She could feel Cord's eyes on her in the darkness.

Then, just as the car turned into the long, winding driveway, he spoke, so low that he was barely audible—but the message was clear.

"It *will* happen, *dushka*. When you are truly honest with yourself. Believe it."

And somehow, despite her fierce resolutions, she did.

Chapter Nineteen

MARILEE awoke the next morning, after a very restless night, to see that Cord's bed was empty. Again he had chosen to sleep elsewhere. And although she felt a wave of loneliness, she knew it was best, for it was becoming increasingly difficult to resist the hunger raging within her.

She no longer hated Cord, nor did she fear him. They had grown close, despite the tense situation they were in. Yet she knew she had to leave him—not only to find her father, but also to avoid rolling headlong into a relationship that could only lead to a broken heart. And if the ransom were not paid soon, she would have to find a way to escape.

He did not come to her at all that day, and when Serge brought in her food trays at breakfast and lunch, he refused to answer any questions as to Cord's whereabouts. But when he was still not back by dinner, Serge reluctantly confided that he was away on business, and he had no idea when he would return. His orders were to keep her locked in her room until he came back. She would not have freedom to roam the house or the estate.

189

"That must mean that after last night, Monsieur Devane made arrangements to pay the ransom, and Cord has gone to get it!" Marilee cried excitedly.

Serge would make no further comment and left, securing the door behind him.

Once more Marilee found herself alone, facing an empty, haunting night. However, she could not help feeling fired by excitement, thinking ahead to when she would be free. No doubt she would be sent back to Spain to stay with the Coltranes until the turmoil in Russia was over and her father was free to come to her. But that was not what she intended. She was not going to sit idly by any longer, waiting for life to happen to her. The first thing she planned was to go to Russia and, somehow, find her father.

However, it was not going to be easy to forget Cord Brandt.

Cord—handsome, charming, provocative, tantalizing. He was the kind of man she thought she'd never have in her life. Being honest with herself, Marilee knew she wanted him—terribly. Although no man had ever possessed her, she knew instinctively that when Cord finally took her for his own, it would exceed even her dreams.

But would it happen?

She knew she could not merely give herself to him for the sake of passion or pleasure.

And Cord was not the marrying kind.

Even if *she* would consider marrying *him*.

So, for the time being, she could only lie awake, resisting sleep, for sleep brought tormenting dreams of tender kisses and intimate caresses . . . leaving her lost and hungry and aching for fulfillment.

Cord did not come the next day, but late in the evening, when she was lying in bed reading a book Serge had found for her, she heard the key turning in the lock and sat up expectantly.

He came into the room like a breath of fresh air, and Marilee's heart skipped a beat at the sight of him.

Their eyes met and held, but there was no time to ponder the electricity charging between them. He crossed the room, sat down in a chair beside her bed, and said brusquely, "I have news. It's not what either of us hoped for."

She was afraid to ask what he meant, staring at him with anticipation.

He explained that Monsieur Devane had admitted that Drakar could not be located. He and some of his friends, out of respect for Drakar and their sympathy for Czar Nicholas, had tried to raise the ransom among themselves. They were not successful.

Marilee's eyes widened with horror as she listened, then her hand flew to her throat. "But what does all this mean? If they can't find my father and they can't raise the money, you'll be told to kill me, won't you?"

"That won't happen, believe me," he assured her quickly.

She shook her head slowly. "You can't say that my life isn't in danger if the ransom isn't paid."

"I told you I wasn't going to let anything happen to you, and I'm not," he said almost angrily. I wish I could just let you go, but I can't. Be patient, Marilee," he urged her softly. "Many people are working on this. Try not to worry."

"Well, why don't you go to the Coltranes for the

money?'' she demanded. "They will pay it, I'm sure.''

"The ransom is not really the point," he explained. "It never was. The *source* of the ransom was what mattered, as far as the Bolsheviks are concerned. Frankly, I doubt they'd have taken money from Devane and his people. They want what your father took with him when he went into hiding—and they want *him*. They also know that the money was smuggled out by a woman who, I'm told, is your father's mistress.''

Cord paused for her to absorb that bit of information. Marilee merely shrugged. He went on. "She was captured and tortured, but she refused to talk. She escaped from a hospital where she was being treated for her wounds, and they think she's found her way to your father or the protection of the Whites. But the reason the Bolsheviks want that money is because they know it will be used to try and free the Czar.''

"But if they can't find my father, and if they can't get word to him that he has to swap the money for me, what will happen?''

Cord took a deep breath, let it out slowly. "You will be held hostage until either Drakar or the money is found.''

Marilee contemplated all she'd been told, then asked, "Can you tell me if my aunt, or any of the Coltranes, knows that I've been kidnapped?''

"No. The original note, which demanded *her* ransom—before we discovered you were kidnapped by mistake—was intercepted before it was delivered. We've since learned she's gone to London to visit your uncle. So far, they don't suspect you're missing, and you can believe it has been emphasized to the Whites that the Coltranes are not to be told."

"So we wait," she declared with a shrug of resignation.

He nodded quietly. "Does it have to be so bad? I think you've found out I'm not the ogre you originally thought I was."

She wondered what his reaction would be if he knew just what she did think of him, that it was all she could do to refrain from throwing herself into his warm, strong arms.

Forcing such thoughts aside, she agreed that the situation was not all bad. "While I don't agree with your philosophies, and I still think you are all lying about my father, I realize that you're only doing as you're told. I'd like to think of you as a friend."

He laughed gently, getting to his feet. "Well, then, if I'm to remain your friend, I'd best take my leave before I give in to temptation and crawl into that bed with you."

Marilee felt her cheeks flame as a shiver of delight coursed through her body. "Yes," she said in a barely audible voice as she retrieved her book and tried once more to concentrate on what she was reading, "I think that would be best."

As soon as he closed the door behind him, she threw the book across the room and burst into tears.

Cord made sure that they had enjoyable days, and they spent long hours walking about the estate while she told him of her childhood memories of Daniberry.

One warm fall afternoon they were in one of the forgotten gardens, sitting on a wrought-iron bench beneath the bare arms of a weeping willow tree. Marilee began to talk, sharing stories of cherished times here with her father.

She also told him about the Coltranes—their exploits, tragedies, and triumphs. He listened raptly. "Maybe one day someone will write a saga about the Coltranes," he commented.

"Maybe we'd better wait and see how *my* story turns out. Maybe that will be the end of the saga," she said soberly.

He drew her close, his breath warm on her face. "God, I hope not, Marilee," he whispered fervently. "I hope the Coltranes never end—that you and I never end."

"All things end," she said nervously. "There has to be an ending in order to have a new beginning."

He devoured her with his eyes as his hands moved possessively up her back, tracing the curve of her spine, the swell of her hips. He pressed her closer, and she felt his hardness as he held her against him. "I think we've begun, my little *dushka*," he murmured huskily. "I don't want to think about where it ends. Not now . . ."

His mouth claimed hers in a searing kiss that left them both shaken.

Mustering every ounce of self-control she possessed, Marilee pulled out of his embrace. She glanced about nervously, afraid that someone was watching. "We'd better go inside. This . . . this isn't right," she stammered, turning toward the chalet.

"It *is* right," he argued, following after her.

"What's wrong is that you're too immature to accept it."

She was not about to be goaded into a fight. "Like all the women before me, Herr Brandt? Did they accept your kisses and everything that goes with them? Did they fall into your arms like eager little puppies?" she asked, tossing her head.

He pretended to ponder her question as he fell into step beside her. She allowed him to take her hand. Finally he sighed. "Yes, I guess they did. I truly can't remember ever being turned down. Not even once. You're quite a challenge, Fräulein Mikhailonov. Maybe that's why you're driving me crazy."

"Oh, really?" She gave him a mock look of wonder. "Then why don't you let me go?"

She broke into a run toward the house, laughing as he followed right behind her. He allowed her to gain a lead, then he grabbed her just as she sprinted into the deserted rose garden. He lunged, grabbing her about her waist and bringing her down with him, laughing, to the ground.

But the laughter stopped when he kissed her. Marilee tried to roll away, but he held her tight and rolled with her until they rested beneath a large shrub that hid them from anyone who might be about.

"Marilee, I want you . . ." he declared, cupping her face in his hands and forcing her to look directly at him. "And you want me. Damn this pretending—damn me sleeping in another bed, or on the floor outside your door, lying awake all night in pain from wanting you more than I've ever wanted a woman in my life!"

"But that's only because you can't have me, and—"

"Dammit, stop playing!" He gave her a shake, then he kissed her again, almost bruising her lips. "Why are you denying us the little bit of pleasure we can take in an otherwise cruel and lonely world? Who's to say either one of us will ever get out of this alive? Why are you torturing me? Torturing yourself?"

Why am I, indeed? Marilee asked herself as her gaze burned into his. Dear God, she *did* want him—fiercely. She, too, suffered physical agony each time they were apart.

She closed her eyes against the emotions running wild within her. Then they both stiffened at the sound of Serge's frantic voice.

"Brandt! Brandt! Where are you?"

Cord sprang to a crouch as he drew his pistol. Holding a finger to his lips, he motioned Marilee to remain where she was and not make a sound.

Then he waited.

Serge's voice came closer. "Brandt! Where the hell are you?"

Finally Cord decided it was safe to call out to him.

"You must come at once," Serge said. "We've got a visitor—"

"What?" Cord roared, glancing about wildly. "Who the hell got through the security posted at the entrance? We weren't expecting anybody."

"A woman," Serge informed him, almost apologetically. "She had the necessary papers to get through security. She's a Zealot. From Zurich."

Cord's eyes narrowed. *Dammit,* he cursed under his breath. It could only be *her.*

"She said . . ." Serge paused to take a deep breath,

knowing his comrade was not going to like what he was about to hear.

But Cord finished for him. "She said her name was Elenore. Goddammit!" he swore again. Marilee felt as though she'd been dashed with ice water. Scrambling to her feet, she joined them as Cord instructed Serge to take her back to her quarters.

He reached out and caressed her cheek, murmuring, "Don't worry. It's not what you're thinking."

Her cinnamon eyes flashed with fire. Although he had never owned up to the fact, Marilee knew he'd been looking for Elenore that night in the cellar. The kisses, the caresses that had awakened her to never-before-experienced passion had been meant for Elenore. And now she had to remind herself that no matter how she felt when he held her in his arms, he was still the enemy—and so was his lover. "How the hell do you know what I'm thinking?" she snapped coldly, hurrying to where Serge was waiting.

Cord watched them go, shaking his head in disgust. Damn! He did not need Elenore to show up—not now. Not when he had almost gained Marilee's trust and confidence.

And maybe, most importantly, her *love*.

Chapter Twenty

SERGE had left Elenore in the custody of one of the other guards. He was not about to give her the freedom to roam about. She paced up and down anxiously, every so often giving the man watching her a glare to let him know she was greatly vexed by his presence.

He merely ignored her.

All the weeks of thinking about Cordell being alone somewhere with another woman had been torture. There was no denying that Marilee was beautiful, and Elenore was all too aware of Cordell's appeal.

She jumped at the sound of the door opening, then screamed at the sight of Cordell walking into the room. "Oh, my darling, how I've missed you!" she cried excitedly. She threw herself upon him with such eagerness he was almost caught off-balance, and began to shower his face with kisses.

The guard smirked.

Cord saw him watching and hissed angrily in Elenore's ear before pushing her back, "Not now, goddammit!"

To the guard, he snapped, "It's okay. You can leave."

As soon as they were alone, Elenore attempted to throw herself at Cord again, but he held her away from him. "What are you doing here?" he demanded. "You had no business—"

She was indignant, masking her humiliation with anger. "Oh, yes, I did!" she blazed. "I had permission. I can prove it."

"Just tell me why you're here."

She tossed the remnants of her pride to the wind and tried once more to wrap her arms about his neck. As he stiffened, she smiled coquettishly. "If you keep pushing me away, darling, I'm not going to tell you, and I think you'll want to know, since I bring very important orders."

"And how did you get here?" Cord persisted.

"By train," she said airily. "An automobile provided by friends in Paris. What difference does it make?" She stood on tiptoe to playfully bestow a kiss on the tip of his nose. "I'm here. We're together again. Aren't you glad to see me?"

She was too damn close, Cord decided, triggering heated memories of the passionate hours they'd shared. After just having been agonizingly aroused by Marilee, he was in no mood for teasing. He unwound her arms from about his neck and held her wrists. Giving her a gentle shake, he commanded firmly, "No games, sweetheart. Just tell me why you're here, and we'll play later, all right?" He had no intention of taking up with her again, not when Marilee had come to mean so much to him. But he wasn't about to let Elenore know that. Not yet, anyway.

She pouted silently for a moment. "All right. Business first," she then said.

He released her and she sat down on the one piece of furniture left in the room—a divan—and patted the seat beside her.

He remained standing.

She sighed. "Oh, Cord, for heaven's sake! What is wrong with you? Being around that namby-pamby little virgin princess has made you positively stodgy!"

He stood with his feet slightly apart, his arms folded across his chest. "Just give me the orders, Elenore."

She paused for effect, then gave up. "Oh, very well. I'll tell you. Drakar Mikhailonov cannot be located. The ransom will not be paid. The kidnapping was a failure. As I knew it would be," she finished with a triumphant grin.

Cord felt a tremor of foreboding. If there was no ransom, what would happen to Marilee? Surely they had not ordered that she be killed, because he'd be damned if he'd let that happen.

Keeping his voice even so as not to betray his inner turmoil, he urged, "So what happens now? And why was it necessary for you to come here? I report to headquarters regularly."

Her gaze was warm with desire. "Because I persuaded them to let me come to you. I've nowhere else to go, and you don't know how badly I've missed you."

He ignored her last words and snapped, "Well, you aren't staying here. And if there's to be no ransom, then I'm getting out, too. Just give me the damn orders, Elenore, so I can find out what the hell is going on around here." He held out his hand impatiently.

She took an envelope from her bag and gave it to him, swallowing her rage at his coldness.

He scanned the lines quickly. He was to take Marilee to Petrograd, where she would be bait for Drakar. The Bolsheviks believed that sooner or later he would hear that his daughter was being held hostage, and he would come out of hiding to save her. Cord did not like their plan. He knew that once he turned Marilee over to them, her fate would be out of his hands.

"Is something wrong?" Elenore asked sharply, seeing the way his brow furrowed. "I thought you'd be pleased. You won't have to keep staying here. You can send Marilee on to Petrograd, and you and I can return to Switzerland together, and—"

"Where's Rudolf?" he interrupted.

She shrugged. "He got worried that the Coltranes would eventually find out Marilee is missing and trace everything to him, and he'd get the blame and go to prison. So he left for Russia with Hanisch Lutzstein and the others in preparation for the Bolshevik take-over—leaving *me* behind," she added testily.

"And your mother? What about her?"

Another shrug. "He had her committed to an asylum. The way she drinks, that's where she belongs, because she can't be left alone, and I'm not going to get stuck with her. I've got my own life to live."

But not with me, he yearned to tell her, feeling no guilt or regret. He had never promised her anything, never professed his love for her. He gave her pleasure and got pleasure in return. That's all it was, and all it could ever be. She might be a hell of a beautiful woman, and a wild, wanton tigress in bed, but it ended there. Elenore had no depth. There was nothing to experience or share with her once their passion was spent.

She started toward him, but he backed away in the direction of the door. "I need to make some inquiries about all this," he told her.

"So do that." She nodded. "But first, don't you have a few moments for me? It's been a long time, darling, and I've missed you . . ."

"Later." He turned to walk out.

Suddenly she sprang at him, pressing herself against his broad back and crying furiously, "Oh, Cord, my darling! How can you treat me like this after all we've meant to each other? How can you forget all the hours we made such beautiful love? I can't believe you've turned to Marilee, that she could give you more than me . . ."

He knew she was nearing hysteria. Soon, someone would hear her, maybe even Marilee. Damn, he couldn't risk that. Not now. Not when he needed her to trust him more than ever before.

With forced resignation, he turned and took Elenore in his arms. As he'd hoped, she yielded. "No," he was able to say honestly, "I haven't forgot what we shared, Elenore, but you've got to realize these are tense times. I've other things on my mind right now than making love to you or any other woman. There are things I've got to do. Arrangements have to be made, and—"

"Oh, darling, darling." She stood on tiptoe, smiling up at him as she trembled with anticipation. "You know I understand. We're on the same side, remember?''

''And you remember I've got a job to do, and that job comes first.''

He released her, and she stepped back, now staring up at him petulantly. ''Go, then. Do what you must do. Then come back to me, because I want to show you just how much I've missed you.''

She threw her arms around his neck and kissed him long and hard. After a few seconds Cord realized that he wanted to respond. It had been a long time. Elenore *was* a desirable woman. Marilee had unknowingly driven him crazy with wanting her. He felt himself becoming aroused, not caring that it was Elenore and not Marilee, whom he truly desired. He pulled her close, wanting to feel her large, firm breasts against his chest, knowing how she'd always liked to feel his erection against her.

Boldly she reached to touch him, and the ache grew worse.

''When?'' she whispered huskily, her tongue running across his lips as she continued to caress him through his trousers, now proud and sure of herself. ''When can we be together, darling? When can I show you how much I've missed you? When can I make you tear me to pieces with your desire . . .''

''Dammit, Elenore!'' How he wished he could take her then and there. The desire was so goddamn fierce he was aching.

''Promise me,'' she begged.

''I'm not promising anything.'' He managed to pull away from her and open the door behind him. He yelled to the guard, who was hovering outside. ''Take her to the sun porch downstairs and see that she's comfortable. Give her anything she wants, but keep her there.''

Elenore's expression was stormy. "I'll not forgive you if you don't come to me tonight," she whispered. "Now go do what must be done to carry out your orders, and then we'll make our own plans to go back to Zurich, where we'll be safe . . . and happy."

Serge was waiting anxiously to hear what was going on, why Elenore had shown up unannounced.

"She has a way of manipulating people into doing what she wants," Cord told him furiously. "Obviously she persuaded someone to let her bring important information.

"Where's Marilee, by the way?" he asked suddenly.

"I took her to her room. She's all right."

They went to the kitchen, poured a cup of coffee, and sat at the table to discuss the situation.

Serge agreed that Marilee should not be turned over to the Bolsheviks. "But what do we do? If you don't obey, they'll take her away from us, and you can believe they'll figure out that we're counterrevolutionaries—which means we'll be executed," he finished grimly.

Cord sighed. "I know that. So there's only one thing to do. I'll get in touch with our people tonight for approval to go underground. It will mean confiding everything to Marilee so she'll cooperate, but I was getting close to telling her, anyway."

Serge smiled knowingly. "Yes, I would say you've been getting close to a lot of things—like falling in love."

Cord looked at him sharply, but then he could not help grinning. "It shows?"

Serge nodded. "It shows."

Cord downed his coffee in one gulp, pushed back his chair, and stood up. "I'll slip out around midnight, and when I return, we'll be able to make firm plans to get out of here."

He started out of the room. "I've got a feeling that it's not easy to get rid of *her,*" Serge said pointedly.

Cord nodded curtly, continuing on his way.

He found Marilee in her room, standing at the window with a pensive expression on her face. She did not turn when he entered. He walked over to stand behind her, wrapping his arms about her, his chin resting on top of her head as he held her close.

Still she did not move, and they stood together in silence. Then she finally whispered, "It *was* her, wasn't it?"

He knew what she meant, just as he knew she'd figured out long ago he'd mistaken her for Elenore that night in the basement of Rudolf's castle. Yes, he'd thought she was Elenore—but only for an instant, because once his mouth had pressed against her sweet, tender lips, he'd known it was the kiss of a stranger— a woman hungry for love and affection. It was only later, when he'd had time to think about the warm and wonderful curves of her body, the way she'd clung to him for just an instant, that he knew she was fire waiting to be ignited—that not only was there a hot, burning spirit of desire, but also a sweetness yet untasted, a sweetness that would eventually work its way into his very soul.

"Yes," he whispered quietly, his arms tightening about her. "I was waiting for Elenore. She was supposed to meet me there that night. I found out later that Rudolf had locked her in with his mother."

Her laugh was tinged with bitterness. "Yes, and then when he got drunk and I had to run away from him, I found my way to you instead."

"And was it so bad?" he asked quietly.

She turned to face him, entwining her arms about his neck. "In fact, I think I knew it was you, before it was . . ." She shook her head in wonder, a sad smile touching her lips. "Oh, but that doesn't make sense, does it? You can't understand what it was like, my dreams haunted by a faceless man who held me and took me to heights of unknown pleasure, unknowingly searching for so long to find that man, and then there you were, and—"

He silenced her with a kiss.

Yes, he knew, for in his own way he, too, had harbored a dream of a love yet undiscovered. And quietly, like a thief in the night, she had stolen into his world, his being, and his heart, to make him want and love her as he'd never wanted or loved a woman before.

Lifting her in his arms, he carried her to the bed and laid her down, then he stretched out beside her and gathered her close. His hands moved up and down her body, and she arched even nearer, wanting to meld into him. Their eyes met and held, blazing with passion and the love they could not deny.

Cord could restrain himself no longer. He lifted her skirt, caressing her thighs and leaving a path of fire as he danced his fingertips higher.

Marilee knew she was dangerously close to reaching a point of no return, yet she could not forget that he was the enemy and she, the prisoner. Was he merely using her to satiate his lust? Was she no more to him than Elenore had been?

But exactly what had Elenore meant to him?

Marilee reached to still his caressing hand, shrinking away from him.

"I must know . . ." She met his questioning gaze. "What was she to you? And why is she here if she means nothing more?"

Cord felt a deep wrenching inside. With a ragged sigh, he rolled away from her, staring up at the ceiling in frustration. He should have known she would demand an explanation.

"I know you won't believe me, but she meant nothing to me, Marilee," he finally said. "She's attractive. She was there when I needed a woman. It was never more than that."

"And I'm to believe that *I* mean more?" Marilee got up and went to stand at the window.

He made no move to stop her, but continued to stare up at the ceiling, his arms folded behind his head. "Yes, because despite the situation we unfortunately find ourselves in, you do mean a lot to me, Marilee," he said miserably.

"And I'm to believe it's all over between you and Elenore?" she asked sarcastically.

"Nothing ever really began," he said tiredly.

"Then why is she here?" she asked once more.

He sat up then. "She's a revolutionary, Marilee. Like me. That's where I met her—at the Wolfa in Zurich, where a group called the Zealots gathered.

She came here today because she has orders from the Bolsheviks concerning you.''

Marilee whirled around, her eyes wide with hope. ''My father!'' she cried. ''They've found him? And he's paying the ransom, and . . .'' Her voice faded as she saw his expression of dismay.

''I'm afraid not.'' He hated to tell her, but he had no choice. ''They've finally decided that the plan to ransom you has failed. So now they want you turned over to them in Russia, to make your father come out of hiding.''

Marilee's heart began to pound with excitement and anticipation. Going to Russia meant being nearer to her father. He was a smart man—he and his comrades would find a way to rescue her. She was far more likely to get out of her predicament there than where she was now. But one prickling question remained— what about her growing feelings for Cord? Despite the fact that he was the enemy, she could not deny how much she cared for him.

She knelt before him, and he cupped her face in his hands. She gazed up at him through tears of joy and trepidation. ''You'll take me there, then? We'll have time to know each other even better, to grow closer. Maybe you will embrace my father's beliefs, and—''

''Marilee, stop it!'' He could not stand to listen any longer. The time had come for her to learn the truth.

He took a deep breath as she watched him anxiously. ''Marilee, there's something I have to tell you—''

''Oh, isn't this sweet?''

They both looked up at Elenore.

"What the hell are you doing here?" Cord demanded. "I gave orders that you were to be kept on the sun porch."

Elenore's eyes narrowed. They were filled with such venomous loathing that Marilee wondered how she could ever have believed Elenore was her friend.

"So this is why there is talk at headquarters that you are becoming weak!" Elenore lashed out at Cord. "I'd heard rumors from the comrades that you were weakening for this icy little virgin, but I was too stupid to believe it. What secret does she possess that makes you such a fool, Cord? What is it she does that I can't do better?"

Cord grabbed her arm and steered her out, coolly declaring, "I don't have to explain anything to you." The door closed behind them.

For a few moments, Marilee could only stand there in bewilderment. But then she came to her senses with a white-hot flash of realization.

It did not matter that Cord was the enemy.

That had nothing to do with the fact that she was falling in love with him.

And no matter what it took, she was not going to lose him to Elenore.

Chapter Twenty-one

For the first time in her life Marilee knew what she wanted, and nothing was going to stand in her way.

But when afternoon faded into evening, she could not deny the prickling feeling that something was wrong.

Serge brought her dinner tray, and she saw the worried look in his eyes when she inquired about Cord, and noticed his evasive tone when he told her that Cord was away on business.

Blocking his escape, she asked, "What kind of business did Cord have to take care of, Serge? Is he making plans for us to leave?"

Serge paled. "I don't know what you're talking about."

"Yes, you do." She gave him a confident smile. "I already know that the ransom won't be paid because your leaders can't locate my father, and they want me taken to Russia. So you can tell me where Cord has gone—and why."

Serge shook his head. "He'll be in to see you when he returns, I'm sure."

He tried to move around her, but she remained where she was.

"Has Elenore left?" she asked curtly.

Serge drew in his breath and let it out slowly. "No. She's still here. I think Brandt went for her orders, as well. I assume," he added nervously, "that he told you she's one of us?"

"Oh, yes." Marilee nodded, frowning. "I was taken in by her, just like her brother. They both made a fool of me, but I'm wiser now."

She stepped aside, then asked softly, "Tell me, where is she staying? I have a right to know. It *is* my home."

"The sun porch on the first floor," he answered readily.

Marilee hoped she was able to hide her anger. That room had been her mother's favorite! To quarter a coldhearted, lying vixen like Elenore there was a sacrilege. But she was not about to say so, not to Serge, anyway.

He started to pass once more. "If you need anything—"

"I do!" Marilee interrupted quickly, feeling a sudden need to see Elenore. But first she had to get by Serge and down the stairs.

He looked at her expectantly. "Yes?"

"Uh, wine!" She snapped her fingers. "I'd like a bottle of Chablis with my dinner. I'm sure Cord would enjoy a glass later. Would you mind terribly?" She opened the door with a beseeching expression, then turned and walked back toward the toilet alcove with its brocade dressing screen, pretending to be in a hurry.

"I need to wash up," she called over her shoulder as she disappeared behind the screen. "Just leave the bottle and two glasses beside my tray.

"And I'm so grateful," she added sweetly.

Serge hurried out, relieved to have been spared further interrogation.

Marilee waited a few moments, then peered out from behind the dressing screen. She smiled in triumph as she realized her plan had apparently worked. He had thought she would be in her toilet, and he was in a hurry, so he had left the door ajar!

She moved quickly.

Tiptoeing out of the room, she glanced about furtively to make sure there were no other guards. Then she stealthily made her way to the front stairway, knowing that Serge would have gone the back way.

She was almost at the entrance foyer when suddenly the front door swung open and Cord walked in.

She dropped to her knees behind the thick mahogany balusters and he failed to see her as he strode quickly and purposefully down the hallway toward the rear of the house.

Marilee felt a sudden wave of fury as she realized that he was headed for the sun porch!

She stood up and forced herself to continue slowly on her way despite the urge to run and burst in on them.

Cord, unaware that Marilee was following him to the sun porch, unlocked the door and stepped inside.

Elenore had been waiting for him ever since he had left her there long hours earlier with a stern warning she was to stay there and keep quiet until he could report to headquarters and confirm the orders she had brought.

She was lying on a wicker chaise, covered with a down comforter. Her hair was loose and flowing around her shoulders, and she lay with her eyes half closed. "I've missed you," she said huskily.

Cord was uneasy at once. Her shoulders were bare. Then she confirmed his suspicions by throwing back the comforter and lazily standing up—completely naked.

"I've been waiting for this moment." Her tongue flicked provocatively across her moist, wet lips, and she moved with seductive grace to where he stood.

Cord did not move.

Despite his reservations, he could not help being aroused.

Her large, firm breasts had always enticed him.

Her waist was narrow and her hips were wide and curved.

Merely watching her move across the floor made him instantly erect.

She stood before him, scant feet away, and paused to spread her legs, in a pose meant to tease and torment. "For you, my darling. All for you. I know you want me. Take me here. Now!" she commanded.

Cord bit down on his lip, the nerves in his jaw tensing. Goddammit, he loved Marilee, but love had nothing to do with the way his insides were on fire now. Elenore had always been a good and satisfying lover, and it had been too long since he'd had her or any other woman.

And he could not, would not, apologize for being a man.

She curved her forefinger toward him, urging him to follow as she backed toward the chaise.

She lay down, spreading her thighs yet wider, caressing herself. "For you, darling. All for you. Take me . . ."

With a deep, agonizing groan of surrender, Cord went to her and lay down on top of her, his lips claiming hers.

Marilee rounded the corner—and stopped dead still. She could see that the door to the sun porch was ajar.

All was silent from within.

Had she made a mistake? she wondered. Had Cord perhaps turned and gone up the back steps? Was he, this very moment, discovering that she was missing?

Well, all she wanted was a few moments alone with Elenore to get a few things off her chest. For too long she had allowed others to manipulate her. Now she wanted to tell Elenore just what a two-faced bitch she was for having connived with her lying, cowardly brother.

And yes, she had to admit that she yearned to tell Elenore of that night in the basement, how wonderful Cord's kisses had tasted. By God, she wanted to have the delicious revenge of seeing the look on Elenore's face when she told her that she intended to have Cord—for always.

Taking a deep breath, she tiptoed quietly to the door, pushed it open—and froze in horror.

Without a word, she turned and fled as quickly and quietly as she had come.

Cord and Elenore, lost in their wild and wanton passion, were totally unaware of her presence.

Marilee ran into the nearest room, a large storage closet that her mother had used for arranging flowers. Now it was empty, and Marilee sank to the floor in the darkness and allowed the tears to come.

First she was overwhelmed with sorrow and heartache to think how Cord had made a fool of her. She had never been any more to him than just another body to give him pleasure. And he obviously wanted Elenore more, for it had been to her he had gone first—not to culminate the passion *they* had shared earlier in the day.

But the sorrow and heartache quickly turned into boiling fury, such as she'd never known before.

Damn him!

Damn him straight to hell!

No more would he make a fool of her.

No more would anyone make a fool of her.

She had been used for the last time in her life.

And now, she realized wildly, she had a chance to escape.

Cord was busy with his animal lust.

Serge was, no doubt, relaxing outside her door, confident that she was safely locked inside.

No one knew she was free, so all she had to do was get out of the house and away from the estate.

But then where?

She thought a moment, trying to think rationally.

She knew Elenore had driven an automobile, for she had seen it parked in the circular driveway in front of the house.

Marilee chewed her lip anxiously. While she had never actually driven a car, she had watched others and felt she could handle it. In her present state of desperation, she felt she could do anything.

Stepping from the closet, she saw by a nearby window that darkness had fallen outside. All she had to do was get in the car and make her way quietly to the overgrown back road which led to the site of a winery her father had planned to build. From there a rough, curving road led to yet another back road. Taking that route, she knew she could reach the main road to Paris undetected. By the time she was discovered missing, she would be well on her way.

She smiled confidently to herself as she made her way out. She would not remain in Paris. She would go from there to the German border, to somehow find her way to Russia. Surely there were subversives along the way, and if she were smart and careful, she could make contact with the underground.

A ripple of fear ran up her spine as she left Daniberry for what might well be the last time, but Marilee would not look back.

No matter what the future held, she was determined not to fail.

She was, after all, a *Coltrane,* and that, she thought with satisfaction, was a legacy that would give her the courage to survive.

Cord lay spent and despondent as he pondered the price he was paying for a few moments of pleasure.

No matter that in his mind the mouth he'd kissed had been Marilee's, and the body he'd caressed had been hers.

And no matter that at the moment of final release he had actually been with *her.*

For when all was said and done, he found himself looking down at Elenore and wishing he'd had the strength to resist.

"Now I know what a black widow spider's mate feels like," he muttered to himself, getting to his feet and gathering his clothes.

A dreamy look on her face, Elenore raised up on one elbow to ask, "What did you say, darling?"

His response was cold. "I said I've got to go."

She reached out to clutch his arm, but he jerked away from her grasp. She frowned. "I don't like you treating me this way, Cordell," she said. "What's wrong?"

A little warning bell went off inside, and Cord told himself that the last thing he needed was to make Elenore angry. He was going to have a big enough problem as it was getting Marilee out of there and to safety without Elenore causing trouble.

With great effort, he leaned over to brush his lips against hers one more time. "I'm sorry. I don't mean to be so cross. It's just that I've a lot to do, and it wasn't on my schedule to be seduced by a beautiful woman." He winked.

Elenore yawned and stretched, pleased as a warm kitten. "Well, do what you must, darling, but hurry. This might've been a splendid place in its day, but it's depressing now, and I want to get back to Switzerland."

She sat up suddenly. "Have you given any thought as to where you'd like for us to settle till we decide on the future?"

Cord groaned inwardly, but with great effort he continued to be amiable. "No. No, I haven't. I just want to carry out my present orders, and then we'll talk about it.'' He kissed her again and left, promising to return whenever he could.

He rushed down the hall and up the stairs, wishing he had never taken time to check on Elenore. It had been Marilee he'd yearned to see the instant he returned, and now nearly a half hour had passed.

Serge was dozing, his chair propped against the wall just outside Marilee's door. At the sound of someone running up the steps, he was instantly alert, hand at his holster. He sighed with relief to see Cord. ''It's about time you're back. She was asking about you a while ago, and I didn't know what to tell her except that you'd gone away on business.''

Cord drew him across the landing so they would not be overheard should Marilee be awake. Then he hastened to confide, ''I confirmed orders from the Bolsheviks to proceed at once to Petrograd with Marilee and turn her over there. I also confirmed with the Whites that once we leave here, we will leave our course and be met by comrades near the German border ready to take us underground.''

''And will you tell Marilee the truth now?'' Serge wanted to know.

''Yes, yes,'' Cord said quickly. ''Have you heard her moving around lately?''

''No. I took her dinner tray to her, and she asked for a bottle of wine. When I took that in, she was in her toilet, so I locked the door and haven't been in since.''

Cord took a key from his pocket and let himself into the room.

Darkness greeted him, and he whispered her name

softly, thinking she was asleep. When there was no response, he turned on a lamp.

The first thing he saw was the dinner tray on the table—untouched—and the full bottle of wine beside it.

He knew.

Before he ran across the room to the toilet and dressing alcove, he knew that Marilee had escaped.

The automobile bumped along slowly, for Marilee was not altogether confident in her driving.

Straining to see in the moonlight, she was relieved to be able to make out the overgrown path to the winery. She had walked it so many times and knew every curve. With a pounding heart, she turned the automobile in that direction.

She was frightened, but her fierce determination would see her through this night.

Cord Brandt would have to face the consequences for allowing her to escape, and oh, how she wished those consequences would be great—and painful—as painful as the aching of her broken heart.

Chapter Twenty-two

S ERGE was distraught as he tried to figure out how Marilee had slipped by him. "It had to have been when I went for the wine. She'd gone into her toilet alcove, and I saw no need to lock the door. And when I came back, I thought it would be rude to call out to her, so I just left the wine and locked the door behind me. But how was I to know she was planning to escape?" He looked at Cord helplessly. "You had let her roam about the château, and she'd made no attempt to leave."

Cord was deep in thought. "Serge, you've got to remember that those times I was usually with her, and besides, there wasn't another woman around. Elenore showing up just made her angrier than I realized."

Serge sighed and shook his head. "She's out there, in the middle of the night, all alone. We know she took that automobile, but the guard at the gate says she never passed him. That means she has to be somewhere on the estate."

Cord nodded absently. He already had every available man out searching the grounds. Did Marilee even know how to drive? Stubborn and determined as she was, he was sure she would not let a little thing like that stop her. No, she would keep on going, trying to make her way to—where?

He snapped his fingers, his blue eyes suddenly glowing with hope. "She'll head for the border. She'll try to make it all the way to Russia."

Serge looked at him doubtfully. "How can you be so sure?"

"Where else would she go? The authorities? Oh, no. She realizes there's a war going on, and she'd be detained somewhere, then sent back to the Coltranes in Spain. She doesn't want that. She's torn over what she was told about her father, and she's determined to find him and prove it was all a lie." He nodded firmly and smiled to himself. "Yes, she'll head for the border, all right, and she knows the countryside. She'll know which way to go."

Serge pointed out, "That still doesn't explain how she got off the estate without the guard at the front gate seeing her pass. He's a good man. He swears he didn't doze off, and I believe him."

"So do I," Cord agreed, his mind whirling as he tried to figure out what to do next.

They were standing on the marble terrace that overlooked the rolling, moonlit lawn. Suddenly a guard appeared, running and calling excitedly. Cord recognized him as one of his own men, and he and Serge hurried to meet him.

"The old road, at the back . . ." He paused to catch his breath.

Cord knew where he meant, for he had made it his business to go over the estate. "The one that goes to the winery Mikhailonov planned to build? But it's overgrown with weeds, and—''

"Yes, yes," the guard agreed quickly, "but she made it through. We found weeds mashed down, and tracks. We followed, thinking maybe she had stalled somewhere, but she made it to the back road, and she's probably on the main highway into Paris by now."

Cord trusted the man. "We have to get her into the hands of the Whites before the Bolsheviks find out she's gone. I'm going to get word to them to intercept her before she gets to Paris. I can, if I leave now, but there's Elenore to be dealt with. She mustn't know about any of this."

He turned to Serge and gripped his shoulders. "Take her back to the Bolshevik headquarters, and only then tell them all that Marilee has escaped. If Elenore puts up a fuss, tell her I've gone and I'm not coming back. She'll go with you then."

Serge smiled at Cord. "You know, I've a feeling this is for the best. You never wanted to turn Marilee over to them, anyway."

Cord grinned. "More than that, my friend. I had no intention of doing so, no matter the consequences."

Marilee was leaning over the steering wheel, her fingers gripping it so tightly they ached. She struggled for total concentration, fighting against thoughts of Cord. Yet no matter how hard she tried, his face continued to appear before her in the moonlight—his blue eyes laughing or warm with desire, his tousled blond hair entwined around her loving fingertips. God, she had fallen in love with him without even realizing it! But oh, how painfully quick that love had turned into loathing and hate!

She could not help pondering what her fate might have been had she not happened upon Cord and Elenore lying naked together, in the wild throes of their passion. Would she have gone on loving him and believing that he loved her?

A shudder of revulsion went through her, and she could only soothe her aching heart with the conviction that she was far better off to have learned the truth. Now she could get on with her life, and be all the wiser for the experience.

She drove on wearily. Her immediate hope was to find a friendly farmer who would give her shelter till she could make plans to continue her journey to Russia.

Suddenly she rounded a curve and saw that the road ahead was blocked by three automobiles. A line of men faced her, and she saw that they were all carrying guns. With a cry of fear and defeat, she could do nothing but brake to a stop, then wait for them to descend upon her.

Damn! Damn! Damn! she cursed. So close, yet so far! To taste freedom, to actually dream of making her way to Russia and finding her father had been too good to be true.

Chapter Twenty-three

THE door on her side swung open, and a man with a German accent said crisply, "Please get out. You've no cause to be frightened. We mean you no harm."

She obeyed, her frustration quickly giving way to renewed courage. With her head held high, she glared at him. "What right do you have to stop me? Who do you think you are?"

Her captor grinned. She could see that he had a kind face. "Who I am," he said gently, "who *we* are, will depend on who *you* are. I ask that you tell the truth."

Lifting her chin yet higher, Marilee disclosed her identity.

His grin grew broader. She saw the men around him relax and lower their rifles.

Still wary, Marilee asked cautiously, "Will you please tell me what this is all about?"

"Are you, by chance, Drakar Mikhailonov's daughter?" their leader asked.

She nodded, beginning to tremble. Dear God, don't let them be Bolsheviks, she silently prayed.

"You have nothing to fear," he told her, signaling one of the men to get in the car. "Come with us. We've been looking for you."

She shook her head, still bewildered. "But why? Who are you?"

He led her to one of the cars. "You'll be told everything later, but for now, suffice it to say that we'd heard you were in this area, being held hostage by the Bolsheviks. We heard from one of our spies tonight that you had escaped, so we were watching the roads to try and intercept you before they got to you first."

She gasped, tears of joy stinging her eyes. "Then, then you are . . . counterrevolutionaries. And you know my father?"

"Ah, yes, we know Drakar well," he assured her. "But allow me to introduce myself. I am Vladimir Dubovitsky. We have a long journey ahead, for we're taking you all the way to Russia. There will be much time for answering all your questions, but let's be on our way. These woods will be crawling with Bolshevik supporters by daylight, and we want to distance ourselves as quickly as possible."

Marilee was no longer afraid. Although she had no proof that he was telling the truth, she had no choice but to put her fate in his hands. Something told her that she was safe.

Vladimir helped her into the rear seat of one of the three cars that formed their convoy, and he settled in beside her. When they were on their way, he explained they would keep to the back roads, skirting Paris and the Allied troops. "We're on our way to a little town called Mantes-la-Jolie on the Seine. From there we take a small boat to Le Havre, where a ship will be waiting to take us on to Russia. We're disguised as fishermen. You will be given clothes to dress as one also.''

Marilee listened, nodding at everything he said. Finally she could restrain herself no longer. ''You've got to tell me about my father! I've got to know he's all right.''

The man driving turned his head ever so slightly to give her a look of sympathy. She felt a chill of foreboding.

''Drakar, as far as we know,'' Vladimir began, ''is fine. I will try to tell you all that we know at this time.''

''Yes, please,'' she urged. ''I've been told some terrible lies about him, that he stole money from the Czar, and the Bolsheviks demanded it be returned as my ransom, because they fear he'll use it to help Nicholas escape.''

''Only part of that is true,'' he said. ''Actually, your father didn't steal anything when he slipped away from the Imperial train in Pskov and went underground.''

''I don't believe he ever deserted the Czar. He and Nicholas were like brothers. They grew up together. They—''

''I know all that, Marilee.'' He covered her hand with his. ''Your father is not a coward. He was ordered to leave the Czar. We knew the end was near, and he could do more for Nicholas by leaving him than by staying to become a general of the Provisional Government, something he did not believe in. So, with Nicholas's blessing, he left the train in the middle of the night and slipped away to join other advisers and officers who planned to start a counterrevolution. They are known as Whites. So are we. Is it becoming clearer to you now?''

She nodded vigorously. ''But what about the money? Why was he accused of stealing that?''

Vladimir's voice suddenly took on an amused tone, and she saw the two men in the front seat exchange smiles. ''Did you know your father had a *lubovnitsa?*'' he asked.

Marilee recognized the Russian word for ''lover.'' Quietly, she responded, ''No. But I'm not surprised. After all, my mother died when I was born. It's hardly likely my father would spend the rest of his life in celibacy.''

''Actually, Irina was more than Drakar's *lubovnitsa*. It was said they were going to be married,'' Vladimir explained.

Marilee was glad to know that her father had found happiness in his life, for she was only too aware of how bereft he had been when her mother died. Kitty had even confided once her fear that he would take his own life in his grief. ''Go on,'' she urged amiably. ''Tell me about this special woman who was able to heal my father's grief.''

''Ahh, Irina *was* special,'' he assured.

''Was?'' Marilee tensed. ''Is she dead?''

''We hope not,'' he said quickly. Then he went on to relate the entire story, how Drakar had melded into the underground and Irina had subsequently smuggled much gold from the Imperial treasury to him. She had been a respected member of the royal court, with access to the Romanov jewels and treasure, so it had been easy for her to slip out a little at a time. Caught with the last bit she was smuggling, she had been tortured, but had refused to tell where Drakar and the other counterrevolutionaries were hiding.

His respect and admiration apparent, Vladimir told how Irina had been in a hospital, recuperating from her injuries at the hands of fiendish Bolshevik guards, when she somehow managed to escape.

"She has not been heard from since," he finished with a shrug. "We can only assume she made her way to your father and is with him now."

"And where is he?" Marilee demanded. "You said he was one of you—a White. So why is it you don't know where he is? Why is it the Bolsheviks don't know? I was supposed to be taken to them as bait to get him to come out of hiding, but I escaped before that could happen. Where is he, that no one seems to be able to locate him?"

Vladimir sighed heavily. "Your father has been captured by the Bolsheviks. He came out of the underground to make contact after hearing you were being held a hostage, and they took him prisoner."

"Oh, dear God!" Her hand flew to her throat, and she felt herself swaying.

Vladimir put his arm around her. "Take comfort in the knowledge that he probably won't be harmed, because he's worth more to them alive than dead. Your father was quite respected. If they execute him, he'll become a martyr to the people, and you can be assured the Bolsheviks don't want that.

"Besides," he hastened to add, "from first accounts, Irina was not captured. The details are still filtering in from our contacts in Russia, but from all we've been able to learn so far, he was alone. Evidently he was wary of a trap, because he didn't have the gold with him. So we can only believe that Irina has it, and that she's in hiding somewhere.''

Marilee demanded fiercely, ''Well, what are your people doing about it? Why aren't you trying to free him instead of wasting your time with me? The Bolsheviks won't be interested in me now that they've got my father.''

''You're wrong,'' he contradicted her. ''You're still a valuable hostage to his followers, like Irina. They'd figure she would not stand back if she knew you were being tortured as she was. She'd come forth with the gold, because that's what your father would tell her to do. I'm afraid you're still important to the Bolsheviks, my dear. And it's best we get you underground and keep you there.

''Now just settle back and enjoy the ride,'' he finished. ''You're safe now.''

Marilee leaned back against the seat, but she was anything but relaxed as she chewed her lower lip thoughtfully, forming a plan.

The night rushed by.

On the horizon, lavender fingers touched the darkness.

The little village of Mantes-la-Jolie was still asleep as their convoy reached the waterfront. Vladimir draped his long wool coat around Marilee's shoulders as he urged her to hurry to where a tiny fishing boat was waiting.

The crew had had advance notice of their important cargo and shoved off as soon as Marilee came on

board. They headed straight into the morning wind—
their destination, Russia.

She was given the clothes of a fisherman. She
tucked her hair, still short from her Irene Castle bob,
beneath a woolen cap. From a distance she easily
passed as just another crew member.

In the little galley below decks, coffee was waiting,
as well as bread and eggs, and Marilee ate and drank
heartily, realizing she had been famished.

"So tell me," she said to Vladimir. "What is the
news in Russia? I'm afraid my *captor* did not tell me
much."

Vladimir had been watching her, delighted that she
seemed so fit and well. He did not miss the sarcasm
in her voice when she said "captor," referring to
Brandt. He, like the other Whites stationed in France,
had heard the rumors that the usually stern and cold
Cordell Brandt was falling in love with his Russian-
American hostage. He knew, also, that Cord had not
yet confided his true identity as a counterspy to her,
and his orders were that she not be told now. It was
obvious that she still harbored resentment toward him.

Vladimir proceeded to tell her that the Bolsheviks
were in power. She was not surprised, knowing that
revolution had been imminent.

Vladimir recounted everything.

On the night of October 23, 1917, Lenin, his beard
shaved and wearing a wig, had made his way secretly
into Petrograd for a meeting with the Bolshevik Central Committee. He had demanded an immediate re-
bellion, and the other party leaders had agreed that
an armed uprising had become necessary.

On November 6, the Bolsheviks had struck. The

cruiser *Aurora*, flying their red flag, had put down anchor in the River Neva opposite the Winter Palace. Armed Bolshevik squads quickly and methodically took over all public buildings, telephone exchanges, bridges, banks, and railway stations.

Kerensky, the leader of the Provisional Government, had left the following day by car, accompanied by another car, which flew the American flag. They had moved without incident through streets packed with Bolshevik soldiers, heading south to attempt to get help from the army. But at nine o'clock that night, the *Aurora* had fired a single blank shell, and the women's battalion within Malachite Hall of the Winter Palace, which had been protecting the remaining ministers of the Provisional Government, surrendered.

Two hours later, shells whistled across the river, hitting the palace and doing slight damage to plaster.

At exactly 2:10 A.M. on the morning of November 8, the ministers surrendered.

"It was almost without incident," Vladimir told Marilee pensively. "From what our people have related to us, nothing really changed. Restaurants and cinemas and stores on the Nevsky Prospekt stayed open and streetcars continued to run in most of the city. There was even a performance of the ballet at the Mariinsky Theater." He shook his head incredulously.

"So the danger is not to the Russian people as a whole," Marilee mused aloud bitterly, "only to those who support the Czar, like you and your followers . . . and *my* father," she added grimly.

"True." He went on to describe how even before

the Bolshevik revolution, there were those who were secretly planning to liberate the Imperial family. Both in Moscow and Petrograd, there were strong monarchist organizations with substantial funds that were anxious to attempt a rescue. "But the problem is planning, not money," he hastened to explain. "The Czar himself is an obstacle, because whenever escape is mentioned to him, he refuses to allow the family to be separated. This, of course, presents a problem. It won't be easy to successfully free, at one time, a number of women and a sick and handicapped boy. It would require many loyal soldiers, much food, and many horses and carriages."

Marilee could well understand their predicament. "Then the Whites are in constant contact with the Czar?"

"At first, yes," he replied. "Right after the Imperial family arrived in Tobolsk, agents were sent to Siberia. Former officers using assumed names got off the train in Tyumen and boarded the river steamers for Tobolsk. Then they mingled with merchants and shopkeepers and asked questions. Servants passed freely in and out of the governor's house, where the family was being held, with letters and gifts and messages. Then the guards put a stop to it. Contact now is difficult.

"Another problem with rescue," he added, "is that there are too many groups that are jealous of each other. We're trying to formulate one solid counterrevolutionary faction."

"What happens to the Czar and his family if they aren't rescued now that the Bolsheviks have seized power?"

Vladimir spread his hands in a gesture of helplessness. "Who can say? The truth is, Lenin and the Bolsheviks might be in control, but their position is precarious as long as they don't have peace. We think they'll use the Czar as a bargaining tool. How, we can't be sure. All we are sure of is that we've got to free him and his family before it's too late."

Marilee could agree with that. She knew it was important, for Nicholas was in a precarious situation.

But so was her father.

And while Vladimir and his group of Whites might be intent on rescuing the Czar and the Imperial family, she had plans of her own—to find her father and help him escape from the Bolsheviks.

How to go about doing that, she was not sure, for it would require much more knowledge of the situation. Once they reached their destination, she would endeavor to learn everything she could about the circumstances of his capture. She also wanted to find Irina.

But for the time being, Marilee could only take solace in the fact that she was now free.

The fact that her heart was still held captive by Cord Brandt was something she would not allow her tortured mind to dwell upon.

Chapter Twenty-four

Spain
February 1918

COLT Coltrane sat on the sofa before the crackling fire, staring into the flames as he sipped absently from the snifter of brandy he held.

Beside him, Jade reread the letter from the embassy in Zurich, her eyes filled with tears. "I don't believe it." She shook her head. "It's a nightmare. It has to be."

"We've known she was missing for over three months. At least now we know the reason," Colt said.

Jade handed the letter over to Kit and cried, "If only I hadn't run away like I did, in the middle of the night. I deserted her. I left her in the hands of those . . . those fanatics!" She burst into tears once more.

Kurt moved to give his mother-in-law a sympathetic hug. "You have no way of knowing all that, Jade. You've nothing to feel guilty about. Hell, we all thought Rudolf was in love with her. How were you to know he was a traitor? *A goddman Bolshevik!*" he could not help cursing angrily.

"I should've checked on her before going to London to meet Colt. But I missed him so, and I thought she was in good hands. I even thought she'd be better off if I just got out of her business and let nature take it course." Jade gave a bitter laugh. "Oh, how stupid I was!"

There was a sound in the doorway, and they all looked up as Valerie pushed Travis's wheelchair through. Still pale from the leg wound he'd suffered in the war, Travis asked, "Is there further news?"

"I've a call in to the embassy," Colt told him, "but they probably won't know any more than they did when they wrote this letter."

Travis shook his head sadly. "I still can't believe it. They thought they were kidnapping Mother, got Marilee instead, and it took us this long to find out the whole story."

Kit spoke for the first time. "What I want to know is why she didn't come back here when she escaped. What happened to her after she ran away from Daniberry?"

Jade sighed. "All we know is what the embassy tells us, that she just disappeared and hasn't been heard from since. We wouldn't even know this much if Rudolf's sister hadn't confessed everything when they kept interrogating her."

"And what about Rudolf?" Travis asked, then slammed his fist into his palm. "Oh, I'd love to get my hands on that bastard!"

"We all would, Travis," Kurt pointed out grimly.

"Looking for Rudolf isn't going to help us find Marilee," Colt said. "That girl admitted he turned her over to some of those Bolsheviks in Zurich who called themselves the Zurich Zealots, then went with the rest of them into Russia to take part in the November revolution. She swears she hasn't heard from him since.''

"Oh, I can believe that," Kurt agreed. "That's the reason she talked, in my opinion. She was mad because her brother took off and left her to take the blame for everything.''

Jade quickly pointed out, "Don't forget it says in the letter that she named her former lover as the actual kidnapper. A man named Cordell Brandt.''

Kit smiled knowingly. "And I've got a feeling that Elenore also confessed because she's bitter over losing her lover to Marilee.''

Colt, Kurt, and Travis laughed together. The women exchanged mutual glances of suspicion.

"Marilee?" Travis hooted. "To think of her as a femme fatale is ludicrous at best. Granted, she's pretty, but she's not the type to go around snatching men away from women.''

"You never know." Kit continued to smile. "Still waters run deep.''

"Enough of this," Jade said wearily. "I think it's time we decided what to do about it. We can't just sit back and do nothing.''

Valerie spoke for the first time. "I think she's in Russia.''

They all looked at her curiously.

She nodded, her blue eyes shining. "I think she went to look for her father. You might not like my saying this, but the truth is—I don't think Marilee ever felt like she was a real part of this family.''

"Now, Valerie, that's a serious thing to say. You

haven't been in the family long enough to sit in judgment like that,'' Travis rebuked her gently.

Valerie lifted her chin defiantly. "Oh, yes, I have. I've heard all of you talk, teasing her in ways you thought were harmless, but Marilee didn't take it that way. I'm an outsider, and maybe I see things differently. I just got the feeling Marilee never felt like she belonged.''

"Well, I don't think—'' Jade began.

"I agree with Valerie,'' Kurt said. "You don't realize it, but you never considered her one of you because you never considered her grandmother Travis Coltrane's legal wife. And you seem to forget that it doesn't matter that Marilee Barbeau was not *legally* a Coltrane. She gave birth to your patriarch's daughter, your half sister, Dani.'' Kurt nodded respectfully at Colt.

Colt said nothing, keeping his gaze on the fire.

"And,'' Kurt went on, "you all, whether you like hearing it or not, made Marilee feel like an outsider.''

"So you're saying that's why she chose to go to Russia instead of returning here when she escaped her kidnappers?'' Kit asked stiffly.

"Exactly,'' he replied. "To Marilee, Drakar is the only family she's got.''

"I say we go after her,'' Travis declared.

"What?'' Colt and Kurt cried in unison.

"We go after her,'' Travis repeated. "Chances are that Uncle Drakar is dead by now. So what happens to Marilee? I think it's time we showed her that she *is* a Coltrane and that her home is here, with all of us. The only way to do that is to go after her.''

"You aren't going anywhere,'' Jade said sharply,

pointing to his bandaged leg. "A German bullet has put you out of the war, my son."

Valerie could not contain her relief, and patted her stomach. "We need you more, Travis. Me and Travis Coltrane the Third."

"Or Katherine Wright Coltrane." He smiled and reached for her hand, pressing it to his lips tenderly. Then he looked from his father to his brother-in-law. "There's nothing stopping you two from going, is there?" he challenged them.

"Oh, for heaven's sake!" Jade cried. "Travis, are you out of your mind? They can't just go traipsing off to Russia. It'd be like looking for a needle in a haystack."

"It's certainly better than sitting back and doing nothing, Mother," Kit said. "And it's not as though Dad doesn't have some political connections and influence." She looked at him. "Isn't that so? You can find out where Uncle Drakar's friends are, can't you? It seems likely she would've found her way to them."

Colt nodded, his lips pursed thoughtfully. "The embassy did not go into a lot of detail, because they didn't want to put everything in writing. There's too much danger of interception. But I can go to Zurich and find out exactly how much they do know. Kit's right, it is reasonable to assume Marilee would make her way to the Whites."

He declared wryly, "The Bolsheviks are betraying nearly every political slogan that brought them to power. They promised freedom of the individual and instead censored the press, forbade strikes, and set up a secret police. While they undertook to respect the rights of minority states, they already had an army on the move to crush the independent republic of the Ukraine. They cried for a freely elected Constituent Assembly, and now they've had it abolished by force."

Kurt asked the question burning on everyone's lips. "So what happens next?"

Based on what he'd been told by the American Embassy on his last visit, Colt said, "There's only one way the Bolsheviks can redeem themselves and make good their promises. They've got to come to terms with the Germans. They can have no hope of their own survival unless they bring the war to an end."

Jade went to stand beside him, her emerald eyes flashing with anger and resentment. "They screamed 'Bread and Peace,' but all Russia will get is famine and civil war."

"Yes," Colt mused quietly. "That's right. But they're also getting something they hadn't bargained for."

Everyone looked at him expectantly.

"The Bolsheviks are about to meet an adversary they hadn't counted on—the Coltranes."

Jade laughed. "God help them."

It was resolved.

Colt would use all his political influence to learn as much as possible about where the Whites were headquartered. He would then send out inquiries about Marilee.

Then he and Kurt would proceed to Russia and do their best to bring her home—where, they all agreed, she belonged.

Marilee was a Coltrane, and they would all stand together.

Chapter Twenty-five

Tobolsk, Russia
February 1918

MARILEE had traveled to Tyumen with Vladimir Dubovitsky and the other Whites. When they had arrived in early December, she had made it quite clear she intended to work with them, doing everything possible to rescue her father from his Bolshevik captors.

Marilee and Vladimir were told that recent information indicated that Drakar was being held somewhere in the same vicinity as the Imperial family—a heavily guarded little town called Tobolsk, where the Tobol and Irtysh rivers joined.

Marilee and Vladimir were told that the Bolsheviks still wanted the gold returned. Irina had been seen in the area, and they felt it was just a matter of time until she tried to buy her lover's freedom with the gold despite contrary orders from the Whites.

The village of Tobolsk was no more than log houses, whitewashed churches, and a few commercial buildings. They had been told that the Czar and his family were being held in the governor's house. A high wooden fence had been built around it.

It was decided that Marilee could best obtain information by finding work in a restaurant frequented by newly assigned soldiers. She was hired and given a room above the restaurant where she could live. Vladimir and his soldiers returned to the White underground, maintaining cautious communication.

Marilee settled down into her routine. The restaurant was open nearly all the time, for there was nowhere else to go during the harsh winter months.

She could not remember such brutal weather in her whole life. The temperature had dropped to nearly seventy degrees below zero, and the rivers were frozen several feet deep. The world was a sculpture of ice and snow. Yet the smoldering intensity of her determination provided all the fuel she needed to survive—and succeed.

She had decided to use a more Russian name, and called herself Natasha Kievsky. She quickly became a favorite with the soldiers, who found her beautiful and vivacious. She did not, however, allow the teasing to go too far. She demanded respect, and she got it.

There were, of course, constant invitations from the young soldiers for dinner or a trip into Tyumen for dancing and theater when they had a pass. She knew the time would eventually come when it would be necessary to get closer to one of the soldiers in order to gain important information, but she also knew that she had to be both patient and discreet. Nothing of value could be learned from an ordinary soldier.

One Saturday night an officer walked in whom Marilee had never seen before. She knew at once that he was someone important when the soldiers instantly fell silent.

He scanned the room with narrow, suspicious eyes as he unfastened his greatcoat. He hung it on a hook by the door and Marilee saw that he wore stiff shoulder straps with bright metallic lace. She moved closer and saw that the straps had two longitudinal colored stripes down the center and three five-pointed stars. He was a lieutenant colonel!

He was tall and heavyset, with piercing black eyes. Marilee found him attractive, but in a formidable way. She took a deep breath, hoping she did not appear overly anxious as she made her way toward him. It was her first encounter with an officer, and he could prove a valuable contact.

He looked up at her coldly, but she did not flinch. Giving him her warmest smile, she spoke to him in fluent Russian. "Good evening, sir. My name is Natasha Kievsky. What is your pleasure?"

"You! I'll have you naked and served to me on a platter," he said mockingly in French.

Keeping her composure, Marilee answered him in French. "I'm sorry, sir, but *I* am not on the menu tonight. Perhaps you'd like to try our special—a platter of nice smoked cod and our best iced vodka."

He blinked, then he threw back his head and laughed. "I never thought a restaurant servant would be so learned. Can you forgive me?"

"Of course." She laughed with him. "If I weren't able to overlook a lot of things, I'd never last in this job, believe me."

They became friends at once. He introduced himself as Boris Gorchakov and said he had only recently been assigned to the 2nd Regiment. By the time the evening ended, he had asked her to join him at his quarters for a nightcap. Marilee demurely refused, knowing he would be back. Somehow she sensed he was important, and that he might just be the officer with whom she would have to pretend romance to get the information she—and the Whites—needed.

Boris came into the restaurant every night. He always sat alone. It was as if it was understood that Gorchakov did not want company.

Every evening he extended the same invitation to Marilee when she got off work. "I have an apartment of my own just across the way. It's not much, but it's warm and cozy, and I keep a supply of good caviar you won't find elsewhere in this miserable place."

Marilee continued to refuse but flirted with him mercilessly. She began to wear her peasant blouse a bit lower, affording him a view of delicious cleavage when she leaned to place his drink in front of him. She did not miss the way he drew in his breath sharply, and knew she had achieved the effect she wanted. After a few nights she did not move away when he reached to touch her; instead she smiled warmly as his hand moved from her waist to trace the swell of her hips beneath her skirt. His looks became more intimate, and he began to trail his fingers down her arm, brushing now and then across her breast as she served him.

A few times, when business was slow, she had dared to sit down at his table and chat. She let him do the talking, not wanting to arouse his suspicion that she might be a spy. At first he only tried to persuade her to go home with him. But then, as they became closer friends, he began to unwind and confide his problems—how miserable he was in his post, how he'd rather be in battle, how he wished the damnable war would just end so he could get on with his life. She learned that he was hard-core Bolshevik and felt that the Czar and his family should be exiled to the deepest regions of Siberia instead of being kept in a fine house at great expense to the government.

One night, when he was in an extremely talkative mood, Marilee dared ask, "How does the Imperial family act? Do they seem happy?"

He flashed her an accusing look. "What do you care? Are you sympathetic to the Imperialist dogs?"

"No, no." She shook her head quickly and reached to cover his hand with hers. "I just thought maybe they might be complaining."

He grunted and slouched back in his chair. "No," he admitted, "they don't complain. To be honest, I try not to be around them that much. I seldom see them. One of the soldiers said the four Grand Duchesses are acting out little plays. The boy joins in. The Empress knits and sews, and the Czar writes letters and reads."

Marilee squeezed his hand and asked, "So what do you do all day to keep yourself busy?"

He shrugged and took a sip of his vodka. Then he looked from her bosom to her face and gave her a suggestive wink. "I count the hours till I can see you, *dushka*. And I wonder how long you are going to make me suffer for your company in a more private place, where we can really get to know each other."

She squirmed in her chair playfully. "Oh, tell me," she continued to tease him. "What do you do?"

Relaxed by the vodka, and feeling that he had no reason to be on guard with her, he said casually, "Oh, we have some prisoners to keep an eye on. Some radical counterrevolutionaries. Whites, they call themselves." He sneered. "I call them sons of bitches and say they should be shot."

Marilee straightened in her chair and put her hand to her throat. "You mean there are dangerous prisoners kept around here? I didn't know—"

"No one knows," he hissed, suddenly realizing that he had said too much. "Forget what I just told you."

He reached to squeeze her arm so hard that she winced with the pain and cried, "Boris, please stop. You're hurting me."

He released her but continued to glare at her. "You ask too many questions, *dushka*. I must be careful. It is not wise to trust anyone these days."

Her heart was pounding. She now knew that headquarters had been right. There were political prisoners being held near Tobolsk, and there was every reason to believe that her father was one of them. Now, more than ever, she had to gain Boris's confidence and learn as much as possible from him.

Taking a deep breath, Marilee leaned forward and gave him her most beguiling smile as she huskily whispered, "You can trust me, my sweet, because I trust you. If I didn't, I wouldn't accept your invitation to have a drink with you at your apartment later tonight."

He looked at her silently for a few seconds. Then,

when he realized that she was quite serious, his rugged face took on a happy glow. "Yes, yes, you can trust me, Natasha. I am your friend. I want to be *more,*" he added meaningfully.

"Time will tell." She winked.

The rest of the evening passed in a blur. No matter what it took, she would find out if her father was being held prisoner, and where.

It was nearly closing time when Boris signaled to her. "I'm going to leave now," he said, paying her for his drinks and giving her a generous tip. "I want to make sure I've got a nice fire burning and some caviar and chilled vodka waiting. Maybe I'll even make us a tray of fish and cheese. Would you like that?"

"Anything." She leaned to pick up the money from the table and looked at him through lowered lashes. She let her breast brush against his arm and heard his soft gasp. "Anything, Boris. I do want to get to know you better."

As he left, Marilee stared after him. She was going to have to be on guard, lest she find herself in a situation from which there would be no escape.

He returned promptly when the restaurant closed, and Marilee gathered her thick wool cape about her and prepared to step out into the frigid night.

And then she stopped dead in her tracks.

Could it be?

She blinked as she saw two men crossing the street and coming toward the restaurant. The wind was blowing mercilessly and snow was whipping about them. She told herself she was wrong, that she had mistaken the second man for someone else.

He could not be Cord Brandt.

Not here.

He looked up as he stepped onto the wooden boardwalk, and her heart leaped to her mouth. It was Cord. He was about to speak, but then he stiffened. The bearded man with him was a stranger to her, and it was he who asked, disappointed, "Is the restaurant closed for the night? We've come a long way, and—"

"It is closed!" Boris snapped abruptly, annoyed by the way one of them was looking at Natasha. He started to walk by them, pulling her with him

Marilee could not move. Dear God, what was Cord doing here? What did it mean?

"Natasha!" Boris said coldly, giving her hand a tug. "Come with me. Now."

Cord blinked, mouthing the name silently.

Suddenly she came to life. She knew that if she continued to stand there, she risked being exposed. She allowed Boris to pull her along and refused to look back.

"I've seen that one with the beard before. I think he's a subversive. I've got men checking to find out what business he has here, though there is little doubt," Boris added with a sneer.

"And what might that be?" Marilee asked.

"Why, they're here to try to free the Czar, of course. We've been watching how they pour into the village—former officers of the Czar using assumed names, secretive visitors with precise Petrograd accents mingling with shopkeepers and merchants. They ask questions and make promises, and then disappear.

"It's not as easy to make contact with the Imperial

family now. Still, we're always alert to strangers—
especially when we know for a fact that they're
Whites,'' he finished angrily.

Dear Lord, where on earth did he get that idea?
She could not vouch for the man with him, but she
knew that Cord Brandt was a Bolshevik through and
through. "What makes you think they are Whites?''
she asked, keeping her tone casual.

"What else could they be?'' He led her down an
alley beside a general store, then up a narrow stairway to a single door.

As he fumbled for a key, Marilee dared to probe
him further. "But the other one. What about him?
Why do you think he's White?''

Boris pushed the door open, and they were greeted
by the cozy warmth of a softly burning fire in the
grate. He turned to take her in his arms. "Don't worry
about him, *dushka,*'' he said thickly, his lips nuzzling
her face. "That is work for me to do tomorrow. Tonight, you have only to worry about *me*—and how
much I adore you.''

Marilee took a deep breath. Swallowing against the
bile of revulsion that rose in her throat, she lifted her
lips for his kiss.

Thoughts of Cord Brandt would have to wait till
later. Now she had to become the world's greatest
actress—and remind herself every single second that
she was doing it to find a way to free the father she
adored.

Chapter Twenty-six

MARILEE knew that accepting Boris's invitation to go to his apartment meant he would think she had finally given up all her reservations and was ready to go to bed with him—just as she also knew she had no intention of doing so. She would have to be very tactful, lest he get mad. All she wanted was to gain his confidence and get him to talk. Although it was a big risk, she was banking on him passing out before he got too amorous—or determined. All evening she had ordered his drinks doubled and paid the difference in his bill out of her own pocket. She knew that vodka sneaked up on a person, and Boris Gorchakov was just arrogant enough to think he had no limit.

"So, you like my place?" Boris asked as he moved to a sideboard where there was yet more vodka. Without waiting for her to respond, he went on. "When I received my orders for this obscene outpost, I was determined to have my privacy. No barracks for me."

Marilee glanced around the huge room. It was like an attic, with eaves and tiny arched windows. The floor was wooden and worn, and the furniture was sparse. In a far corner was the sleeping area, where a muslin curtain hung from ceiling to floor to conceal, she supposed, a bed.

"Nice," she said finally, taking the glass of vodka he held out to her.

He downed his drink in one gulp, his black eyes shining as he leered at her over the rim. Then he threw the glass into the fireplace and lunged for her. "Ahh, but not as nice as *you, dushka!*"

Marilee lost her balance as his huge arms wrapped around her, spilling her drink down the front of the cape she was still wearing.

She gasped, "Oh, Boris, look what you've made me do," pretending to be more dismayed than she was. Actually, she was glad for the excuse to slow things down a bit.

He dropped his arms and apologized. "I'm sorry, so sorry. I've just waited so long for this moment, Natasha. Come, let me get something to dry—"

"No, no, it's all right. I'll just take it off and hang it by the fire. You can get me a fresh drink, though."

He turned to oblige her, and she took her time draping the garment on a chair. Then she sat down on the sofa and patted the seat beside her. With the grin of a small boy about to be given a cookie, he took his place. Then, as he started to embrace her again, Marilee quickly lifted her glass. "To us and to our friendship."

"Ahh, I gladly drink to that." After clicking his glass against hers, Boris downed his vodka. He then reached for her again, but this time he carefully took her drink and set it on the floor.

His hands seemed to be everywhere at once, his lips devouring. It was all she could do to keep from shoving him away in revulsion. As it was, she could only lie there, accepting his kisses and caresses. Try as she might, she could not respond.

But Boris was too drunk to notice. He was, Marilee thought disgustedly, like a big, sloppy hog, grunting and snorting as he thrust himself against her. Finally she could stand no more. She mustered every ounce of strength she possessed to push him away. "Please, darling, please. You rush me! I worked all day, and I'm starving. You promised me caviar, and—"

"And you've been promising me something for weeks now," he snarled, reaching for her again.

His arrogance stung her, and despite her resolve, Marilee could not let it go by. "I promised you nothing!" she retorted hotly, wriggling out from beneath him. "And if this is all you want from me, then I've made a mistake in considering you a friend."

She got to her feet and reached for her cape, knowing that he would never let her leave.

She was right.

As she'd expected, Boris was right behind her, clutching her shoulders. "I am so sorry, Natasha. So sorry. It is only that you drive me crazy. You're so beautiful . . ." He began to rain kisses on the back of her neck.

"Then do not rush me!" She whirled around, her eyes flashing. "I'm not an animal, Boris. I'm a woman, and I want tenderness.

"Besides," she added with a coquettish smile, "*I* can also be tender . . . when I've had enough vodka."

At that, Boris whirled around to get fresh drinks for them both.

When they were again settled on the sofa, Marilee

snuggled close to him. "I want to be more to you than just someone to lay with, Boris," she said softly.

She did not miss the way he caught his breath at her remark.

Turning to face him, she asked, "What is it? Did I say something wrong?"

"Well . . ." he said hesitantly, "I think I should tell you—it cannot be . . ." His voice trailed off apologetically.

She blinked in feigned confusion. "I don't understand."

He would not look at her. "I'm married," he mumbled.

"Well, did you think *I* wanted marriage?" Marilee asked.

Suddenly a hopeful gleam appeared in his black eyes. "But what *did* you mean?"

She gave an exaggerated sigh. "How did you ever get to be a high-ranking officer when you're so naive, Boris Gorchakov? I don't expect you to marry me merely because we sleep together. I am only saying that I want to be more to you than just pleasure for one night." She began to dance her fingertips up and down his arm. "I want us to make each other happy for as long as you are here."

"That . . . that is fine with me!" He grinned.

He started to set his glass aside, but she stopped him. "What I want is for us to get to know each other better, Boris. I did not come here tonight just to crawl into bed with you. You must be patient and slow and loving, or I'll find a soldier who will be."

His eyes darkened. He did not like the game she was playing, but he realized that he would have to go along with her rules if he wanted her in his bed with him every night. And oh, how he did. "Very well," he growled. "What is it you want me to do?"

She snuggled against him again. "Oh, talk to me. Tell me about yourself. Tell me about the wonderful lover I'm going to have for a long, long time."

Flattered by her interest, he began to tell Marilee about his past, his prowess as a Red soldier, and his great work in the Bolshevik revolution. She even learned that his wife lived in Petrograd and they had two small daughters.

Then she dared to begin her interrogation. "Tell me about your work now."

Boris shrugged. "It is not so interesting. I don't like being around the governor's house and the Imperial family, because I loathe them and everything they represent. So I spend most of my time at our stockade for political prisoners."

"That sounds dangerous." She forced a little shiver. "Do you have many terribly evil men there?"

He sneered. "Since when is a White dangerous? They are all cowards, hiding underground like rabbits, afraid to come out and say who they are. We get them in prison, and they snivel and cower."

"*All* of them?" she pressed. "How many do you have there?"

As he had been bragging about himself, he had been drinking constantly. His words were starting to slur, and Marilee knew he would not be alert much longer.

He narrowed his eyes in thoughtful contemplation. "Oh, less than a dozen."

"And they are all cowards?" she challenged him.

"Then why do they need you? If you are as brave and courageous as you say, why do they waste your talents on sniveling men? Why don't they send you into battle?"

She knew that, sober, he would have become angry at such a remark, but with so much vodka flowing in his veins, he merely snickered. "Oh, they aren't all cowards. There are a few that are quite formidable, and that is why Lenin himself ordered me to be in charge!" He pounded himself on his chest proudly for emphasis.

Marilee took a deep breath and pushed on, trying to sound mildly disinterested. "Oh, really? Which ones? Do you have any important prisoners?"

"Oh, yes," he replied quickly. "We have the infamous Drakar Mikhailonov, who . . ."

The rest of his words were lost in the sudden roaring that exploded in her ears. Dear God, it was true! They did hold her father prisoner—and so very, very near.

She felt herself sinking into a deep void. Only with great effort was she finally able to give herself a mental shake and return to the present. He had grown silent, and she feared he had noticed her reaction. Making her voice as normal as possible, she turned to look at him. "I'm sorry. I guess I'm more tired than I thought. What were you saying—"

Then she saw that he had finally passed out.

His head lolled to one side, and his hand was slowly dropping. She reached for the glass he held in his hand and caught it just before it crashed to the floor.

The confirmation of her father's imprisonment and

seeing Cord, both in the span of a few hours, were just too much to comprehend. She needed time to think things out, to decide what she should do next.

Quietly, she got up and reached for her cape and crept toward the door. Then, as an afterthought, so that Boris would not be too angry when he woke up and realized she had left him, she took a blanket from the end of the sofa and tucked it about him. He would think she had been angry because he had passed out, and he would be the one to apologize.

Then she left and hurried through the frigid night to her own quarters, where, only because of the vodka she'd consumed, she was able to finally fall asleep.

She was awakened by an urgent knock on her door. Opening heavy eyelids, she glanced about groggily in the lavender light that spilled through a corner window.

The knocking continued.

"Who is it?" she called irritably, thinking it was probably old Micar, the man who cleaned up the tavern, wanting help. Occasionally she'd come to his aid after a particularly busy night when there was much to be done, but if he was awakening her before good daylight to help, she was not going to be very obliging.

There was no response.

She threw back the covers, snatched up her robe, and padded barefoot across the cold wooden floor. Outside, the world was a white glaze.

"Micar, you've got a nerve—"

She jerked open the door and froze.

Cord stepped in and slammed the door behind him.

He took her in his arms and gave her a rough shake. "What the hell are you doing here? I couldn't believe my eyes when I saw you last night! Dammit, Marilee, you're going to get yourself killed!"

Her shock was quickly overcome by fury, and she began to struggle and twist in his grasp as she retorted hotly, "And what are *you* doing here? Pretending to be a White when you're a dirty Bolshevik, and—"

He covered her mouth with his hand, wrestling her toward the bed. He threw her down roughly, then fell beside her and held her tightly. "You want to wake the whole village?" he hissed. "Now listen to me, dammit. I've got something to tell you, and you're going to listen."

She managed to bite one of his fingers, and when he yanked his hand away in pain, she cried, "No, damn you, Cord Brandt! *You* listen to *me!*" She was careful to keep her voice down, lest someone hear. She could not risk exposure any more than he could. "I'm an impostor just like you are, because I'm trying to get my father out of prison, and if you reveal my true identity, I'll do the same to you. So it's best you just get the hell out of here and forget you saw me, or that you know anything at all about me."

He stared down at her incredulously, then he suddenly threw back his head and laughed.

"What is so goddamn funny?" she demanded fiercely.

He shook his head and continued to chuckle. "I don't believe this—both of us pretending to be Red, only not at the same time."

She was baffled. "What are you talking about?"

"I'm trying to tell you, little one." He gazed down at her adoringly. "I'm on *your* side. I always have been. I was going to tell you before, when you ran away. I'm not working for the Bolsheviks. I was always working for the counterrevolutionaries—the Whites. My job was to look out for you—to protect you."

"You expect me to believe a lie like that?" she cried indignantly. "What kind of idiot do you take me for? You kidnapped me by mistake, then decided I was valuable, too, because of my father. Then you tried to make me think you were falling in love with me, and then I find you making love, if you can call it that, with Elenore, when earlier you'd been trying to do the same thing with me!"

He stared at her for a few seconds, stunned to finally learn why she had run away. Then he rolled over onto his back to stare up at the ceiling and whisper wretchedly, "I'm sorry. Sorry that you saw . . . sorry that it happened. But it did. She was there to willingly feed the hunger you created."

He rolled over and tried to take her in his arms, but she held back from him. "But you're right," he rushed to say. "I was falling in love with you. I *am* in love with you. And that's why you've got to believe me when I say I want you out of here. Boris Gorchakov is a dangerous man, not one to play games with. Now I want to take you back to Tyumen, where you'll be safe. *I'm* here to get your father out of that prison, and I'll do it, but I can't be bothered worrying about you."

She could not believe the depth of his arrogance. "Go to hell, Cord Brandt!" She sat up and glared at him, trembling in her rage. "I don't believe you. And I swear, if you expose me, then I'll expose you. We'll hang together."

"No, you're wrong." He got to his feet and began to pace beside the bed. "Come with me today to the Whites' headquarters. They'll identify me, and—"

"I said *no!*"

Her voice rose, and she leaped from the bed and pointed to the door. "Get out of here now. Forget you saw me, and forget you knew me."

Cord knew she was serious, just as he knew that then was not the time to try reason. With a helpless shrug, he said, "I am sorry. I'll go, because I know you're angry, but I promise I'm going to make you believe me."

Their eyes met and held. Neither one spoke.

Then, just as Marilee was about to order him once more to leave, there was a soft rap on the door.

They both froze.

Then came the sheepishly apologetic voice of Boris Gorchakov. "Natasha, my sweet, are you awake? I must talk to you, and tell you how sorry I am."

Marilee swayed in terror. It would ruin everything for him to find Cord here. She held a finger to her lips and pointed to the window.

He nodded, not wanting to be discovered.

The window made a loud scraping sound as he opened it.

"Natasha?" Boris called, sounding alarmed. "What's wrong? What's that noise? Are you all right?"

He began to jiggle the doorknob, and Marilee was

grateful that Cord had taken the time to lock it after he had burst in.

"Wait a moment, Boris," she called, making her voice sound groggy, as though he'd awakened her. "You startled me. I knocked something over."

"I'm so sorry," he cried. "Oh, I do apologize . . ."

On and on he rambled miserably through the door, while Marilee anxiously watched Cord scramble through the window and disappear into the frozen morning. It was not a long drop to the ground.

Closing the window after him, took a deep breath, and went to face Boris.

Outside, Cord's booted feet hit the snow with a soft thud. He glanced about in the purple light, blinked against the glare of the sunrise, then hurried on his way.

On the other side of the alley, crouched unseen behind a collection of garbage barrels, Rudolf grinned.

He had somehow known that when he found Cord Brandt, he would find Marilee.

His comrades would take care of the traitorous German.

He would take care of her.

Chapter Twenty-seven

CORD was so angry that it was all he could do to keep from smashing his fist into Vladimir Dubovitsky's face. He wanted to know why Marilee, a woman completely uneducated in the ways of subversion, was being allowed to undertake something as dangerous as manipulating a man like Boris Gorchakov.

And the answers he was getting were making him madder than hell.

"She's aware of the risks, Brandt," Dubovitsky said quietly, after Cord had exploded. "She knows what she's doing."

"No, she doesn't," Cord shouted. "There's no way she can. You need a professional for a job like that. Somebody like that Bolshevik bitch, Elenore Hapsburg. Don't we have anybody like that available?"

"They would not have the same motivation as Marilee, because Marilee is only doing it to try and get her father out of prison," Dubovitsky quickly pointed out.

"And besides," he could not resist goading,

"thanks to you, Elenore proved to be a big disappointment to the Zealots, didn't she?"

Cord let the remark pass. He knew only too well how Elenore had fulfilled the old story about the wrath of a woman scorned.

"She wound up confiding everything to the authorities, but now we're informed that the Coltranes are en route to Russia to try to locate Marilee. We've been asked to help, but, of course, we're keeping her whereabouts confidential until she's completed her mission," Dubovitsky said.

"Well, I just hope they get to her before Boris Gorchakov finds out who she really is," Cord growled.

"Stay out of it, Brandt!" Dubovitsky snapped.

"No! I happen to care about her, and I'm not sitting back and letting her endanger her life just because you bastards believe that the end always justifies the means—no matter who gets hurt in the process!"

He turned to stalk from the room, but on Dubovitsky's signal, the other men present moved to block his path.

Realizing that he was outnumbered, Cord turned back around. "Okay, what else is on your mind? I'd like to get back to Tobolsk and keep an eye on things."

"That's what I'm trying to tell you, Brandt," Dubovitsky informed him coldly. "We *do* mind."

Cord's eyes narrowed. "There's no way you can stop me, except by force, and I wouldn't advise that." He slipped his hand inside his fur parka, touching his gun.

Dubovitsky was well aware that he was armed. "We have people watching her. You'll only complicate matters if you get involved. You could even jeopardize Marilee's position yourself,'' he said placatingly.

''No.'' Cord shook his head firmly. ''I wouldn't do that.''

''But you said you went to her room over the restaurant. That was taking a hell of a big chance. What if you were seen? You never should have made personal contact with her.''

''Who's going to be out wandering around at dawn in this freezing weather?'' he replied fiercely. ''Besides, I had to see her. I wanted to know what she was doing with a goddamn Bolshevik officer, and she sure as hell needed to know I wasn't just spying for them, pretending to be a White.

''It wouldn't have had to be that way,'' he added angrily, ''if you'd have let both of us know what was going on.''

Dubovitsky let that pass. It had not been entirely his decision to keep that information confidential. Instead he said sharply, ''You didn't accomplish anything, because you said she didn't believe you. You'd have been wiser to contact us to find out what was going on and keep your distance from her. You had no business acting on your own that way. It was dangerous.''

Cord finally exploded. ''Let me tell you something! I'm not just some patriotic private citizen out to do my good deed for the fucking counterrevolution! I'm every bit as good at what I do as you and the other bastards in this room!''

Dubovitsky was sitting behind a makeshift desk, and he shrank back in his chair as Cord leaned menacingly toward him. The men standing behind him moved warily forward.

"I've got a big stake in this war, Dubovitsky. I've got my own personal vendetta against the Bolshevik pigs, remember? One of Lenin's insane followers killed my mother in a butcher shop in Petrograd with a knife because she didn't agree with what he was orating about that day. And then the bastards shot my father down in cold blood when he tried to take his revenge on the maniac.

"My father had taken my mother out of Russia," he went on, moving away from the desk. "They had lived in Germany since they married, but she'd gone back when her father died to clear out the home place. It was their last day there. I was away at Oxford when I got the news. Then I knew it had become my goddamn war, too. That's why I'm in it. For revenge. And you and everybody else know it. I've never pretended that it was for anything else."

Dubovitsky reached to pat his shoulder in understanding. "We know that, Brandt, and you're one of our best men. Just don't let your heart rule your head and make you do something stupid, all right?"

Cord's anger returned. "I'm not some lovesick schoolboy. I know what I'm doing. And all I ask of you is to pull Marilee off her assignment. Get her out of there, and then tell her who the hell I really am, so she'll trust me."

Dubovitsky exchanged concerned glances with the others. He would have liked to be able to order him not to return to Tobolsk, to send him somewhere else that he might be useful, but knew he'd never consent. "Very well," he said finally. "Go back there. Keep an eye on her—but from a distance. Remember that you could jeopardize not only her life, but yours as well, not to mention other Whites in the area.''

''And what about backing me up on who I am?''

Dubovitsky shook his head sadly. ''We can't do that now. It would only complicate matters. Let her do what has to be done, then she can be told everything. She needs to put her sole concentration on deceiving Lieutenant Colonel Gorchakov, not on sorting out the feelings that will be provoked by learning the truth about you. That is the decision of those in authority.''

Cord knew it was no use to argue anymore, and besides, he was anxious to get back. Wanting just to end the meeting, he pretended to concede. ''All right,'' he said finally. ''I've got no choice but to play by your rules . . . for now.''

''For now . . .'' Dubovitsky echoed, nodding. ''Then go. And we will be in contact. But remember, your original assignment was just to be in Tobolsk in case you're needed.''

Cord nodded and hurried on his way.

He was not yet sure how he would do it. He knew only that there was no way he was going to allow Marilee to be hurt.

And he also wanted to make sure she didn't get herself into a situation she couldn't get out of, one that would haunt her for the rest of her life.

Boris Gorchakov stared at the portrait of Lenin which hung behind his desk in the tiny room he used for an office. He templed his fingers to keep himself from hitting something. His teeth were clenched so tightly his jawbones ached. The roaring in his head was not only from too much vodka the night before.

He had awakened to realize that Natasha was gone, but when he saw how she'd tucked the blanket around him, he'd dared to hope she might harbor no hard feelings. Still, he had known he would not rest easy until he could be sure.

He had a deep, burning desire for her, an ache in his loins like a gnawing hunger. He had to have her.

So he had hurried into the frigid morning and made his way to her place above the restaurant to let her know how much he regretted the way the night before had so abruptly ended. He wanted to make sure that another date was made for the evening to come. This time, he swore, he would not overindulge in vodka. He would be awake, aware, and very, very passionate.

But when he heard the strange noises coming from within her room after he had knocked, he felt that something was not quite right. Even though she had graciously accepted his apology, assured him she was not angry, and even agreed to see him that night, she had not invited him into her room. He had passed off her reluctance as fear of being caught entertaining a man in her private quarters. He could understand that, and was not anxious to be seen there, anyway. So he had gone on his way, happily counting the hours till he could be with her again, this time to prove to her what a man he could be. How he would make her glad she was a woman!

He arrived at his office to find a dark-haired man waiting to see him. He said he had no time for him, but the man got his full attention with one statement.

"Natasha is not her real name."

He ushered him into his office, past the surprised gaze of his staff assistant. Once the door had closed behind them, Boris grabbed the man by his shirt and slammed him up against the wall. "Tell me who you are and why you are here, before I lose my patience and kill you . . . comrade," he added with a sneer.

"Natasha is not Natasha," the man repeated, his eyes bulging in fear. Boris Gorchakov was a huge man who could easily crush a man's throat with the squeeze of one large hand. "She . . . is . . . daughter of . . . Drakar . . . Mikhailonov."

Hearing that, Boris emitted a loud, guttural snarl; then he lifted him up and threw him into a chair. "Talk!" he commanded. "And if you cannot prove what you say, then you will die this very day."

The lieutenant colonel spun around in his chair and faced Lenin's portrait.

Rudolf was not about to say anything more until the officer got hold of himself. He knew it had to be very disconcerting to a man in his position to hear that he had been betrayed by a woman, especially one who turned out to be a *spy*.

Rudolf had thought the situation over carefully. After following Brandt and watching as he prepared to leave Marilee's room, he had decided there was no need to follow him to the Whites. He could get caught himself, for the trail to their headquarters was heavily guarded. Besides, he felt it much more important to let Gorchakov know he was being deceived—and dangerously.

"So," Gorchakov said finally, spinning around to face him, this time with a cold smile touching his lips. "My little Natasha is actually the daughter of Drakar Mikhailonov. What a fool she has made of me."

"Oh, no, sir," Rudolf hastened to reassure him. "You had no way of knowing. It was only by accident that I discovered her little scheme—*and* Brandt's," he added with a vehement grunt.

"You see," he hurried to explain, "I became suspicious of Brandt when I heard that Marilee had escaped from Daniberry. Then, when my sister betrayed all of us, I knew it had to be because she was angry at him for becoming romantically involved with his hostage. So I started trailing him, spending all my time and energy tracking him down, and it paid off."

"You did well, Citizen Rudolf," Gorchakov grunted. "And because you've proved yourself to be so competent, I will leave it to you to decide what happens next."

Rudolf was almost shaking with happiness. *He* would be in control of their fate.

Gorchakov asked, "Shall I send soldiers to arrest her and throw her in jail with her father? Brandt, as well? We could torture them both, or execute them as an example to other spies in Tobolsk."

"No, no," Rudolf was quick to disagree. "We don't want to alert the rest of the Whites as to what's going on. It has to be done quietly, and quickly, before word leaks out."

"Go on."

"When do you see her again?"

"Tonight."

"Good. Act as though you suspect nothing. We can be sure that Brandt will be watching her like a hawk. We'll set a trap for him at your place, and then we'll have them both. We'll take him off to jail, and her, too . . . *after,"* he finished with a suggestive wink, "I get my reward for a job well done."

Gorchakov grinned, a lascivious gleam in his black eyes. "Ah, yes. You deserve to have your fill of her, and then it will be *my* turn."

Rudolf kept a smile pasted on his face, but he was actually repulsed by the thought of Gorchakov with Marilee. He would not admit it to anyone, but he realized that he had, somewhere along the way, fallen in love with Marilee Mikhailonov.

He wanted his reward, all right, but not only for a few days and nights. He wanted her for always.

But for the moment, he cared only about getting her away from Cord Brandt and Boris Gorchakov . . .

. . . and having her all to himself.

Chapter Twenty-eight

MARILEE was so nervous that she had spilled two trays of drinks, and Miklos, the restaurant owner, was scowling. She knew that this night there would be no turning back. She had to extract the information she needed from Boris, and whether or not she'd be able to successfully stave off his lusty advances remained to be seen. Her only defense, she had decided, was to find something to get angry about. Then she could storm out of his place and continue to hold him at bay while the Whites finalized their plans for the escape.

Still, she knew she could not get through the evening with her nerves so frazzled. Dealing with Boris was enough to worry about without the added stress of finding out that Cord Brandt was around. Damn him! Didn't he have sense enough to know that as soon as possible, she would turn him in as a spy? Just as *she* was wise enough to know that he would do the same to her! That was why tonight had to be the night, no matter what. To wait any longer was to invite exposure.

Boris usually appeared late in the evening. So far, she had not seen Cord. Maybe, she dared to hope, he had heeded her warning and would leave her alone. But she was so on edge that she began to sneak little sips from an opened bottle of kirsch in the back room of the restaurant. Gradually, she felt a little more sure of herself.

When Boris walked in, she was startled to see him because it was still early. He did not take a table. He paused only long enough to unfasten his chin strap and remove his khaki cap. Then he gave her an affectionate, eager grin and walked purposefully across the room to Miklos.

She watched as the two spoke, and did not like the smirk on Miklos's face when he looked in her direction. Then they shook hands, and Boris headed her way.

"What was that all about?" she asked, feeling a bit piqued.

He leaned to kiss her cheek boldly, then he whispered happily, "Get your things, *milochka*. You are free for the rest of the night."

"But—" She shook her head, bewildered. Dear Lord, not so soon! She needed time to get herself together. She just wasn't ready for the evening's performance!

"What is it?" He stiffened, glowering down at her. He was perhaps two heads taller than she. "You aren't pleased that I was able to get you excused early? You aren't as happy as I am that we can now be together longer than planned? What kind of game are you playing with my heart, Natasha?"

"You're wrong!" She shook her head again. By God, she could not wilt now. Forcing a smile, she stood on tiptoe to brush his lips with her own. "I'm just surprised he agreed. Miklos can be difficult, and—"

"You forget who I am," Boris roared, happy once

more, "but he does not! Now get your things, and let's be on our way. I have a nice fire, and I've even prepared a little dinner for you to make up for last night."

She sucked in her breath and turned, wincing as he laughed lustily and gave her a playful pat on her bottom.

Hurrying to the back room, she pulled her boots on over her shoes with shaky hands, pausing now and then to sip more kirsch. Then, reaching for her cape, she took a deep breath. This was it. There was no turning back.

As she walked out, she had a sudden, stabbing wish.

Her Uncle Colt had called her weak.

But, despite her apprehension, she knew that she had never felt stronger.

The Coltrane blood was flowing, and how she wished the Coltranes knew it.

The woman stood in the kitchen doorway and watched as Boris left with the lovely young girl.

The woman's job was to keep the bar glasses washed. When the basket on the floor at the end of the long wooden bar was filled with dirty glassware, she would take it into the back room to carefully scrub and polish the glasses. The clean glasses would be placed in yet another basket, ready to go back to the shelves behind the bar.

The basket was filled, but she did not move. She had just seen Boris Gorchakov enter.

She now knew that Marilee was in his clutches. Where was Cord Brandt? She was powerless to do anything to help, and—

"You! You want your rubles tonight?"

Miklos was glaring down at her, his hands on his hips.

She scurried forward and retrieved the basket, then hurried into the back without saying a word.

Miklos watched her for a few seconds. She was a strange one. She had begged for the job, and didn't care what he paid her, she said, as long as she got something to eat. She stayed to herself, kept her head down, and never looked anybody in the eye. He wondered why she was staring after the Russian officer and Natasha. He grunted. It didn't matter, she had gone back to work.

Irina felt like crying out, but long ago she had learned to swallow her tears and keep on going. But how she cringed to think of poor Marilee in the clutches of that fiend—and all to try and save her father.

Cord was the only one who knew Irina's true identity. She had not even let the other Whites know where she was. They were afraid she was going to use the gold she had hidden to buy her beloved Drakar's freedom. She was sorely tempted—but she knew he did not want that. It was to be used only for the purpose intended—on behalf of the Czar and the Imperial family. Drakar had given her explicit orders to stay hidden, along with the gold.

Through the gossip of the underground she had heard of Marilee's abduction and the Bolsheviks' demand for ransom—but it had been too late for her to do anything. She knew that Cord Brandt was working as a counterspy, and had managed to contact him. She had then helped him to find Marilee.

But now she had no way to contact him, and oh, how she needed him! Marilee was in trouble, and if Cord didn't return soon, Irina knew she'd have no choice but to try to do something about the situation.

She took the basket back out and set it on the bar for one of the tenders to put away. Then she returned to the kitchen and paced about nervously as she tried to decide what she should do. Finally she decided that she had no choice but to make her way to Lieutenant Colonel Gorchakov's quarters to be nearby should Marilee find he was more than she could handle.

It had begun to snow, but the flakes were large and soft, and the wind wasn't blowing, so it would not be too difficult to walk the short distance. Irina wrapped her worn woolen coat about her and made sure the little knife she kept strapped to her ankle inside her right boot was secured. Then she opened the back door of the restaurant.

Just as she stepped outside, a figure loomed out of the alley and grabbed her. She was terrified until she recognized Cord Brandt's intense face.

"Something's happened," he said in a rush, pushing her back inside. "What is it?"

She told him that Gorchakov had shown up early and gotten Miklos's permission for Marilee to leave.

He swore. "How long have they been gone?"

"Nearly forty-five minutes, I think," Irina said reluctantly.

"Where?" He started to shake her. "Where does the bastard live?"

She told him, and he immediately turned to go. She caught his sleeve and cried, "Cord, what are you going to do?"

"Get her out of there, goddammit."

"But she needs time—"

"For what?" He whipped about angrily. "To get him to tell her the best time to break her father out of jail? You really think she can do that, Irina? Maybe she's cunning enough, but I doubt it, especially when that reprobate has got other things on his mind. He's not going to waste time on conversation tonight. You can bet your hidden Imperial gold on that,'' he could not resist adding.

"You don't understand, Cord. Drakar himself ordered me to keep it hidden until it could be used to free the Czar and his family.'' She suddenly gave in to her tears. "Nobody knows what I've suffered to keep my promise.''

He patted her awkwardly. "Yes, they do, Irina. Everyone knows that they tortured you, and that you didn't give in, and everyone respects you for that, including me. Forgive me if you thought I was being unkind. Drakar is a lucky man.''

He gave her a quick hug. "I'm getting her out of there, one way or another.''

She followed him to the door. "But then where will you take her?''

"To where I met you,'' he replied, then disappeared into the night.

Irina stared after him for a few seconds, then closed the door and leaned against it, offering up a silent prayer for the people she loved.

Outside, where there was no sound except for the snow gently falling, a lone figure appeared from the shadows . . . and stealthily followed Cord Brandt's footsteps into the shimmering night.

Chapter Twenty-nine

Boris stood behind Marilee to take her cape, and when it dropped from her shoulders, he kissed the back of her neck. She stiffened, but he did not notice, for he had waited so very long for this moment.

He clamped both hands on her breasts and pressed her back against him, his lips nuzzling her skin as he moaned against her ear, "Oh, *milochka,* my *darling.* You are driving me crazy. Never have I wanted a woman more. I must have you . . ."

He spun her around and covered her mouth with his lips in a clumsy but determined kiss. Marilee tried to endure, but when he forced his tongue into her mouth and clamped a thick hand between her legs, she could stand it no longer.

Jerking away from him, she cried, "Boris, what's wrong with you? How dare you just . . . *maul* me this way, the second we walk through the door? What do you think I am?"

"A beautiful, desirable woman," he declared hotly, reaching for her again. She stepped back.

"I want you desperately," he cried. "Don't you know that? Why do you torture me?"

"In time!" she said sharply. "You promised me dinner, and I'm famished."

"Yes." He nodded and moved to the little kitchen area. "You're right. I'm sorry. I'm rushing things, but I just want you so much. We'll eat first . . ." He began rattling things around. "And then we'll go to bed, where we'll be nice and warm, and I'll make it so good for you, my dear Natasha, so good."

He turned to give her an adoring gaze, and she managed a tight little smile.

He held out a drink to her. "You'll like this. I got it especially for you. It's called *Palusookhoye*, a nice champagne."

She took it eagerly and gulped it down, then asked for a refill. Then she watched, her mind whirling, as he scooped some sort of stew from a large pot on the stove.

"You should recognize this," he told her. "It's *pelmeni*, very popular in Siberia, made of reindeer meat."

Marilee shuddered. It did not smell very good, but she had no intention of eating, anyway. She was on her third glass of *Palusookhoye*, feeling just daring enough to pretend idle conversation. "You have such a dangerous job. I worry about you all the time. What if some of your prisoners escape? Isn't that a frightening possibility?"

Boris's back was turned, and he was glad she could not see the knowing smile that touched his lips. The little vixen. He would play her game, but only for a little while, because he intended to have his fill of her before Rudolf arrived. He had told Rudolf to wait till near midnight. A glance at the clock told him he had nearly two hours. That was why he had arranged to bring her here early, so there would be time for him to do what his loins commanded so hungrily.

Finally he replied, "Well, not really, Natasha." He feigned indifference.

"But every jail is vulnerable somehow," she persisted. "Each has a weakness."

"Of course." He shrugged. "I suppose if we have one, it would be around daylight, when there's so much going on—the changing of the guard, inspections, the prisoners receiving their breakfast trays in their cells. I've made a note to put more guards on duty then, but I don't really worry about it."

He could not resist giving her a probing look. "Why do you?"

She looked up at him coquettishly through lowered lashes and laughed softly. "Why, no reason really, except to reassure myself that you're safe. We've become so close. I don't want anything to happen to you, Boris."

"And nothing will, I promise you."

He filled two bowls with *pelmeni,* then set them down on the table, gesturing for her to join him. "Let's not waste any more time, Natasha, darling. The fire is burning down, and we'll be much warmer in bed."

Marilee sucked in her breath and sat down. There was no chance that he would pass out this night, because he wasn't even drinking. She pointed to the bottle he'd placed on the table. "Aren't you joining me?"

"No, I'm determined to make up for last night. I want all my senses to be keen tonight so I can make sure that you receive all the pleasure I have to give you.''

Marilee was afraid she was going to be sick.

''Eat.'' He gestured impatiently. ''You said you were famished.''

Marilee knew it was time. She had quite easily learned when the jail was most vulnerable. More information than that she could not expect. Giving her plate a shove, she declared petulantly, ''I don't like reindeer meat.''

Boris raised an eyebrow. ''Oh, really? Well, that's all I have. Eat it or go hungry, but make up your mind, because I'm ready to go to bed.''

''Well, I'm not!'' she cried indignantly, ready to start an argument so she could storm out and be finished with him forevermore.

Getting to her feet, she snapped, ''I must say, sir, that you are not a very polite host. Not only do you not ask me in advance about my food preferences, but when you learn you've prepared something I don't like, you don't even care. If that's your attitude, then I doubt you'd have any regard for my preferences in your bed, and—''

''Oh, but I do care!'' he said with a roar, leaping to his feet so quickly that his chair tipped over and hit the floor with a bang. ''And now I'll show you. I promise that you'll not only like it, little *milochka*, you will beg for second helpings.''

''No . . .'' She tried to stand, but he was too quick for her. He grabbed her and lifted her in his arms. Then he carried her across the room and threw her on the bed.

Terror rose bitterly in her throat as she watched him quickly pull off his clothing.

"No . . ." she repeated. She tried to get up, but he threw her back down roughly. "No, you can't do this . . ."

"Oh, yes, I can!" He laughed, then fell on top of her, straddling her as he began to tear at her dress.

She fought with every ounce of strength she possessed, but she was no match for him. When she was completely naked and totally vulnerable beneath him, he glared down at her with lust-filled eyes. "Now, you treacherous little vixen, you're going to find out what happens to women stupid enough to think they can fool Boris Gorchakov."

He tried to spread her legs with his knee, and Marilee twisted from side to side, clawing out at him.

He slapped her, then he backhanded her. "Goddamn you!" he bellowed. "Stop fighting. I will have you again and again, as much as I want."

He tried to slap her into submission as he continued to rant. "And I am going to love every second I am fucking Drakar Mikhailonov's daughter!"

Marilee froze in sudden shock. He knew who she was!

He took advantage of her momentary stillness and was about to enter her when she came alive at just the last second and caught him off guard. She threw him off-balance, and he fell to the floor with a mighty thud.

Scrambling off the other side of the bed, she raced across the room, not caring that it was freezing outside or that she was naked. All she knew was that she had to reach that door and escape.

Boris was scrambling to his feet. Marilee was so terrified that she tripped and fell, and he was on top of her at once.

"I'll take you right here!" he screamed. "On your knees like the bitch you are!"

He attempted to mount her, but she fell forward, screaming in terror.

Boris had lost patience. He knew he was running out of time, and that if she kept on yelling someone might come to demand what was going on.

He fastened his huge hands around her throat and squeezed.

Marilee felt herself choking. The world was getting darker, and she was getting dizzy. Suddenly the yawning blackness of oblivion gave her momentary peace.

Satisfied that she was merely unconscious, Boris picked her up and threw her down on the bed roughly. Then he positioned her for his pleasure and prepared to proceed.

So intent was he on his lust that he had not heard the scraping at the lock, nor was he aware when the door quietly opened.

He did not even notice the sudden blast of cold air as Cord Brandt let himself in.

Boris knew nothing until he heard a whistling sound.

But there was no time to wonder what was happening. He felt an explosion of pain at the base of his skull, then he slipped into unconsciousness.

Chapter Thirty

CORD rushed to Marilee's side and lifted her in his arms. He whispered her name, cold dread seizing his heart at the thought that Boris might have killed her.

He laid her down on the bed and saw with great relief that she was breathing. He then tapped her cheek in an attempt to bring her around.

Her eyes opened slowly. She coughed and gasped, shaking her head to dispel the roaring in her ears. Then she looked up and awareness dawned in her eyes. "You! What—"

He cut her off. "Are you all right, Marilee? Did he hurt you?"

Then the nightmare came flooding back to her. She turned her head to see Boris lying in a heap on the floor.

In answer to her unspoken question, Cord told her, "No, he's not dead, just unconscious. We've got to get out of here before he wakes up. I'll tie and gag him, to give us extra time before he sounds an alarm. Try to get yourself together."

Marilee suddenly realized she was naked, and immediately began to fumble for her clothing, suddenly feeling terribly self-conscious. But Cord was not paying any attention. He began to look around for something to tie Boris with, finally settling on his belt.

"Hurry up," he snapped when he saw she was still not dressed.

Her gratitude was fast turning into humiliation and fury. "I'm not going anywhere with you, Herr Brandt," she told him scathingly. "I found out how to get my father out of that prison, and I'm heading for the Whites to enlist their help. If you try to stop me, I'll scream to high heaven, so help me, because nothing is going to stop me now."

Cord was bent over Boris, who was moaning as he started to come around. Glancing over his shoulder at Marilee, Cord gave her a crooked grin. "You still don't believe we're on the same side, do you?"

She shook her head adamantly. "And I don't know what you think you're accomplishing by trying to convince me otherwise."

He stood and came toward her. When she backed away, he grabbed her and held her tightly against him. "Because I love you, Marilee . . ." he declared fiercely. His blue eyes searched her face for some sign of trust. "I think I've loved you since that first night I held you in my arms—"

"When you thought I was someone else!" She gave him a violent shove and darted for the door. He had been about to kiss her, and for one instant she had almost let him, even wanted him to. She knew that if she did not get away from him quickly, she would succumb to the desire burning within her.

Cord started after her, and they both froze as the

door suddenly opened. Rudolf was standing there with a pointed gun.

Cord muttered an oath and Marilee gasped. Rudolf was the last person either of them had expected to see.

He stepped inside, grinning in triumph. Pursing his lips, he made a smacking sound in Marilee's direction. Then he scowled as he saw Boris trussed up on the floor.

"Untie him. At once," he commanded tersely.

Cord could not argue with the gun aimed right at him. He only wished he could get his hands on his own. Rudolf sensed what he was thinking and ordered him to unbuckle his holster and toss it aside before he proceeded. He had no choice but to obey.

He freed Boris, who was rubbing the back of his head and groaning. Rudolf asked him if he was all right, and he blinked dizzily. Then he said that if he had a little vodka he would be just fine.

"Get it!" Rudolf ordered Marilee.

"Get it yourself!" she retorted, instinctively moving closer to Cord.

Boris struggled to his feet.

Rudolf continued to point his gun at Cord and Marilee. He watched as Boris staggered over to a cabinet and grabbed a bottle of vodka, then held it to his lips and drank eagerly.

Boris wiped his lips with the back of his hand; then he turned and glared furiously at Cord. "You . . ." he snarled, ". . . will wish you were dead before I and my men are through with you."

"I had my orders," Cord said, pretending that he was still on the side of the Bolsheviks. "In case you don't know who I am, I was one of the leaders of the Zurich Zealots in charge of the abduction of Marilee Mikhailonov. She escaped. I was sent to track her down and bring her back. You were about to rape her. You think she's worth anything to us once you rip her to pieces?''

He spoke so coolly that with each word Marilee hated him all the more. "You bastard," she said between clenched teeth. "You goddamn bastard!"

He winced ever so slightly, hating what he had to do but knowing that it was necessary to save their lives. "So what?" He grinned arrogantly. "Can I help it if I don't like seconds?"

She slapped him then, losing all control. He just stood there and forced himself to laugh.

"Enough of that!" Rudolf exploded. To Boris, he cried, "He's lying. He's a traitor to our cause. I've been in on this from the beginning. He fell in love with her when he was holding her for ransom in France. That's why my sister got mad and told the enemy everything. He'd been trifling with her, too. He's no good as an agent, and he can't be trusted. All he wants is Marilee, and you promised her to me . . ." His voice trailed off in a whine.

Marilee was repulsed. "I'd rather die than have you touch me, you spineless little coward!"

"No!" he said, a grim expression on his face. "You won't die, Marilee. You're going to learn to love me, the way I love you. I'm going to be so good to you, you'll beg me to take you again and again . . ." His eyes had taken on a glassy look, and he spoke thickly, as if in a trance.

Marilee told him he was crazy.

Boris snickered. "I really don't think she wants any part of you, Rudolf. Maybe we'd better reconsider our agreement."

Rudolf's eyes grew darker, and the hand holding the gun began to tremble slightly, as though he were fighting an inner battle to keep from turning it on Boris. "What did you say?" he demanded.

"I said . . ." Boris paused to lift the bottle to his mouth once more and take a long swallow. "I said that perhaps we should reconsider our little bargain. Our little Natasha, or I should say *Marilee,* doesn't seem to want any part of you."

"Well, she sure as hell doesn't want *you!*" Rudolf cried, indignant.

Cord almost made his move. Rudolf lost his concentration for one split second, but just as he started to leap forward, Rudolf lifted the gun once more and snarled, "I'll kill you, Brandt. I swear it."

Then he looked at Marilee. "Gorchakov would have your father executed. Brandt is a traitor and can't be trusted. He made a fool of my sister. He'll do the same to you, if you let him. *I* am the only one you can trust, Marilee. I am only here because I love you."

Marilee threw back her head and laughed. "You fool! I'd rather die than have you love me! Love your cause, Bolshevik," she went on contemptuously. "It's a worthy cause for your lust."

He winced, as though he'd been slapped like Brandt. His eyes narrowed. Brandt and Gorchakov both snickered, which only served to infuriate him all the more. "Enough!" he shrieked, enraged. "You're coming with me. Get your cape. Now."

To Gorchakov, he said, "Brandt is all yours. We're leaving."

"You wait a damn minute!" Boris stopped laughing, his mouth suddenly grim as he set the bottle aside and started toward Rudolf. "I think you forget who I am! *You* take orders from *me, Citizen* Hapsburg. I say what will happen. You are going nowhere."

The two Bolsheviks had their backs turned to the door, and were unaware of the movement behind them.

But Cord and Marilee saw—and remained frozen.

Cord contained a sigh of relief as Irina slipped quickly and quietly inside the room, holding a knife at her side.

Marilee was puzzled. She had seen the woman at the restaurant, washing glasses. Who was she, and why had she come? Yet another Bolshevik? But if she were also the enemy, why was she sneaking up behind Boris with a knife?

And then there was no more time to wonder, as the blade arced through the air and sliced through the back of Boris's thick neck.

Cord lunged, knocking the gun from Rudolf's hand and punching him in the face.

Both men crumpled to the floor simultaneously.

Boris lay in a rapidly forming pool of his own blood, his eyes already glazed as death gripped him.

Marilee stood watching in astonished silence as Cord spoke to the woman.

"You got here just in time." He gave her a quick hug, then said tersely, "We've all got to get out of here. Rudolf may have men stationed nearby who will be suspicious when he doesn't return."

"There was nobody about outside," she told him. "It's snowing pretty hard, and all's quiet."

Marilee wondered what the stranger's part was in all this. If she was a friend of Cord's, why had she just murdered a Bolshevik?

She noticed that, despite having just killed, the woman had almost an ethereal air about her. The shadows in her eyes revealed that she had obviously suffered and endured much in life. Yet she was lovely, and the smile she bestowed on Cord was compassionate and caring.

Another of his women, no doubt, Marilee fumed. But it did not matter to her.

She began to inch toward the door. Cord's back was turned as he knelt to tie Rudolf. He did not notice the way Marilee was stealthily moving, but the woman saw. "Please don't leave us, Marilee. We mean you no harm," she said quietly.

Cord leaped up just as Marilee started to run. He blocked her path, then grabbed her and held her as she began to struggle.

She tried to scream, but he clamped a hand over her mouth. "Stop it! You've nothing to fear from her. That's Irina."

Irina!

Marilee's eyes widened above Cord's hand, and he released her. She turned to the woman in awe. "Irina. You . . . you're my father's . . . friend."

Irina smiled through her tears. "You can trust me, Marilee. I swear it. And Cord, too. He's always been on your side."

Marilee looked from one to the other, still wary.

"But we've got to get out of here," Irina reminded

them. "Come. We'll go to the special cabin. We can talk there."

She took her hand, but Marilee hesitated.

Cord nodded to Irina, who stepped back obligingly. Then he put his hands on Marilee's shoulders, forcing her to look up at him. He could see the indecision in her cinnamon eyes, but he sensed her desire to believe. "I've always been your friend," he said huskily, "but I want to be much more, if you'll let me."

Then he kissed her.

Marilee answered that kiss, her arms going about him. She was overcome with joy as what she had wanted for so long came true.

Chapter Thirty-one

IT was nearly midnight when they reached the little cabin deep in the snowy woods. Cord immediately built a roaring fire in the grate, and Irina retrieved a hidden bottle of brandy and poured them all drinks. Then she and Marilee curled up with thick wool blankets on one of the cots and began to talk.

Irina told Marilee how she had met Drakar many years earlier. Gradually, they realized that they had fallen in love. They had been about to confide their betrothal to Marilee before making a formal announcement, when the political situation in Russia worsened and interrupted their plans. "I like to think you would have approved," Irina finished, holding both of Marilee's hands in hers. "Though I'd never met you, I felt somehow that we'd be close, good friends."

"Of course I'd have given you my blessings," Marilee assured her. She already liked Irina very much and admired her for her courage.

Irina's smile was hesitant. "You wouldn't have felt that your father's remarrying would be disloyal to your mother's memory?"

Marilee shook her head vehemently. "No. Absolutely not. I know my father loved my mother in a special way, and I'm glad that you were able to take away his sadness.

"But wait!" she cried suddenly, laughing nervously. "We've got to stop talking this way, as though it's all over. It's just the beginning. We're going to get him out of that jail, and then we'll all get on with our lives."

Cord turned from the fireplace, speaking for the first time since they'd arrived at the cabin. "Marilee, getting Drakar out of there isn't so easy. I've spied all around that place. It's crawling with guards."

"But that's what I've been trying to tell both of you," she cried excitedly, tossing aside the blankets and scrambling to her feet to explain what she had learned from Boris.

She looked from one to the other. "Don't you see? He wouldn't have told me that if he had thought I'd actually be able to do anything about it. He knew who I was and was just stringing me along till Rudolf got there. But now he's dead, and Rudolf is tied up and stuffed under the bed where nobody will find him until long after we've freed my father and gotten away from here."

Cord and Irina looked at each other thoughtfully. Then they exchanged smiles, and Cord spoke for both of them when he declared, "It can work, but we have to do it today. Once Gorchakov's body is discovered and Rudolf is found, they'll be looking for us, and security will be extremely tight all over."

Irina leaped up from the cot. "I'll get the message

through. We won't need many men to help us. The fewer the better.''

Cord agreed. ''And see if they can send somebody who knows something about the inside of that place. I've looked around enough to know it's got a back entrance, but as far as I could tell, it's not used. If we can slip inside without being seen, there's a chance we might not encounter any guards at all, if they're busy outside with roll call.''

''What about the other prisoners?'' Irina wanted to know. ''Do we take them with us?''

''We'll free them all, but they'll have to go their own way. It's safer to separate.''

Irina grinned and reached for her cape. ''I'd better get going.''

''Maybe I'd better go, Irina,'' Cord quickly offered.

''Oh, no.'' She shook her head, her eyes shining. It had been a long, long time since she'd felt so good. ''I want to be the one to take this message in. It's not that far to the next post, anyway.''

She got to the door, then said with a wink, ''Besides, I think you two need some time alone together.''

''Yeah,'' Cord agreed firmly, walking toward Marilee. ''We sure do.''

The door closed behind Irina as he took Marilee in his arms. Their bodies melded together and they trembled with the intensity of their passion. He kissed her until she was breathless. Lifting her, he carried her to the cot. He gently laid her down and whispered, ''God only knows how I've waited for this moment, Marilee.''

They gazed feverishly at each other as Cord slowly began to strip off his clothes. When he flung his shirt aside, she marveled at his rock-hard chest and the sinewy muscles of his arms. Her fingertips ached to dance in the thick mat of chest hairs that curled down to—

She shuddered with heated anticipation.

His trousers fell, and he kicked them aside and stood naked before her. Marilee gasped at the sight of his erection, and she reached out to touch him.

He could stand it no longer. With a deep groan, he helped her remove her clothes. Then he stretched out beside her to gather her close, his hands moving up and down her hot, eager body. He cupped her full, round buttocks and squeezed, then moved to softly knead the flesh of her breasts. All the time his lips were nibbling, tasting, devouring, finally settling upon one ripe, taut nipple to suck hungrily.

Marilee's back arched as she moved yet closer, wanting only to be consumed by him. Her fingers weaved through his thick, blond hair, and she lifted one leg to cross over his hip so that his massive organ began to tease between her thighs. She felt her own moisture, the quivering within her belly that cried for yet more of the delicious wonders unfolding.

"Take me," she begged. "Oh, Cord, my darling, take me, all of me, again and again. Never, ever stop. I want you . . ."

He raised his head, then suddenly, almost roughly, cupped her face in one strong hand and squeezed ever so gently, forcing her to meet his burning blue eyes. "I want more than that from you, Marilee. I don't want just your body, your sex. I want your love . . ." he said hoarsely.

"And you have it," she cried, thrusting her whole body toward him. "For always, Cord. I love you . . ."

He entered her then, and she gasped with momentary pain. Then discomfort yielded to pleasure, and her cries were not of torment but of joy and ecstasy. The crescendo was building, higher and higher, and she thought she would surely die from the sheer wonder of it all.

And then the ultimate explosion came, and her nails dug into the flesh of his back as he pushed yet harder and took her to even greater pinnacles of delight.

He reached his own zenith, then held her for long, precious moments before whispering, "Never like this, my darling, never like this . . ."

She knew what he meant, knew that there was never a time before quite as wonderful, that their shared love made every experience before fade to nothingness.

"Together," he said, his lips moving to claim hers once more, "and forever."

And she sealed his proclamation with her own fervent kiss.

They made love again, reveling with wonder that their joy could be repeated so passionately and so quickly, laughingly admitting that they were each ready for yet another earth-shattering experience.

But the night was passing quickly. There were plans to be made—not only for what would happen at dawn, but for the immediate future as well.

When Irina returned, she brought with her three men they had never seen before. The newcomers introduced themselves as Odar, Kievan, and Sthrom. Marilee had changed into men's clothing—thick trou-

sers and shirt, a heavy greatcoat, a fur cap, and heavy
mittens. With a woolen scarf pulled across her lower
face, she was ready for their mission.

Cord led the way, having memorized the path that
would take them through the hard-packed snow and
up the ridge that overlooked what had once been a
small monastery in the hills. Squat and flat-topped, it
was surrounded by a fence. One gate faced the road
leading up from the village. Circled by ice-crusted
hillocks as the building was, the Bolshevik soldiers
hardly worried about escape attempts.

Odar knew the monastery well. He confirmed Cord's
observation that there was indeed a back door that was
not in use. "There's a tiny courtyard that the monks were
able to use for meditation only in the summer months.
Since the Bolsheviks took the place over to use as a prison,
the back plot hasn't been used."

He went on to describe the way in from the rear.
"There's a steep, rocky ledge back there. With ropes,
we can climb down easily enough."

Cord nodded approval. "If the front is vulnerable,
the back should be totally unguarded. It's the last
place they'd expect somebody to come in."

Marilee asked quickly, "But how do we get back
out again? If an alarm is sounded, won't we be a
perfect target climbing those ropes?"

"We aren't going to worry about sneaking out,
sweetheart," he told her. "Once we free everybody,
we move as fast as possible and scatter."

"Not exactly," Irina said in a strange, almost apologetic voice. They all turned to stare at her expectantly.

She took a deep breath and let it out slowly. "If

we succeed, Vladimir said we are to take Drakar to our outpost near Petrograd to await further orders.''

Marilee blinked, surprised. ''But why? All I want to do is get him out of the country. To go right into the middle of the Bolsheviks is insane! I assumed that the Whites would take us underground and smuggle us through to the Allies.''

''Those are the orders,'' Irina said almost angrily.

Cord squeezed Marilee's hand. ''We'll obey them. Evidently they're working on a plan to get both of you out of the country.''

''I don't like it,'' she protested. ''We'd be better off heading south, and—''

Cord cut her off. ''We'll follow orders, Marilee, the way we're supposed to. It's too risky striking out on our own, and besides, your father and Irina are very important. The Bolsheviks will go after them with everything they've got.''

She supposed he was right, but she knew she would not rest easy until they were all out of Russia. With a sigh, she conceded. ''Very well. We follow orders.''

Cord motioned for them to move on.

At the top of the ridge, they stared down at the monastery below, making sure all was quiet. Sure enough, as Boris had said, it seemed that there were no guards about. All they saw was two sentries at the front gate.

Odar and Kievan dropped two ropes down the ledge, a distance of nearly thirty feet. Sthrom shimmied down, then waited while Odar descended. Then Irina made her way, followed by Marilee. Finally

Cord went down, leaving Kievan at the top to help them when they made their ascent.

Odar led them toward the building. The back door was locked, but a boarded window was quickly ripped open. He scrambled inside, and in seconds, they heard the bolt within sliding; then the door opened.

Odar had told them the cells would be downstairs, in what had once been a little winery for the monks. They groped their way stealthily through a dark narrow passageway. When they reached the bowels of the monastery, they were relieved to find a small torch that illuminated the ring of small chambers around them.

"Keys!" Odar whispered hoarsely, pointing to a rusty ring hanging beneath the torch.

"Here!" someone cried. They saw bony fingers clutching a barred window. "Dear God, here! Here!"

"You must be silent!" Cord said as loudly as he dared. "Be patient, and we'll get you all out."

Marilee began to run from one cell door to the other, whispering feverishly, "Drakar Mikhailonov! Which one of you is my father . . ."

"Marilee. . . ."

She turned slowly, afraid that it was all a dream, that she would turn around and there would be no one there.

But he *was* real.

He staggered stiffly toward her, his arms held open. She ran to him and was folded against his chest, and they clung together for long, emotional moments, unashamedly crying tears of joy.

Marilee felt a hand on her shoulder and reluctantly drew back from her father's embrace to see Cord's anxious face in the torchlight. "We've got to go now. There were only six other prisoners, which explains the lack of security, but we're taking chances to hang around.''

''Brandt!'' Drakar grinned, his dark eyes flashing. ''I should've known you'd be behind this. Bless you!''

Marilee shivered with delight to think that now she had all the proof she ever needed that Cord Brandt was exactly who and what he had professed to be.

And dear God, how she loved him!

Drakar looked at Marilee once more, still unable to believe she was really there. ''I don't know how this came to be,'' he said in wonder, ''and I'm sure it's a long story, but bless both of you, and—'' He froze, as the final surprise hit him.

His arms dropped from about Marilee, and with sudden renewed strength, he rushed to Irina and gathered her in his arms, his wasted body shuddering with sobs of joy.

Beside her, Cord whispered, ''I wanted so badly to tell you so many things, like how your father found happiness.''

''I'm happy for him,'' Marilee said with all honesty. As much as her parents had loved each other, she knew her mother would not have wanted her father to spend the rest of his life alone.

Cord spun her about and kissed her, then declared, ''And there's no doubt about ours, either, Marilee. Now let's get the hell out of here and see what the Whites have got planned for us, all right?''

She met his glorious, loving smile with one of her own, and hand in hand, they hurried on their way.

Chapter Thirty-two

OUTSIDE, the other freed prisoners scattered in the misty, crystal light. They would make contact with White soldiers later. For the time being, they wanted only to distance themselves from the prison before they were discovered missing.

Marilee, her hand tucked in her father's, with Irina on his other side, fell in behind Cord, Odar, Kievan, and Sthrom as they began their arduous journey. There was so much she wanted to tell Drakar, so many questions to be answered, but she knew there was no time for conversation right now. They had to keep trudging along, moving as fast as possible in the biting cold.

Finally they reached the frozen Irtysh River, where ice boats would speed them along to sleighs waiting farther north.

That night they found shelter in the barn of a White sympathizer, where vodka and hot, spiced tea waited, as well as gruel and smoked meats. Marilee was impressed that their route was so well planned, that so many preparations had been made so quickly.

Drakar smiled. ''That's why we'll ultimately overthrow the Bolsheviks, Marilee, because we're better organized than they think. We have people like Irina who are dedicated, and Odar, Kievan, and Sthrom.

"And Cord Brandt." He nodded appreciatively to where Cord listened quietly.

"But it's over now for you," she said confidently, pretending not to notice the way the others exchanged uneasy glances. She would not let herself consider the possibility that he would not be leaving Russia with her. "Daniberry will still be there after the war. Till it's over, we're going to find a place where we can just be together in peace . . . and love."

She looked at Irina, who would not meet her gaze, then at Cord, who also glanced away.

Drakar sipped his vodka in silence.

Marilee felt a stab of foreboding. Finally she could contain her fears no longer and cried, "What is this? Why are you all acting so strange? We're leaving together, aren't we? *All* of us? We're getting out of this land of ice and snow and bloodshed, and we're all going to make a new life together, aren't we?"

She grabbed her father's arm. "You've done your share. We've been denied so much of each other, and now we can all be a family and—" Her voice cracked; she could not go on.

Drakar was silent for a moment as she leaned her head against his shoulder and cried quietly. Then, without looking at Irina, who was watching anxiously, he hugged Marilee against him. "You're right. I've missed out on so much with you. We'll all make a new life . . . together."

Only then did he look at Irina for confirmation, but she glanced away, unable to speak.

"Promise me!" Marilee cried desperately. "Promise me you'll leave with me. Dear God, I don't know where we'll go, but just promise you'll leave Russia with me, and that we'll find peace together."

He lowered his head and closed his eyes. She was his daughter, the daughter he had never really known. She deserved this time, and so, perhaps, did he. "I promise," he whispered tremulously.

Cord looked at Irina as she got to her feet and slipped out of the barn and into the white night. Drakar did not see her leave. Cord did not go after her—it was not his place to do so. Irina was a complex person, and although there was no doubt that she loved Drakar with every beat of her heart, she had suffered terribly at the hands of the vicious Bolsheviks. She wanted revenge and justice, not only for herself, but for her people.

Drakar realized later that she was gone. When he went to Cord, distraught, Cord could only say, "It was the way she wanted it. We all do what we have to do."

Marilee was asleep. Drakar looked at her and sighed. "She's my daughter. I owe her a stable life. I guess I couldn't expect Irina to understand that."

"Like I said," Cord responded. "We all do what we have to do."

Drakar gave him a strange look, then asked bluntly, "Are you in love with her?"

Cord nodded with a smile. "Oh, yes. I think I loved her before I even knew her."

Drakar shook his head. "I don't understand."

"I don't expect you to." He was not about to try

to explain that night in the castle cellar, back in Zurich. It seemed a lifetime ago.

Drakar seemed pleased. "Then you'll be leaving with us. I thought perhaps we'd go to Spain. The Coltranes have a large ranch there, and we can stay till the war is over. I only wish that something was resolved with Nicholas and his family. I feel like I'm deserting them, and—"

"You've done all you can," Cord quickly interjected. "Just concentrate on your own future, Mikhailonov. God knows, you've given enough of yourself to Russia and the cause."

Drakar looked at Marilee fondly, and his words were barely audible. "Have I, Brandt? Who can judge me?"

He went and lay down in a pile of straw on the far side of the barn, wanting to be alone with his memories . . . and his doubts.

The next morning he was awakened by Marilee's frantic shaking.

He looked up at her groggily and saw the distraught look on her face. "It's all right, honey. She's gone, but I guess I never could've expected her to leave with us. Maybe one day she'll change her mind and—"

"It's not only Irina," she told him in a dead, dull voice.

He held her at arm's length, searching her face, unwilling to believe what he knew she was about to tell him.

"Cord's gone, too. It's just you and me, Poppa."

They clung to each other for long, miserable moments; then Marilee spoke for them both as she quietly declared, "I guess I thought when you loved someone as much as I love Cord Brandt, they just had to love you back. But I was a fool. He loved his cause more.''

Drakar nodded, his spirit broken. He had not known such emptiness, such grief, since the day his beloved Dani had died.

Odar traveled with them all the way to Petrograd, confiding that when Irina had slipped away to follow her destiny, she had entrusted him with the final orders for their delivery. But he waited until they actually arrived in the city before informing them that they were to go to the Kshessinskaya Palace.

Drakar stared at him, wide-eyed and openmouthed. ''Are you mad? That's the headquarters of the Central and Petrograd committees of the Bolshevik Party! What is this? Some kind of trick?'' He drew Marilee into a protective embrace. He wished he had a weapon, for now he was sure they had been betrayed.

Odar was quick to assure him otherwise. ''No. It was orders from our leaders that Irina passed along to me. You are being granted political immunity, and officials of the United States government are waiting for you there. Trust me, please.''

Drakar sighed. ''I guess I have no choice, Odar, but I swear . . .'' He lifted his chin. ''If you have betrayed us, you'd better pray they execute me quickly, or so help me, I'll cut your heart out.''

Odar grinned confidently. ''Just go inside and find out for yourself, my friend. And Godspeed.''

Then he disappeared into the crowds along Gorky Prospekt, to return to the Whites—and the cause.

Drakar and Marilee looked across at the tiled facade of the elegant palace which formerly belonged to the ballerina Mathilde Kshessinskaya, mistress of Nicholas II.

Marilee asked fearfully, "What do we do now?" She felt guilty because she no longer really cared. In time she knew she would feel differently, but for the moment, she could only grieve for her lost love.

Somberly, Drakar took her hand and started walking. "We follow destiny, my daughter. We have no choice."

They no sooner had reached the front steps of the palace than they were surrounded by guards and ushered within. Marilee was terrified and clung to her father, sure that at any moment they were going to be shot and killed. Dear God, was this why Cord had abandoned her and run away in the night? Had he known this was all a trick? And had Irina known, as well? If so, then she hoped it would end quickly, for to think of the two people they had loved and trusted betraying them was worse than facing death.

They were taken into what was once a ballroom but was now a waiting room for those seeking to be heard by the Central Committee. They were shoved roughly into a corner, their guards glowering at them contemptuously. Marilee bit back her tears, proud of the way her father arrogantly met their hateful looks.

"Bastards," he hissed. "Bolshevik bastards!"

"Do not press your luck," one of the guards threatened. "I may lose my patience and give you the knife in your belly you deserve!"

Then, like a giant sunbeam swooping down upon them from heaven above, a great bronze door opened. She heard her name called lovingly, and Marilee looked up to see Colt and Kurt rushing toward her, with Travis close behind, limping from his war injury.

Later she could not remember running to meet them, for it was as though some angelic hand carried her forward, until she was wrapped in their arms and everyone was crying with joy.

Drakar was welcomed into the fold, and then they were taken into yet another room, where Colt endeavored to tell them that he had arranged for them to be taken out of the country with political asylum. "We're all going back to Spain—together!" he shouted triumphantly.

"I can't believe it," Marilee said over and over as they were hastily fed, then given a change of clothes. "I didn't think I'd ever see any of you again."

Travis gave her a loving, lopsided grin. "Hey, did you really think you could get rid of us so easily? Once a Coltrane, always a Coltrane, Marilee. Don't ever forget that."

"How can I?" She laughed through her tears. Then she turned to her uncle and cried vehemently, "How could I have ever thought I wasn't one of you?"

"That was our fault," Colt told her gruffly, "but we've a lifetime to make up for that. For now, just hurry and let's be on our way. The river is frozen, but we've got ice sleds waiting to get us to the train.

"We don't want to impose on our hosts any longer than necessary," he added sardonically.

When they were ready, they were taken by cold-eyed Bolshevik guards to where several ice sleds were lined up in procession. Marilee was relieved to see American soldiers waiting to go with them.

She was about to be helped into one of the sleighs

when suddenly Drakar called out to her in such a pained voice that she stepped back in alarm, afraid he'd been injured.

He was staring down at her with haunted, desperate eyes, swinging his head from side to side. Never had she seen such misery etched on a face. In a voice so wretched that it was almost unrecognizable, he told her hoarsely, "Forgive me, my darling, but I can't go with you."

She met his forlorn, anguished gaze and did not have to ask any questions. Nor would she argue with him. She knew. In that instant she knew that he had made a decision from which there was no turning back.

"Godspeed," he said chokingly with a small wave. "We'll meet again one day, Marilee. Here . . . or where your mother waits . . ."

And then he was gone, melting quickly into the crowd before the guards had time to realize he was gone. Within moments he would be snatched under the protective wing of the Whites and on his way back to Irina . . . and his destiny. For, as he'd said, he had no choice.

Marilee felt Colt's hand on her arm and knew it was time to go. He did not speak, and she was glad, for what was there to say? It was decreed by fate.

They were about to leave the shore, to skim along the ice to where the trains ran. Marilee felt her tears freezing upon her cheeks but she did not try to hold them back. Yet she knew she did not weep for her father. He would find Irina and his happiness, and that was best for him. She could not begrudge his joy.

She cried instead for herself, for she had known love only to have it snatched away. Cord, like her father and Irina, had loved the cause more. He was dedicated to defeating the Bolsheviks, and she supposed she could not fault him for it.

But oh, dear Lord, how she loved him . . . and always would.

She felt a strong arm about her, silently thanked Colt for his understanding comfort.

Then she heard words that made her whirl around.

Cord had slipped silently into the sleigh to take his place beside her. All the love within him was mirrored on his smiling face as he declared fervently, "You, my darling, are the cause I dedicate my life to. I love you so . . ."

And she welcomed his embrace, and his love, and his kiss of eternal devotion.

Sometimes, Marilee realized thankfully, there was a choice, after all.

Epilogue

THEY stood together on a windswept hill, overlooking the azure Mediterranean sea.

There were no orchestras or flower-bedecked carriages. There was no huge gathering of important guests.

There were only the bride and groom, a padre to hear their vows, and a family to share their moment of love . . . and triumph.

Marilee was radiantly lovely in a gown of white lace; Cord was strikingly handsome in his suit of beige linen.

In the Spanish morning's ethereal mist, memories were stirred, and the presence of loving ghosts were felt as they drifted down from heaven to witness the final triumph of love.

There was the ghost of Travis Coltrane—who with his devoted wife, Kitty, became legend in their days of love and war.

Present also was the tenacious spirit of Marilee Barbeau, to see her granddaughter wed, and the loving shadow of Dani Coltrane Mikhailonov, who made her mark in love and splendor . . . and would live forever in her daughter's heart.

Colt Coltrane stood proudly, reminded of his own initiation into the Coltrane birthright as he lived through his days of love and fury, then found love and dreams with his beloved Jade.

Next to them stood their son, John Travis Coltrane the Second, and his lovely wife, Valerie, and their legacy to the saga—John Travis the Third.

Nearby were Kit and Kurt, who found love and honor, with their son and daughter beside them.

It had all begun nearly sixty years ago, in a small town in North Carolina at the dawn of the War Between the States, and had moved on so gloriously to that hilltop in Spain.

The padre pronounced the couple man and wife, then closed the brief service with the age-old benediction requested by Marilee:

"Lord, dismiss us with thy blessing, hope, and comfort from above; Let us each, thy peace possessing, triumph in redeeming love."*

And the Coltrane saga would forever live on in the hearts of all who were privileged to know them.

*Benediction, Robert Hawker, 1753–1827